JOSHUA AND THE

ARROW REALM

Donna Galanti

Paperback ISBN: 978-0-9968904-9-6 ePUB ISBN: 978-1-945107-36-8
Mobi ISBN: 978-1-945107-37-5

Published by Tantrum Books for Month9Books, Raleigh, NC 27609
Cover Illustrated by Deranged Doctor Designs
Title designed by Victoria Faye
Cover designed by Najla Qamber.
Map illustrated by A. L. Sirois

To the real Joshua Cooper, as always.

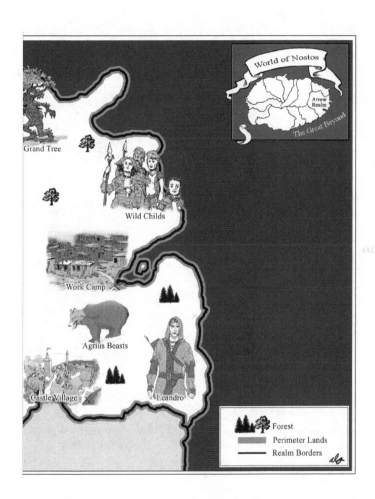

… and when the Olympian heirs at long last act with goodness in their hearts, an Oracle will arise to restore their full power and shut down the Lightning Road forevermore …

JOSHUA AND THE

ARROW REALM

Chapter One

"On your mark. Get set. Go!" We hurtled down the crusty ice-covered slope under a midnight moon. Charlie raced the faster sled, but I knew every dip and bump of this hill. I veered toward a ramp I'd made the day before he arrived from France and launched off it. He yelled a French curse at me and I laughed, now in the lead. The trees and creek disappeared. The fort Finn and I built last summer, before we got kidnapped to another world, was a white blob. I zoomed past it, picking up speed, and headed for the frozen pond at the bottom of the hill, wishing Finn were here with us too, but he was visiting his grandparents for winter break.

The star-studded sky hung over us, and the full moon reflected off the glittering snow before dashing behind rolling clouds. Light sleet slapped my cheeks. I skidded left and flipped over. Charlie grinned at me as he passed, his long legs trailing off the back of his sled. He rocketed to the pond, spraying my face with snow. "*Au revoir,* Joshua!"

His black hair and red scarf flew up, a splash of color in the white tundra. I threw myself on my sled and raced after him. He was going to win! It was okay. I wanted to make every minute fun for Charlie because he was in a rough spot. His American dad got some fancy job in Boston and the whole family was moving here, but Charlie's younger brother and mom stayed behind in France for a few months to pack the house. For now, Charlie had to deal with his dad, a new school, and a new country. At least his dad thought it'd be good for him to hang with his one American friend over winter break since they just moved here. If Charlie needed cheering, he came to the right place. He was like a brother and brothers let each other win, didn't they?

A faint rumble groaned through the whistling wind.

Boom!

Thunder ripped the sky overhead.

Charlie reached the frozen pond, spinning across it. "Woohoo! I win! You Americans can't beat us at speed!"

Lightning flashed. It zinged across the pine trees like brilliant sunlight. A seed of terror flickered inside me.

Boom! Boom!

Another flash scorched the sky.

Charlie's smile fell to a frown as he raced across the ice, peering up into the swirling clouds.

We both knew what lightning could do.

Suddenly, sneaking outside for a moonlit sled ride before Bo Chez got home from his monthly poker game didn't seem so smart.

The sleet turned to snow. Icicles flew off trees like glass splinters, shattering on the hard snow. As I shot toward the pond, a tree on the edge moved. Its branches swayed in the swirling snow.

It wasn't a tree, but a girl! She stumbled through the mad flurry, arms outstretched.

"Charlie, look!"

Gusts snatched the words away as my sled hit the ice and careened out of control on the bumpy surface. The girl staggered and fell onto the pond. I twisted my sled away to avoid hitting her and smashed right into Charlie. With a yelp, he pulled me up, and we clumped toward the girl. We lifted her up, half dragging her back up the hill to the house in the pelting snow and sleet.

"Who is she?" Charlie yelled.

"No idea," I yelled back.

He said more, but his words were lost in the wind.

My lungs burned with the cold and effort. There was only one reason someone would appear with lightning— to steal us. This girl might appear like a waif unprepared for a storm but I couldn't trust that's all she was.

I considered leaving her out in the storm, but the inevitable guilt and wanting answers won out. Charlie wrenched the back door to the kitchen open, and we hauled Mystery Girl inside. The wind pummeled us with angry flakes as I pushed the door shut, leaving the arctic freeze behind. The girl slumped in our arms, and I lowered her down on a chair.

"Watch her," I said, ripping off my gloves and hat. "And call Bo Chez!" I threw him the cordless phone and pointed at my grandfather's cell phone number on the fridge. Charlie nodded with a startled look as I ran into the dining room to grab Bo Chez's lightning orb from the case over the fireplace. It was the one weapon we'd kept from Nostos that worked on Earth. I'd used it before to take the Child Collector down. I'd do it again.

My hands shook as they had almost five months ago when I'd taken the orb for the first time without knowing its power but needing it to help rescue my kidnapped friend, Finn. This time, I understood its power. It glowed blue in my shaking hand. I squeezed it hard then shoved it in my front snow pants pocket. Suddenly, I remembered Apollo's flute and Leandro's bow—gifts from my friends when I left the Lost Realm—and pulled them out from the cabinet of the built-in bookcase. They might come in handy too. I blew on the flute. A squeal piped out. I still had no enchanting musical power with it here on Earth, but the world of Nostos was another thing. I ran back into the kitchen with my stash.

"It went right to voicemail," Charlie said in a shaky voice, placing the phone down. "*Mon Dieu*! What now?" He looked from me to the girl, who sat with her chin on her chest. I glanced at the stove clock: *9:42 p.m.* Bo Chez would be home by ten o'clock, and he was never late. He'd be in the car right now. Sometimes, he'd forget to take his phone off silent after playing cards. He'd be here soon. Now, we faced more trouble than just disobeying his orders not to go outside.

Thunder grumbled and stopped. A brief flare of lightning cut across the backyard. Were more strangers coming? I shoved aside the kitchen curtains and scanned the whiteout. The tops of the pine trees poked through the storm until a wall of snow shrouded them. A howl shrieked around the house. The predicted storm had hit early. The weather was always on my radar.

I listened for the sound of breaking glass from an unwelcome intruder but heard only the scratch of sleet on the kitchen windows and the steady tick-tock of the clock. First, I had to know who this girl was and why she came here.

9:45 p.m. Be early, Bo Chez!

"What do we do?" Charlie said.

Taking a deep breath and clutching the orb, I turned back to the girl.

She remained still with her head down. Charlie nudged her shoulder. With a gasp, she looked at us, her fierce expression making me step back. In the soft light over the sink, her long, wet hair appeared the color of dirty dishwater. A thick blade of hair escaped its wooden ponytail clasp and slashed down the side of her face. Her eyes shone like big emerald stones and were fixed on me. She gripped my arm, cold fingers pressing into my wrist.

"Hey!" Charlie tried to un-wrap her fingers but she held on.

"It's okay," I said, pretty sure by now she wasn't a threat.

The girl looked older than me by five years, about seventeen, and as skinny as Charlie. She was dressed in snug pants and a tunic made of animal skin that fell above laced-up, fur-rimmed boots. Her right leg twitched, revealing the top of a knife glinting from a leg holder with a handle wrapped in an oily rag.

The girl shook her dripping hair, and a tangy smell of dying leaves and wet leather lifted from her. She leaned forward. Her suede satchel slid off her shoulder and down the arm of her baggy coat lined with buttons made from birch bark cut into ragged squares. A closer look at her lopsided clothes made me think they'd been cut from a crude pattern and unskillfully sewn with crooked black stitches.

One thing was certain. She wasn't from Earth.

Chapter Two

The wind batted at the windows trying to get in with the snow. I turned on the floor lamp by Bo Chez's corner rocker.

"Joshua." The girl's voice cut like rough timber.

She knew my name!

"Who are you?" I said.

She leaned closer, and her fingers eased off me. Drops of sweat ran down my back as the furnace kicked on, warm air clanking through the vents. I waited for her to speak.

9:50 p.m.

Drip. Drip.

The soft melting of snow from our clothes cut through the rise and fall of the wailing wind. I followed Charlie's lead and ripped off my heavy jacket but left the liner on, tugging my snow pants over my jeans and boots. I slung the bow across my chest and stuffed the flute and orb in my jean pockets. A shiver ran across my chest even though the kitchen was warm.

I stepped closer to her. "Who are you?" I repeated.

"Ash." It came out a rasp.

"Like ashes from a fire?" Charlie said.

"No. The tree." She squeezed her throat. "Got water? I sucked in pine needles when I left home."

Where was home?

Charlie raised his eyebrows at me and I nodded. He filled a glass, hesitated, then placed it in her hands.

"Where'd you come from?" I said.

She pointed up as she gulped down the water.

I wanted an answer but didn't want the truth. "The Lightning Road?"

She stared at me with her bright green eyes and nodded.

I pulled out a kitchen chair out next to her and sat down. She seemed more an escaped prisoner than a bad guy. The fear of being kidnapped back to Nostos as a slave to the heirs of the Greek gods in the Lost Realm clamped me like a vise. Yet ... she didn't seem like a Child Collector here to steal and sell us at auction. Could she have escaped from Nostos to get back home to Earth, like my mother had done?

"Why are you here?" I said.

She sat up straighter, color coming back into her pale cheeks. "For King Apollo."

It took a moment for it to register. The King Apollo I knew died, but his son, who became king—and my friend, Sam, was alive.

"You mean Sam? What's happened to him?" I stood up fast, knocking my chair over.

"Queen Artemis kidnapped him."

"*Mon Dieu!*" Charlie shot me a look as if I knew what we should do.

9:55 p.m. Bo Chez, we need you!

Thoughts flew through my head with what could've happened. We'd left the world of Nostos with the plan for Sam, the new King Apollo, to end corruption in his Lost Realm kingdom, stop Zeus from plundering Earth, and shut down the Lightning Road to Earth forever.

Ash stood, her lips pinched together. "You have to leave with me. Now."

Charlie shook his head like crazy.

"My world depends on it," Ash said in a rising voice. "And your future—the future of all kids."

She wrenched me toward her. The bottom button of her shirt popped open, revealing her waist—and her belt.

"A Child Collector's belt!" Charlie and I both said, jumping back. She folded her palms together, knelt before us, and bowed her head.

"She's not here to hurt us," I said.

"Why? Because she's praying to us like we're Greek gods?" Charlie said, darting his eyes from her to me and back again.

I nodded, hoping I was right. "Where'd you get that belt?"

She raised her arms, clenched a fist, and pulled a hand back as if shooting an arrow.

My stomach trembled inside. It could be only one person. "Say his name," I said, my voice cracking.

She pressed her palms together again and staring into my eyes with those intense green ones, said quietly, "Leandro. He sent me here to bring you back."

Hearing his name jolted me back to a time when I'd blindly trusted Leandro in any event. He'd risked his life many times to help us rescue my friend, Finn, in the Lost Realm last summer while leading me to believe he was a traitor in order to beat the evil Ancient Immortal, Hekate. He got me, Finn, Charlie, and Bo Chez back home. He'd believed in me when I hadn't.

The wind moaned around the house.

9:59 p.m. Any second!

"Charlie, our friends are in trouble. We've got to go with her!"

His eyes widened as he shook his head frantically. "You've done enough. We've done enough. It's their world. Let them figure it out. *S'il vous plaît!*"

"What if they don't figure it out?"

His eyes screwed up. "Then they don't. It's out of our hands." He looked away. Maybe he was right but our friends were asking for our help. How could we do nothing?

Ash stood up with her hand held out. "We need to leave."

Charlie put his hand up. "Wait a minute, *Tree Girl.*" He turned to me. "What if she stole Leandro's belt," his voice dropped to a whisper, "and did something to him?"

"What about the Takers? Hekate? The power mill? The hydriads?"

"What about them?" He threw his hands up.

"Leandro and Apollo saved us from all of them."

Charlie sighed. He was in.

Ash put her fists to her waist, waiting for my decision. She looked out of place in our farmhouse kitchen with her animal-skin clothes and belt of colored squares that transported her between worlds. But she had Leandro's belt. She came to us from the Lightning Road on his orders. She wasn't stealing us away, and my friend Apollo needed help. The decision was clear.

10:01 p.m. Bo Chez, where are you?

Lights flashed in the driveway. Finally!

"Got to tell Bo Chez!" I said.

Ash caught my hand as I bolted out of the kitchen for the front door. "No time."

"*Oui*, we have to tell Bo Chez first!" Charlie said.

"No!" She pulled me back in the kitchen.

I tore away from her. "We can all come with—"

She jerked me back. "No! I can take only one. You!"

"Why?" Then I remembered the Child Collector only transported one of us at a time. It's why he came back again and again to the same spot—to steal more kids.

"Too dangerous," she said. "No room. More might fall off the road!"

"You can't take him without me," Charlie said dragging me back by my shirt.

I stopped him. "Wait! If Apollo's in danger and Leandro sent her to ask for our help, maybe Leandro's in danger too!"

"*D'accord*! But see what your grandfather says!"

Charlie pulled me closer to the front door. Ash stomped her feet and pulled me back in the kitchen. I swayed back and forth between their tug-of-war until she shoved Charlie away and pressed the buttons on her belt.

Click. Jangle. Tap-tap. "I'm home, boys. It's a monster out there!"

"Bo Chez!"

My words were lost when the back door flew open with the raging blizzard. Ash clasped me to her chest as the wind swept up in a funnel, sucking us away.

The last I saw of home was Charlie lunging for me,

yelling *"Attendez!"* and Bo Chez's wide eyes as he ran into the kitchen.

"Patrok!" the girl exclaimed.

Bo Chez reached out to stop us.

Too late.

Charlie, me, and this mystery girl blasted away on a river of fire down the Lightning Road to another world— and another adventure.

Chapter Three

Stars blasted past us on our road of fire then we crash landed. I cracked my elbow on a rock coming off the Lightning Road as Leandro's bow dug painfully into my back. Charlie landed next to me with a whoomph and a shout I'm pretty sure was a French curse word. I scrambled to my feet, hanging on to Charlie, never so glad to see someone in all my life. He'd slipped off the road's edge on the way here, and it took all my strength to hold him up.

"I knew we'd make it." He swiped a hand across his face and fell back into a tree trunk with a big sigh.

Ash stood in a wide stance as if she'd landed in such a confident pose with one hand shielding her eyes from the crackling light of our transport. Hot breezes blew the tang of pine all around me, filling in the cold I'd left behind. No world of white greeted us. Just green woods, a deep purple sky, and the Lightning Gate we'd been transported through.

The gate's blaze spun a web of brilliance then dimmed and died out, leaving us in deep shadows under a rising orange moon. The massive portal filled the small meadow like a tarnished bronze statue that had weathered many storms. Its two Greek columns stood on round stone blocks, and another wider slab overhead connected them. Carved figures and animals moved through the gate's ancient metal as if alive. The scent of blistered tin blew off the door to another world, still standing after 2,000 years. Built with lost Olympian magic, I'd once again traveled through it to rescue another friend.

Across the top crosspiece, giant letters scrolled the last words Charlie and I'd seen from this world before returning home to Earth: *Honor the fire of Zeus that sparks your journey. Adversity breeds true power. Bow to the gods!*

This trip called for true power. I wouldn't be bowing to any gods this time around. As if in response, the lightning orb pulsed in my pocket.

Ash scanned our surroundings. Oak trees loomed over us, their gnarled branches clawing at the stars. Shadows stretched deeper in the dark and twilight rushed down. Harsh voices broke my study of this unfamiliar land.

Charlie darted his head back and forth. "This isn't the Lost Realm. Where—"

"Guards!" Ash yanked my hand and we were off in a new land. We raced between trees, their limbs bowing with our passage as Charlie clung to my shirt. Amber light pierced the ground, revealing the roots of the wooden giants spreading outward from each trunk like two-toed feet. I vaulted over them, panicked they'd rip themselves from the ground and stomp us flat into a mossy grave. Anything was possible in this world. I dared a peek behind me, more terrified to see red eyes of the cadmean beasts staring back than guards. No monster foxes with fire breath chased us down—yet.

A pain in my side forced me to slow down, and I pulled Ash to a stop. Charlie groaned with relief. We'd run far and all was quiet. A good time for questions. "How do you know my grandfather?"

She darted her eyes back and forth. "Patrok?"

"He's Bo Chez to me."

"Not to Leandro. He praised Patrok as a great Olympian Storm Master hero from long ago and for his recent help freeing kid slaves in the Lost Realm."

A hero. Yes. "What happened after we left there?"

"Obviously, nothing good," Charlie said, wiping the back of his neck. "No surprise."

She ignored him and spoke fast. "Apollo angered Zeus by freeing the mortal slaves. Zeus put him on house arrest and banned his land from trading with other realms. It got bad for his people. Apollo was secretly working with Artemis and Poseidon to start a revolution when Artemis turned on us all. Nostos rulers are divided. Some want the Oracle to rise and deliver their ancestor's powers to them and stop looting Earth. Others want things to stay the way they are and seek power for themselves. Enough?"

"Almost. Where are we?"

"Arrow Realm."

"Leandro's land. And these trees—"

"The tallest in all of Nostos. Sky-highs."

She nodded, motioning us along, and said, "Keep talk short on the ground. Artemis's patrol could be about. Above, we can talk all you want."

Charlie shook his head. "Tree Girl, I've got my own questions," he said, flicking a finger at her. "Why isn't Leandro here? Where's Apollo? And what's the plan to save him and get back home?"

"You weren't supposed to be here." This shut him up. She put a finger to her lips and whistled a high-pitched call, the sound reminding me I had Apollo's flute. I drew it out and tested it. The former squeak was replaced by an enchanting melody. Its power was mine again. No butterflies floated down like they had in the Lost Realm. A great *screech* called overhead.

"Korax," Ash whispered. Charlie and I knew that word. We tucked ourselves in the shadows of a tall bush.

The monstrous bird soared in circles overhead. Butterflies were preferable. Maybe Apollo's flute called different flying creatures in each realm—good or deadly. Talons gleamed through the treetops, searching for prey. I sucked in my stomach at the memory of being snatched up by these giant birds and carried away as a slave to the power mill in the Lost Realm. They'd rescued us later on, and we'd ridden on their backs to freedom, but the bad stuff was easier to remember. Charlie backed up into a tree while Ash readied her bow and I gripped mine. Some good it would be against birdzilla with no arrows, but the cries faded and the massive wings flapped away.

"You called it with the flute, didn't you?" Ash said. I shook my head, not sure what had happened. She let it go.

I glanced around. "Who were you whistling to?" Ash scanned the woods but didn't answer me.

Charlie shrugged helplessly at me and chewed on his thumb. I focused on the woods and the forest came alive. Squirrely-things jumped from limb to limb. A swarm of bats flew across the moon in a burst of black smoke. Leaves on the ground rustled. Unseen things scurried across my feet, and I squished my toes together as the scent of mud and earthworms crept up my nose. Yellow eyes peeped out like stars in the black holes of tree trunks. A figure slunk through the shadows low to the ground.

Charlie saw it too, and we backed into a tree, its bark biting into me. Ash put up her hand. "No need to scram and cram."

"This is not the holiday vacation I signed up for, Joshua," Charlie whispered to me.

He was right about that. He'd followed me into danger—again.

The form became the shape of a black dog and sat before us, its fur sticking up in shiny points. The creature's head reached my shoulders. Its thick paws tapped the ground as its massive tail swished. To my shock, Ash removed the Child Collector belt and buckled it around the beast's neck. "For Leandro."

The dog bowed its head and gazed at me with black eyes then spoke. "Joshua of Earth, welcome to Arrow Realm. I am Lore."

Charlie tugged on my shirt. "You understand it?"

I nodded, shocked to have an animal speak to me again. Only on Nostos, with my lightning orb, did I have this power. "Why are we here?"

"Leandro requested it."

"Why?"

"I don't question him. I'm his trusted hound. I do know Queen Artemis has kidnapped King Apollo and is holding him in her dungeon for ransom. She wishes to conquer his kingdom, the Lost Realm."

I got Charlie and Ash up to speed on what was happening.

"Why should we trust you?" I asked the beast.

"Because Leandro is my master and your friend. He

wants to stop the queen but fears she suspects his loyalty. He sent his Wild Child friend here to bring you to this land."

"Wild Child?"

The dog raised a paw at Ash. "Their leader. They live in the Wild Lands. She led you to me and now I'll get you into the castle and out again. Once we free the king."

"Enough talk," Ash said with a toss of her ponytail. "Whatever Lore's told you, you should know enough by now to go with him, malumpus-tongue. I have to get back to my people." She pulled a rag out of her satchel and thrust it at us. "Food. Dried squirrel mash and ache cakes."

I unwrapped it for a peek. A bitter, smoky smell rose up from what appeared to be beef jerky and pancakes. Charlie scrunched up his nose. I split them with him and we stashed them in our pockets.

"Good protein and the acorn in the cakes stops leg cramps," Ash said. I wondered why she told us this when she explained, "If you do lots of running." Charlie blew out a big breath.

"Be quiet and on alert—always. Trust only those you know in your heart." Ash handed me a leather canteen full of water from her bag and turned to leave.

"Wait, Ash, will we see Leandro?" Since I'd said goodbye to him, I didn't think it'd ever happen again. He'd saved my life in the Lost Realm more than once. I wanted the chance to pay him back and prove myself to him—to me.

"If you do, you won't live long," Lore answered for her with a grim tone. "He's the head guard for the queen."

"He guards the queen?" I asked Ash.

She nodded but said nothing.

I slung the canteen across my chest, and it banged against my bow. The great dog pounded a paw to the ground and headed off into the woods, expecting us to follow. Ash motioned for us to go with him, but it was all too quick for me. "Come with us," I said to her.

She shook her head and put a fist to her heart, then spread her palm out to the forest. "My home."

"Can you promise we'll get back home?" Charlie said. "My brother is waiting for me ... Well, sort of."

His words cramped my gut with the memory of home—and Bo Chez's face as we flashed away.

Ash lowered her head. "We don't make promises here. It's too hard when they get broken."

"*Fantastique*," Charlie said. He straightened up. "How do we know this mutt doesn't breathe fire like those nasty foxes in the Lost Realm?"

Lore whirled about and headed back for Charlie, who pressed himself deep into a tree trunk. The giant dog opened his mouth. Spiked teeth chomped in our faces, and he blew out a big stinky breath.

Charlie squished his nose together with his fingers. "Eww, okay."

Lore threw his head back with a snort. "Come on, Reekers."

"What did it say?" Charlie said to me.

"He called us Reekers."

"*Zut*! That's the worst dog breath I ever smelled. Look who reeks."

Ash laughed for the first time. "Trust him." She pointed to Lore. "He'll lead you to Apollo."

"Tree Girl, I don't trust anyone I've known for five minutes," Charlie said.

"You did with me," I reminded him.

"You weren't an ugly dog with stinky breath."

I snorted at that as Ash pointed at me. "Trust."

"Who?"

She moved closer and tapped my chest. "Yourself."

"I'll try."

She stared into my eyes for a long moment. "Try hard."

"I'll help him," Charlie said.

"Let's trust we can get back home alive," I said.

Ash nodded and raised her hand. I lifted mine in return, wondering if we'd ever see her again. She hoisted herself up into a tree and disappeared in the leafy shadows. Charlie and I were left to trot after our guide in this new land. Could we trust him? Ash thought so, and while we'd just met, I trusted her.

And so, Charlie and I followed Lore through the Arrow Realm woods.

As we moved through the forest, it shivered with a heart beating from all that dwelled here. Even its tall pine and oaks leaned in, an army of silent sentries protecting a wild land. Squirrels leaped into branch clutches that caught them in a game, then unfurled to let them go. Shiny eyes followed us from tree holes, as did trilling coos.

The orange moon watched over it all with its fiery eye.

I ran faster toward Apollo—or toward my own death? I'd learned all is not as it seems on Nostos. Death's door could mercifully slam shut just when you were doomed to enter.

Chapter Four

Lore stopped fast and Charlie and I skidded to a stop behind him. Towers jutted up in the distance, stabbing the night sky with jagged rock. Queen Artemis's castle glowered down, daring us to enter.

"What's the plan?" I wiped the sweat off my forehead as Charlie and I chugged some water and tried Ash's food. The salty squirrel jerky had a smoky flavor, and the pancakes were dry but nutty and filling.

A cool breeze chilled my skin, reminding me of the blizzard blowing back home and all we'd left behind.

Lore sniffed, the hair on his back quivering. "Can you swim?"

I asked Charlie who nodded with a frown. Lore stared at us as if deciding we were worthy of his wet task. "We enter the moat, swim to the middle and where the moon aligns with the queen's flag, swim below to an old underground gate that leads to the dungeon. It was used before the moat was dug and filled."

I translated Lore's words to Charlie, who gunned me a look like we'd be crazy to do it.

"How will we get Apollo? Get back out, get him back to his land, and get back to ours?" I asked Lore.

"You must trust me," Lore growled, ears twitching. "Leandro trusts me."

So says the mutt. If Leandro were here, he'd do anything in his power to help us get home again. We had no choice but to trust Lore.

"And he trusts what *you* may be," Lore said with a jerk of his head.

Those words zapped me like a live wire. This was why Leandro brought me back.

Charlie pulled me aside. "*C'est impossible*, Joshua." Lore watched us, his eyes shining like spotlights then he moved away to study the castle towers.

"Nothing's impossible here," I said.

"People lie." Charlie thrust a chin at Lore, who sniffed the ground. "Animals lie. We can find our own way. We did before. You and me."

"And Apollo."

"But he's the reason we came. He helped us alone. Let's do the same." He looked sideways at Lore and edged back toward the path we'd traveled.

I tugged him back. "We rescued Finn and got home last time because we trusted people—and animals. Right?" The more I convinced him, the more I wanted to convince myself.

He didn't answer but stopped moving back and crumpled his skinny shoulders. He'd grown taller in the few months we'd been apart. Even with his slouching, I had to crick my neck up at him, waiting for his answer.

"You can't trust family," Charlie finally whispered. "So why these ... these people?" He picked at a pocket thread on his jeans. He cleared his throat and said, "I don't think my mom wants to follow us to America."

"Oh." My brain switched gears with his words. Guilt coursed through me over getting him caught up in this mess.

"My dad's new job was supposed to make us happy. Their last chance, I heard my dad say. I think he tries too hard at the wrong stuff, you know?" He gave up on the thread and shoved it in his pocket, looking at me with wet eyes. "What if I never see my mom or brother again? Now I'm farther away from them ... and might not get home."

"Friends don't let each other down, right?"

He tightened his lips and nodded.

"Then come on. Apollo would do the same for us. We got home last time. We will again."

He sighed and nodded. "Let's follow the fur ball."

The fur ball had finished sniffing about and waved a paw at us to follow. The closer to the castle we got, the more it looked like a crooked rock pile that'd been smashed together by the hands of some giant. Torches lit the massive wooden door at the end of the bridge arching over the moat. Figures strode back and forth in front of it: guards with snake spears that could blast you to ash.

"How do we unlock Apollo's cell?" I whispered to Lore, as we hunkered down behind a pricker bush. They scraped my skin and I winced, shrinking back. The water on the moat rippled in a black sheen.

"With words," Lore said in a low rumble. "The cells are locked with enchanted spells by guards."

"The queen's slaves?"

"We are all her slaves."

"No way," I said. "Not a slave. Not ever again."

"*Oui!*" Charlie chimed in.

Lore chuffed. "There is always a way."

"Leandro and Apollo were supposed to stop kid slavery after we left last time," I said.

"We need a revolution—or the Oracle—for that to happen." The big dog sniffed me, his ears twitched. "Are you he?"

"Am I who?"

"The Oracle."

I shook my head, sharing our conversation with Charlie.

"If he is the Oracle, you better be on our side," Charlie said to Lore.

Lore snapped his jaws, and Charlie and I both jumped back. "I don't need a hero, you Reekers. I've got my own."

Before I could wonder what Lore meant, Charlie cleared his throat. "We can't swim in that muck. There's got to be another way."

"No other way," Lore growled.

A cloud of bugs flew low across the moat as if they agreed, their wings chopping through gas bubbles sprouting from the silent sludge. Moonlight shone across the water, revealing chunks of algae floating in the scum. A whiff of decaying vegetation attacked my nose. I tried not to gag with the thought of diving into the slime. A frog *barrumphed* a lone croak and the trees bent over the moat, their branches ensnared in the watery grave.

Neither Charlie nor I moved.

"Suit yourself." Lore's hair bristled across his broad body, and his tail thrashed us as he turned toward the water. "The guards change in a moment. Must go while they're distracted."

"If we get in and out and back to the Lightning Gate, we could send Apollo back to the Lost Realm and be home before lunch," I said to Charlie, wishing so bad those words were true.

He looked at me doubtfully. "Or we may never get home."

His words echoed what he'd told me in the auction pit of the Lost Realm when I'd first met him. *I'm not saying you won't find your friend. You might. But we'll never get home again.*

Was that our fate now?

The guards called out the changing of their posts. Lore plunged into the rank water. He swam away fast, his brutish head cruising across the moat's slime. I stared at the sky one last time, our purple portal to freedom, and slid into the briny black, shivering from its cold embrace. A foul stench filled my nose as I pushed slimy algae away. Charlie sighed, and his splash told me he followed close behind.

Something skated across the water toward me, its beady eyes glittering as it grew closer. I swam faster toward Lore to escape the snake, my heart thudding harder with each stroke. It passed behind me and continued on its quest. I tried not to think about what lay below the water and kicked my legs furiously, promising any creature that dared drag me under a good smack in the head. The moat wasn't wide, but crossing it seemed to take an eternity.

Lore threw his snout up in the air. We'd reached the middle of the moat. The queen's flag snapped in the breeze from a tower above, a white pendant ablaze with a fiery black arrow. Our guide disappeared.

The trench swallowed him up. One ripple rose as evidence he'd been there. I took a deep breath of the rotting ooze and sank into the creepy waters. Doom and dark engulfed me as I swam the dank depths lurking with danger—and death.

Chapter Five

I forced myself to open my eyes in the murky realm we pushed through. Lore's body swum ahead, and I focused on his tail and not the gunk flowing around me. The moon tainted everything under the water a sickly color. I pretended we were swimming in sticky soda fizz rather than stinky ick.

Tails flipped past as fish wriggled around me. My lungs burned. I dared a peek behind me. Charlie pushed through the water, his eyes bulging.

The need for air threatened to launch me into full panic. We should be there by now! A yellow light swelled before us. Out of the corner of my eye, something else grew bigger. White chompers gnashed together. A mutant rat! Claws ripped through the water driving the rat toward dinner. Me!

I swam faster. Could the orb work as a weapon under water? No time to find out! The water crushed me. My boots clung to me like mud. My chest screamed for air. Lore's body disappeared into the light. The dog dragged me and Charlie out of the water with his teeth. I cracked my ankle on stone. Pain ripped through me as I scrambled up the steps when a snout exploded through the water. Teeth sliced the air. I screamed, jerking my leg away. Charlie lugged me up the steps, scraping me with every inch. Lore stood and yanked down an iron grate anchored in the ceiling. It bashed into the rat's head before locking into fitted holes in the ground. The beast squealed and swam away.

Shuddering, I sprawled across the steps. The light I'd been swimming toward hadn't come from any torches but from the rock of this watery dungeon entrance. It glowed yellow with sparkly gold flecks.

Charlie panted next to me, hair plastered in black fingers down his forehead. We both reeked like garbage sitting under a blazing summer sun.

"Your scream was not helpful," Lore said to me.

"You didn't tell us giant rats would be in the moat! We have to go back that way?"

"What other monsters can we expect to make friends with, fur ball?" Charlie choked out, as he spit scum from his mouth.

Lore pulled his lips back in a fierce grin. "No time for that." He thumped us each with a paw, and we followed him up the fluorescent steps. I grew dizzy, and my ankle ached as we wound up a twisty set of stairs and out into a hallway. Flickering torches lined the walls. Lore made a sign to stop. We pressed ourselves up against cold, cracked stone. A cobweb brushed my face. I ripped it away, shivering in my damp clothes.

Foul smells of rotten meat and mold overpowered my own stench. My every sense was on alert waiting for guards to come pounding toward us. Ahead, thick bars covered doorways to cells.

Lore stepped out in the middle of the corridor and padded silently ahead as Charlie and I sneaked behind. I peered into each empty cell we passed, hoping to see my friend Apollo, grating my teeth with each *pling* of water seeping from the ceiling. Something rustled. A chain clinked. Then a moan had me running toward the closest cell. There in the shadows huddled a lump in a bed of straw.

I clenched the bars. "Sam? I mean … King Apollo?" I whispered, calling him for the first time by his new name as king.

The lump lifted his head. It was him! His pale face and white hair glowed in the torchlight, eyes wide with surprise. He staggered up, chains rattling from an iron ankle cuff hooked into the wall. His royal purple and gold clothes were torn and streaked with dirt. I hardly recognized him through his filth. He stood as tall as me now, and his once skinny figure was now muscled. Time moved faster here than on Earth.

"Joshua!"

"Leandro sent for me and Charlie to get you out."

He strained at his chains and peered at us. "Charlie?"

"*C'est moi*! This pooch got us in to rescue you," Charlie whispered, poking his nose through the grates. "Hey! Boy, did you get big."

"Leandro's hound got you here?" Apollo said.

I nodded eagerly.

"Back," Lore commanded. He muttered a string of words, and the thick iron latch creaked with the spell and slid across the bars. Charlie and I ran in. Lore spoke another rush of words, and the iron cuff fell off Apollo. He gripped my arms, darting his eyes from me to Charlie.

"My Earth friends!"

"Let's get out of here," I said and quickly explained our plan as Lore paced the dungeon hallway on guard.

As we turned to leave the cell and head back through the rat-infested waters, Lore slid the latch back across the cell with his paw. It locked with a *boom*.

I rushed to the bars. "What are you doing?"

He smiled, dagger teeth etched in torchlight. Foam frothed at the corners of his mouth as he shook with laughter, sending spit flying across my face. "Whatever my queen says, Reekers."

"We never should've trusted this mutt!" Charlie shook the bars of our cell.

"I trust no one. Why should you?" Lore laughed louder.

He was right. I'd trusted Ash, and she'd trusted this beast. Now we were rat-food—or worse. Time to fix that.

I tugged the lightning orb out of my pocket and hid it in my hand as I moved behind Charlie. Sneaking a peek at the crystal, clouds rolled and lightning flashed inside. The orb glowed blue. Electric shocks raced through my hand. Ancient Olympian power throbbed through my fingertips.

I stepped out fast from behind Charlie and flung the orb between the cell bars at Lore. In a blink, he caught the orb between his teeth and lowered it on the floor. The blue faded, and it returned to clear crystal.

My big weapon was gone.

Lore threw his head back and laughed again. I took the opportunity to try to steal back the orb through the cell grates, but he snapped his teeth. Dank breath burst hot across my face as I snatched my fingers away before they got diced. Charlie and I looked at each other in desperation. Apollo sighed and slumped his shoulders.

I tried remembering the spell Lore used to open the cell to no use.

"Forget it, ignorant Reekers," Lore said, padding back and forth in the corridor. "It doesn't work for those *inside* the cell." He let loose a great bellow. His howl rose in pitch, alerting our presence to the keepers of the dungeon. Its sound, echoing around the rock walls, sealed us in.

A cool draft struck me. The torches crackled and spit smoke. Feet slammed down on stone, and the clash of metal whacked the air. Charlie and I backed up to the wall in the shadows, but Apollo stood staring pitifully at the floor.

"*Mon Dieu*, we're done for," Charlie whispered.

"Not yet!" We couldn't fail now that we'd found Apollo. There must be a way out. I cursed myself for not keeping the orb to blow a hole in the rock of our prison. Heavy boots stomped our way, urging me to slide my hands along the damp walls seeking escape, but doom had arrived.

Four guards lined the front of our cell, each with a sword in one hand and a vape snake spear in the other. Chain mail pulled across their chests and they banged their vapes on the floor, the deadly serpent heads hissing at us, ready to strike. Venom goo dripped from their fangs and sizzled on the flagstones. With a collective thrust, the men pointed their swords our way and pierced us with stony stares. A figure pushed through the sentries and bent to pat Lore's head. "Good dog for guarding my belt. Now let's see what you've caught."

I gasped, recognizing the voice. The man drew his sword out, pulled the hood back from his cloak, and turned to face us with a scowl on his face. It was my old friend Leandro. His scowl melted to worry.

He looked as shocked to see me as I was to see him.

Chapter Six

"Leandro!" I ran to the front of the cell and squeezed the bars. "Let us out!"

Charlie rushed to my side. "*Oui*! It's a mistake!"

"A mistake indeed," Leandro said evenly. His eyes darted over the bow slung across my chest—the very bow he'd fashioned for his missing son and given to me when we'd said goodbye in the Lost Realm—and he creased his eyebrows then slid his eyes to the soldiers and raised his sword. "More traitors I see, trying to free your king perhaps?"

"*Non*." Charlie shot me a confused look, but I was just as puzzled.

Lore chuffed. "Oh, yes, Master; that Wild Child let them in."

"Wait! What? *You* let—" I tried to out the traitor when a clear voice called from the end of the dungeon's hall.

"What have we here?"

Leandro's nostrils flared and his sword hand trembled. His hair fell in ropes, flecked with more white now, and the lines in his forehead ran deeper. The last time I'd seen him in the Lost Realm, he was setting out for the Arrow Realm to create a better future for Nostos. Now Artemis had kidnapped Apollo, and Leandro fought on her side. Deeper confusion set in. Had Leandro failed in his mission and sent Ash to ask for our help? Or did Ash steal Leandro's belt to find us and bring us here on her own? Or had Leandro turned to the dark side? Anything was possible on Nostos. One thing I understood quite clear—Lore was no friend.

The guards and Leandro bowed.

"Queen Artemis," Leandro said solemnly, lowering his sword. "I wasn't expecting you."

"Keeps you and your guards alert," the clipped voice shot back.

A tall woman strode toward our cell as the soldiers parted. Her head was covered in a crown of twisty thorns, every prickly point encrusted with blood-red jewels and tinged with gold. Her cropped brown hair framed high cheekbones between short curls and narrowed eyebrows arched over large, brown eyes. Her nose and lips were thin like the rest of her, a face more handsome than pretty. She wore matching plum-colored velvet pants and a hooded tunic that fell to her knees with open slits on either side. A rough-made bracelet of polished braided wood encircled her left wrist. Her white shirt was flecked with gold threads, and billowy sleeves puffed out above her slender hands resting on a burnished metal belt hanging low across her hips. A dagger with an intricate handle dangled from her belt. Form-fitting black leather boots laced up her legs and one foot tapped the floor. The strangest thing about her was the black sunglasses she wore. They had round frames, and the lenses flickered alive with torchlight.

She bent to pick up my lightning orb.

"Hey," Charlie burst out. I shook my head at him but he went on. "That's Joshua's ... you ... you ..." His voice fell to a whisper as blades flashed.

Artemis shot him a withering look then turned the orb admiringly in her hand. "It's been a long while since I've seen one of these. It will go well in my chambers as added protection. Did you pilfer it from a Storm Master, thief?" She turned her head to me.

I nodded. I'd "stolen" it from Bo Chez when I'd been kidnapped as an energy slave on my first Nostos trek. I'd grown-up with adventure tales from Bo Chez about the power of this crystal, and I'd taken it then, desperate for his stories to be true—for it to have real power. I'd found out quickly it did.

She accepted my nod and slid the orb into her tunic pocket. Charlie groaned as our last hope disappeared— again.

"King Apollo, looking as pathetic as usual I see," Artemis said, staring down her nose at him. "No wonder your people have no use for you."

Apollo stared back at her without expression. "Traitorous kin. Your days are numbered too. Zeus will make it so."

"Oh, Zeus has no idea what's coming for him." She smiled grimly. "Neither do you."

Artemis stepped toward Leandro, whose head remained bowed, his hair covering his face. "Leandro, how is it these Barbaros Reekers came into my dungeon and nearly set my prized prisoner free?"

Leandro shifted his feet and raised his head. "I cannot say, my queen. Perhaps they chanced a swim in the moat to the old flooded entrance. I'll have guards seal it off immediately."

She moved closer to him and raised her hand. He stiffened as she traced the long scar on his right cheek. He'd once told me he'd gotten it in a fight when he traveled undercover to find his lost wife and son before being pardoned as a deserter. "Would you like another scar to match this one, guard?"

"No m'lady," Leandro said.

She lowered her hand. "Good. Now open their cell."

Leandro stepped in front of our cell. I clamped my fingers around the bars, breathing in his spicy chocolate scent that brought with it all he'd once meant to me. His eyes, one bluer than the other, squinted at me as he chanted the spell to open our cage. The iron door slid open, and Leandro's fingers brushed mine before I let go of the bars. For a second, I imagined him joining us in the fight against the queen and her men to battle our way out of here.

"Check the Reekers for other weapons and take the bow from the boy," Artemis ordered.

Charlie and I soon found ourselves jabbed in a rough search. Leandro stood there and watched without expression except for the wince that crossed his face when his men ripped the bow from across my chest.

I glanced at Charlie, who hadn't lost his habit for knuckle chewing. He gnawed on one now. Apollo leaned up against the walls with his eyes closed and hands folded. What was wrong with him? He wasn't acting like the king he was meant to become. Even when he'd been only Sam and not the king, he acted more kingly than anyone I'd known. He'd sacrificed his own needs for his people. Now, he stood a shadow of himself, tired and defeated—like a pathetic old man. Like his father had been.

"My family will find me," I burst out to Artemis.

She smiled. "No one will find you."

She cast a bigger stone of doubt in the pit of my stomach that we'd survive this. It fueled my anger. I pointed at Lore, who'd sat up on his haunches next to Artemis. "Yeah? Well, why don't you ask your pet how we got in here."

Charlie stepped forward. "*Oui!* Your mutt led us in."

Artemis looked at Lore and back at me and Charlie, eyebrows raised above the rim of her sunglasses. "My favorite hound? Never. Lore's loyal to me and my head soldier. Isn't that right, Leandro?" She stroked the dog's ears with her long fingers while nodding at Leandro. He bowed but didn't speak.

In a flash, Lore surged forward, grabbed Leandro's sword with his teeth, shoved him into us, and slammed the cell's gate shut. Before the great dog fell back, he transformed into a soldier who twirled the sword and sheathed it, grinning at us like he'd pulled the biggest prank ever.

Chapter Seven

"Good work, Borin," Artemis said, tapping the shoulder of the dog-turned-man who slid the Child Collector's belt from around his neck and buckled it at his waist while sneering at us.

"Thank you, my queen," Borin said and fell in line with the other guards.

Leandro clapped his cloak behind him and strode to the front of the cell, thrusting his fist at Borin. "You!"

"Yes, Leandro," Artemis said with a tight smile, spreading spider-like fingers at her waist. "Borin has been watching you for some time as your trusted hound. You thought he was away for training."

Leandro's shoulders shook. "Why?"

"You came to me from the Lost Realm with the former King Apollo's dying wish for you to be my head soldier, along with his ridiculous plan to stand up against Zeus with Poseidon, free the Reekers, and shut down the

Lightning Road. As if I'd ever let that happen! I have other plans."

"Traitors everywhere," Charlie muttered, crinkling his eyebrows at me. Right now the two of us could only count on each other. There was no counting on Apollo, who remained leaning on the wall with eyes downcast.

Leandro gripped the cell bars as if he wanted to rip them up from the blocks of stone. "What happened to you, my queen? You embraced the idea of change when I first came here! We were on the same side."

"I let you think so." She fingered her braided bracelet back and forth. "I kept you, my enemy, close at hand. Borin eagerly used his ancient power to transform into Lore, and you welcomed this gift of a royal hound from me. It was easy for your watchdog to watch *you* and discover your plans to bring the Oracle here to defeat me." Her lips set in a thin line, and she brushed a curl of hair from her cheek. "Funny how your plans worked out for my own. Now I have the Oracle. He'll come in handy. Wait and see." She smiled, and my insides shuddered as Leandro shot me a knowing look.

The Oracle. She believed. Leandro believed. My mission to save Apollo exploded into something much more, like facing who I truly was—and saving a whole world ... if I survived.

"I thought you trusted me," Leandro said in a low voice.

"Trust you? Ha! You betrayed your own kind by fathering a child with a Reeker and deserted your post as a guard here. My mother once trusted you when she was queen, but you failed in your oath to her." She leaned in closer to him. "You've been following me in the woods, watching me lately. I knew you would betray me now. A traitor is all you'll ever be. Why trust you now?"

Leandro reached a hand through the bars, and Artemis twitched, taking a step back. The soldiers jabbed their vapes toward him, but he kept his hand out toward her and said so quietly I strained to hear, "Because you trusted me once with your heart and soul as a confidant."

"As a princess, you betrayed me then too!" The torchlight flared across Artemis's sunglasses.

Leandro let his hand fall at her anger. "Your mother assigned me as a work camp guard to keep me from you when our friendship was discovered. Not my fault."

"No, but falling in love with a Reeker was. You were the closest thing I ever had to a brother." She paused. "You never came back for me."

"I left to find my family."

"I was your family first."

Leandro bent his head and sighed. "I'm so sorry ... Temi."

Artemis trembled at his nickname for her, and her lip wobbled. She jerked around to command her soldiers. "Keep Leandro locked up with the Reekers until I decide their fate."

She strode down the corridor with my lightning orb and disappeared through the doorway to the castle above. The soldiers snapped to attention and followed the queen. Their marching boots soon faded away, leaving us trapped in our rock cage. Charlie banged on the cell bars, spewing French curses at them. If only cursing had power here.

We'd gotten Leandro imprisoned with us, and we weren't heading home anytime soon. Instead, we awaited our fate, as Artemis put it. What Artemis meant most likely by *fate* in this land of hunters was really *bait*—and bait gets dead.

Heavy despair wrapped around me like fists between the sounds of Charlie's ragged breathing, Apollo's sighs, and the tapping of Leandro's boots as he paced the cell. I stepped toward Leandro but fell back, unsure what to say ... what to ask. When we'd said goodbye in the Lost Realm, he'd flashed away here to his homeland through the Lightning Gate. Now he stood before me again, larger than life, striding back and forth with his hands clasped behind his back.

Suddenly, he stopped and gazed at me, his green-blue eyes shining in the torchlight. "I'm sorry. I got you in this mess. I had to believe."

I swallowed hard. "That I'm the Oracle."

"Yes."

"I-I don't ..." I couldn't put my conflict about being the Oracle into words.

"We'll know in time," Leandro said to reassure me.

"We don't have time!" Charlie shot back.

Leandro cast him a crooked smile. "Merely one of our problems."

"Not your fault, Leandro," Apollo whispered. "This all happened because of me."

We looked at him. He stared ahead with big, sad eyes.

"Zeus turned against me after you left," Apollo continued. "My family turned against me, never believing I was the king my father wanted me to be. My people lost faith in me. The only ones loyal to me now are the korax. I reunited them with their families and improved their living conditions. Funny, the only ones I could help as king were dumb beasts." He sputtered a sad laugh.

"King Poseidon was a friend, but I'd barely begun secret talks with him when Artemis kidnapped me. She turned against me ... I don't know why. She'll probably turn Poseidon against me too. The Oracle … that's a myth. No one is coming to save us." He fingered his filthy purple vest, the royal sun insignia of his land stitched on it. The king's ring, given to him by his dying father, shone bright gold. He pushed his sleeves up and clasped his hands behind his head, revealing the royal tattoo on the inside of his wrist: a yellow sun with a fancy "A" in the middle. He may be a king but he was branded like all Nostos slaves in a prison of his own destiny's making. We were all in the same jail now.

Anger filled my every limb. Anger at trusting Ash and Lore—or Borin. Anger at the queen for imprisoning us and taking my orb. Anger at coming here in the first place. Anger at my friend Apollo, who'd given up hope when we needed it most. As quick as it came, my anger fled, leaving a depressed knot in my chest.

"What happened to you, Apollo?" I said.

He didn't answer.

"After you left, Joshua, Zeus punished Apollo for releasing the Lost Realm slaves," Leandro explained for him. "He shut down the Lightning Road to Earth from every land except the Arrow Realm, which became the main hub of inbound mortal slaves and outbound Child Collectors. I've tried to reason with Artemis to band with Apollo and lead the revolution Nostos needs to free itself from slavery. At first, she was receptive, but now … she's changed." He narrowed his eyes. "I suspected she's been lured to dark forces so I followed her into the woods seeking answers. Now I know she watched me too."

"Did you find any answers?" Charlie said, with a lilt of hope.

"Yes," Leandro said. "That she forces herself to go into the forest she dreads to overcome her terror."

"Terror of what?"

"The woods."

"She's a hunter and afraid of the woods?" I laughed.

But Leandro didn't laugh. He frowned at me. "She's had this fear of the trees trapping her and strangling her to a slow death since she was a child. Her mother made her sleep in the forest alone at the foot of the Black Heart Tree to drum the weakness out of her but it drove her anxiety on. Artemis still forces herself to go there and sleep sometimes to spite her mother, now long dead. I thought Artemis was cured when she returned one morning with a new bracelet she'd made from the branches of the very trees that terrified her."

"So was she cured?" I said.

"I don't know. She still wears her sunglasses. They make her feel safe and invisible from the trees. Or so she told me as younglings." He inhaled sharply and flung his cloak behind him at the memory. "Perhaps she dreads taking the glasses off. I don't know. I do know this: it seems as if the old Artemis is gone, replaced by another ..." He tapped his lips with a knuckle in deep thought.

"What does that have to do with us?" Charlie said. "Let's break out of here. We've got Apollo like we planned. We can go home." He backed up and rammed into the cell bars. They shook but didn't budge.

"They're sunk two feet deep into the stone," Leandro said with a deep sigh. "I know. I *was* the head guard here."

"Call on some of your animal friends to help us then." Charlie rubbed his smashed shoulder.

"We're too far below ground to reach them if they'd even come. Most are loyal to Artemis."

"Joshua, you've got powers here. I mean, *mon Dieu*, they think you're this Oracle. That must mean *something*."

He twisted his fingers around the bars and lowered his head to them. "I'll never see my brother again … even if I do get home."

"Stop," I said. "You will."

But our adventure had grown more complicated.

"Joshua has no powers," Apollo said with watery eyes. "Artemis took his lightning orb."

"You're a king! Don't you have people to call on for help? Could you get them a message somehow?" I said, eager for him to be the take-charge Apollo he was when I knew him as Sam.

He shook his head.

"It was your father's dying wish to help your people, don't you remember?"

"I can't help anyone. I'm powerless."

"You don't need powers to do the right thing. All you need is to believe in yourself." How true those words rang for me as I said them but Apollo didn't respond. I tried once more. "Don't let your father's death be for nothing."

"*Oui*," said Charlie. "At least he apologized to you in the end for how he treated you."

Apollo refused to look at either of us and so I continued to search every crevice of our cell for a spot to tunnel out. Hopelessness filled me but I shook it off, not wanting to believe we were powerless to save ourselves. There must be a way out! Loose stone to pull apart. A hole to make bigger. Something! The heavy stones wouldn't budge.

We were fortified worm food.

Chapter Eight

Apollo talked on as Charlie and I searched for a way out of our rock prison. "My father named me his successor with his dying breaths, but the rightful heir, my cousin, contested it. He said I killed my father. My own father!" I glanced at him in my search. He gazed at the ceiling, nostrils pinched. "My cousin called me weak for wanting to end mortal slavery. He convinced the rest of my family. They all said Leandro was a deserter and not to be trusted as my father's witness to name me as heir. No one stood with me for what was right." He paused and in a quieter voice said, "I failed in my promise to you, Joshua."

"Your cousin sounds like a bully," I said. Charlie agreed. I'd had my share of them at all the different schools we'd moved to over the years. The new kid with only a grandfather for family was great for getting picked on. "There's got to be others on your side. I just know it.

Don't give up, okay?" I said. "We all need to get home where we belong."

Charlie nodded, swatting at a sluggish moth buzzing about his head.

Apollo huddled on the floor, knees to his chest. "Nostos is too corrupt for change. I'm just one person. One person can't change a whole world."

"Yes, they can." Leandro strode to Apollo and pulled him up to face him. "The Oracle can." But he stared at me when he said it.

"He'll die trying," Apollo whispered.

Leandro shook Apollo. "Are *you* going to let Joshua die?"

Tears welled in Apollo's eyes. "It's not up to me. I used to have faith there was an Oracle."

Leandro let Apollo sink back down to the floor. "We need to have faith in something to go on in this doomed world. It's why I sent Ash to bring Joshua here. And Lore. Unfortunately, that didn't work out."

"Obviously. They betrayed us," Charlie said.

"Only Lore. Ash is a friend, and why wouldn't she trust my hound? She trusts me."

"Funny," I said. "Like I thought you betrayed me once."

"Yes, well, we are alike, you and I, young Joshua," Leandro said. "We must pass over what is evident and search deeper—trust our instincts to know the truth."

He held my gaze. Old feelings for him as a leader and a hero surged through me.

"Do you have faith in me?" Leandro asked as if reading my thoughts.

With all my feelings bubbling inside me, I could only nod.

Then a silky voice murmured from the stone walls. "Faith is alive."

We all looked around. "Wha—"

Leandro held up a hand to silence us. "Who said that?"

"A mastermind. And a master of minds," the voice said with a giggle. I pointed to where the voice came from in the wall. Leandro nodded and we sneaked over there.

"It's a crazy prisoner Artemis locked up," Apollo said.

"Perhaps he has information to help," Leandro said.

I nodded and pushed on a two-foot block of stone where the voice came from. Nothing. I tried another stone. Put all my weight behind it. Charlie and Leandro helped. The voice giggled again. We braced our feet and shoved our shoulders into the wall. Charlie grunted, his face straining red. The rock moved an inch. We both gasped in excitement. It must've been used to get through before. We pushed harder. The jagged rock slid forward and fell on the other side.

A man's face bulged through the opening. I jumped back and fell on my butt. His eyes widened, and his giggle spilled into a musical laugh bouncing around our cell.

Leandro reached through the hole and caught the neck of the giggler. "What's so funny?"

The man's eyes bulged bigger. "Nothing, m'lord," his voice croaked. "You need faith to get out of this dread. Faith is alive. Not dead!"

Leandro let go and the man's face popped into our cell. His pale, smooth face beamed with large, bright blue eyes, red cheeks, and a chunky nose. Tufts of white hair stuck out from his head. He looked like an old man trapped in a kid's face.

Charlie jerked back. *"Mon Dieu!* Santa's crazy cousin."

"Faith renders us invincible," Crazy chanted. "No matter the enemies yet to be faced. If doubt enters, our faithful hearts will be erased."

"You're talking nonsense, whoever you are," Leandro said, flinging his cloak behind him.

"No, no. A silly sot they put here to rot … but the truth will be got. Found in the lyric cast to spin my trick." The old man's words and eyes mesmerized me, chaining me in place. His face became a head and an arm with a hand stretched toward us as this strange person squeezed farther through the opening. We all leaned back. The tip of the man's blackened fingernail curled up and pointed at me.

"Are you ready to lead?" His puffy white eyebrows rumpled up but his lips didn't move. His voice echoed inside me.

Maybe, I wanted to say, but my words escaped me. The walls pressed closer and the voices of my friends tumbled together and grew faint.

"You will be tested, faithful one." His voice pierced my head. I put my hands over my ears and closed my eyes to push the dizziness away. "Take the knife of Leandro. 'Tis hidden in his boot. Plunge it through his heart like a poisonous root. What he seeks stands before him, but he cannot see through the gloom. Die he will soon. End his suffering under tonight's moon."

"No! He's my friend." Waves of tiredness beat against me.

"What's he doing to you, Joshua?" Charlie said, pulling me closer. "You leave him alone, you crazy old man."

He didn't. His voice crooned on in my head, making me so sleepy. "A desolate wind crosses our land of sea and stone. You must cross it alone. All will forsake you. Kill them now to end their pitiful life so abhorred. Only the heart of a true warrior can command ancient powers to be restored."

"I won't!"

"Fail to face your destiny and die. Lose faith and die. Are you ready to die?"

"No!" I stumbled.

"Neither am I. Which is why you must."

The cool stone charged up to slap me. Hands pulled me up but couldn't stop the black that rushed in.

Chapter Nine

Blurred faces hovered over me. Cold rattled inside me from the stone floor. I breathed deeply, inhaling a bitter smoke and muck stench. The day's events spun inside me all over again. Hands stood me up as my vision cleared. I shook off Charlie and Leandro's grip. The strange face was gone, but humming floated from the hole in the wall.

"What did you do to him with your spells old man?" Leandro strode to the hole, reaching an arm through to grasp our neighbor's neck again without luck.

"All is well within his well," the voice sang. "The past is leaves in his book yet to be read. A faithful heart will read them all and not get dead."

"I'm fine," I said.

"Fine, fine, fine." The voice giggled. "Your mind is not mine, mine, mine!"

"We're not fine," Charlie muttered.

The humming continued.

"I know what he is," Leandro said, giving up his quest to choke the crazy man. "A rare breed that hides away. He carries the ancient magic of Hypnos. He hypnotizes folk and forces them to do what he wishes."

"According to his riddles I've been forced to listen to, Artemis found him scavenging for roots in the Perimeter Lands," Apollo said from the floor. I'd forgotten he huddled there. "She threatened to flush out his secret cave community there and use them as slaves—and bait—if he didn't do as she ordered. He's the leader of hundreds of cave dwellers in the Perimeter Lands. They're harmless folks unless provoked. Then you risk being hypnotized and waking up tossed in a bog. Artemis uses him to command her soldiers."

"What did he command you to do?" Leandro asked me with eyes of concern. I opened my mouth but couldn't tell him. He put his hands on my shoulders. Their warmth soaked into me, chasing some of the cold away. I wanted to lean into all of his warmness but was frozen with confusion over what happened.

I swigged water from Ash's canteen. My friends waited for an answer. "Nothing," I mumbled.

"And you came here for nothing," Apollo said. "There's no use fighting. It's hopeless."

"Stop saying that." But he just stood there with a sad look on his face. "We didn't come here for nothing."

"*Oui*," Charlie butted in. "We came here for you, King-man."

"I'd listen to your friends, King," Leandro said, crossing his arms. "It all started in the Lost Realm with one boy, one king, and one hope to change our world."

Something stirred inside me with his words—

something bigger than me.

The floor shook. Marching feet hammered our way.

"Here comes the queen's army," sang our neighbor. "Ruled by the mean and smarmy."

Leandro bent down to his boot. "Don't do it," I said. "They'll kill you."

He let his hand fall and straightened. "How did you know?"

"The Hypnos guy told me."

He frowned but there was no more time to talk. Soldiers ripped open the cell and grabbed me and Charlie.

"No!" Apollo came to life and hooked my shirt with his fist. "Take me instead."

"We intend to soon, prisoner, queen's orders, but not yet." A soldier pushed him into the wall and held a knife to Leandro, who struggled to get to us. "You'll be later, traitor. The queen has other plans for you." Then Charlie and I were hauled down the corridor.

"Leandro!" I twisted around, reaching for him while digging my heels into the floor. A soldier thrust a hissing vape in his face and locked the cell.

"I'll find you," he called out. Leandro's face creased with fear, and he clutched the bars next to Apollo, his pale face frozen in a grimace.

We turned the bend and my friends were gone.

They took our neighbor too, who turned out to be a short, fat man in a frayed gray robe. He waved lumpy arms at us, his giggles filling the air like bubbles. "The beasts soon feast!" His high-pitched voice cut into my ears.

"Feast on this." Charlie kicked at Hypnos as we turned another corner, but the old man jumped to the side and Charlie kicked the soldier instead, receiving a hard *whomp* to the head for it. With each step, I grew farther and farther from Leandro and Apollo. We'd met up again only to be separated, and Charlie and I were now on our own. No weapons. No orb. No one to watch over us.

The guards' swords clattered on the walls as we climbed the steps out of the dungeon. The torches crackled from the wind racing through the stairway, and the soldier's vapes hissed back. Out of the corner of my eye, a vape's snake tongue waved near my head. I leaned back, but the soldier's calloused hands choked my wrist, pulling me tight to him as we mounted the stairs. Rough rock scraped my side, ripping across my skin.

"Time to hit the showers, you ignorant Barbaros," my guard grumbled and pushed me along. "You're stinking up the castle!"

Charlie and I soon found ourselves separated, shoved down different corridors. Fear that I'd never see him again zipped through me. His eyes reflected the same thought as he turned the corner. I was pitched headfirst into a cell where I waited until a servant arrived to spray me with water from a thick hose while another cranked a rusty wheel on a wall to pump it in. I sucked in water by surprise, but the cold liquid tasted good and soothed my dry throat. The soldier on guard laughed at me as I was led into another room with a giant rusty fan. A servant pumped a pedal attached to it, and it blew me dry within minutes.

After what seemed like the longest hour of my life, Charlie and I were thrown back together in a corridor. Shivering, we cast grateful glances at one another as we trod in front of our guards. The scent of roasting meat and fresh baked bread clung to the air, stirring my stomach juices like crazy. The clanging of pots mixed with voices. Wood smoke wafted by as we passed a kitchen. The servants stopped their duties, hands in midair, to stare as we were forced along the hall.

"Hurry Reekers, the queen awaits in her personal throne room." My guard gave me a good shake.

Light and shadows crept up the forbidding walls that stretched taller with each step. The echoes of our feet on the hard slab crowded around us until we reached the queen's royal room. Over the doorway, an archer on her horse raced along with the words: *Hunt well or die. Mercy breeds weakness. We live on through wretched flesh. Immortality shall be ours again!*

The soldiers shoved us into a brightly lit room. A tiered chandelier dripped with wax from dozens of lit candles. More candles lined steps, a yawning fireplace, and windowsills. I squinted from the light that burned in blazing streaks and wondered how the heck we were going to get out of this mess.

Chapter Ten

Queen Artemis sat at the end of the room on a massive bronze throne that shimmered in the fire's flickering flames. Colorful tapestries filled with bloody scenes of hunters riding horses through a forest hung from the walls. They chased monstrous beasts—and those beasts chased kids as bait. Sheer terror was painted on the kids' faces as curved teeth snapped at their feet.

I shivered even as sweat broke across my upper lip. Artemis tapped her fingers on the throne and waved us forward. Flames burst across her black sunglasses, her eyes spears of fire. Charlie and I were shoved toward her. Hypnos hung back on the arm of his soldier, humming to himself.

"I've been waiting for you." She pointed at me. A whack from behind forced me on my knees. Charlie fell beside me, breathing heavily.

"Why?" I asked.

A boot to my back knocked my face onto the floor.

"For the love of Olympus, don't question the queen, Reeker fool," a rough voice snarled.

Charlie reached for me, but a swift kick sent him sprawling too. I rubbed my face and sat back on my knees again. The fire's flames crackled and spit at me.

Artemis laughed along with it. "You're going to give me the world, that's why, Oracle."

I kept my mouth shut, not wanting another boot to my back. Hypnos hummed louder. It filled my head with an aching buzz.

Charlie and I found ourselves hauled up, our sleeves pushed aside, and our forearms stamped with the mark of the Arrow Realm slave brand. I tried to wrench away, but the soldier gripped me harder, pressing the stamp deeper into my arm and hissed in my ear. "Do you want a fire brand instead, Reeker?"

I shook my head and let him do his dirty work, becoming a slave on Nostos for the second time. I traced my new mark. A black arrow. It flared across my skin, encircled by a ring of fire. Around the ring read the words: *No escape. Your armor of flesh and bone fuels us on!*

Artemis stood, turning her bracelet back and forth. The light glimmered across her purple velvet tunic and sparkled in her gnarly crown. Her face looked young, but up close, she could be old enough to be my mother. It struck me that her mother had been queen when my mother was imprisoned here, and now I was this queen's prisoner.

"That Wild Child betrayed me like Leandro." She pointed at me. "What do you think should happen to her?"

"Leave her alone," I said.

Artemis smiled with her thin lips. "Don't worry; I

swear by the gods she won't be harmed. I have a special place in my heart for the Wild Childs, like Leandro. You see, the dead father of my daughter was one. Leandro, on the other hand …" She spread her hands out and cocked her head.

"Don't hurt him! He's my … my—" I squeezed my hands to my thighs.

"He's what? Your friend? Your leader?" Her eyes blazed. Charlie glanced at me, chewing on a finger. "Or something else."

"He's my friend. He wants to help your world—my world. Can't you see that?"

Artemis motioned to a soldier, who dragged me and Charlie closer to her.

"I see many things, Joshua." My name on her lips sent a quiver across my chest as she circled me. "Now Hypnos will see into you and you shall give me the world. Come, Hypnos! It's time to do your duty or your people will pay."

Hypnos stopped humming and edged along the wall toward us, pulling on his tufts of hair as his nails *click-clicked* across the rough stone. Charlie pushed up against me as the soldiers crowded us in, their breaths hot on my neck with vapes poised to zap us into ash. The fire's smoke stung my eyes. I grew woozy as the shadows crept taller around me, wanting to suck me up in darkness.

"I don't have anything to give you," I mumbled, trying not to faint. Charlie clamped a hand on my arm as I swayed. I closed my eyes, and when I opened them, Hypnos stood before me with his head bowed and his hands clasped over his big belly.

"You have it all, Reeker boy," Artemis said. Her purple outfit floated before me between the flames. I tried to focus but her fire eyes burned into mine, erasing everything around me. I shut my eyes again to make her go away. Charlie shook me, but it made the dizziness worse.

"What are you doing to him?" Charlie's fingers pressed tight around my arm, then he was pulled away and rough hands held my arms at my side. "Leave him alone. He's been through enough!"

Charlie's shouts faded as words flew like arrows through my head. *Release your powers to the queen. Give them to her or die. Your companions die. Your grandfather dies. Your father dies. Artemis sees all. Now so do I. This will come to pass. Command your powers!*

My father? How could he know my father and grandfather? Uncertainty swam through me in my frozen state. Hands gripped my shoulders, and I opened my eyes to the chubby face of Hypnos. His musty breath curled up my nose.

"You are the Oracle," Artemis said, her voice rising. "The Black Hearted one has prophesied it."

Leandro! Apollo! Where are you? I needed friends who understood this Oracle business.

"Listen to my slave here, Oracle." Her voice flowed over me like warm honey, soft and soothing. I stopped shivering and the hands on me relaxed. "Obey his request. Show your powers and release them to me. You can go back to your little life on Earth with your friends and family. Don't you want that, boy?"

Yes. So tired of fighting these prophecies. So easy to give in.

"No, don't do it, Joshua!" Charlie's words jerked me up. "She'll kill you when she's done. We stick together, *mon ami*!"

"Quiet, Reeker fool," Artemis said and joined Hypnos's side, her sunglasses sucking me in to their black holes.

"Only you carry the powers of the ancient Olympians inside you. Only you can relinquish them to their heirs. Except you'll be handing them over to one heir: me."

Hypnos touched his forehead to mine, once again speaking the queen's ordered words: *You possess the ancient powers. Turn away from them. They are not for you to keep. You are but a vessel. Be honorable. Be wise in your sacrifice. Artemis can rule her people, our world. And you shall have all you desire.*

But I don't know what I want—or who I am.

Give up your free will, and all you care for shall live.

The eyes of Hypnos drilled into mine as his nails dug into me tighter.

What would Bo Chez do? Not give up. Not give in. Nor would Charlie.

Neither would I.

My head cleared. The words faded away. My toes crunched together tight, and my body tensed with new energy.

"No," I said.

The fire's spewing flames died down, and the breath of everyone around me beat like a slow drum roll. Wax from the chandelier dripped onto the flagstones in a steady *tap-tap-tap*. Metal clashed somewhere in the castle as if battling swords cheered me to victory.

Hypnos released my shoulders and smiled before shuffling back to the wall. "He cannot be taken by my powers, m'lady. He is immune."

Charlie moaned, and the soldier behind me snorted. Artemis moved toward me with her hands behind her back and pleated brows.

"Fine. We'll find another way," she said with a smile that filled me with more dread than any frown.

Chapter Eleven

"Come eat, both of you." Artemis gestured to a table along the wall. Servants brought in platters of steaming meat and fresh baked bread. Charlie and I looked at each other.

"It's not poisonous, see?" She sat down at the table, filled a plate with food, and began to eat.

Eat. You want to eat, my friends. So tasty and good for you.

The words filled my head as Hypnos stared at me.

You need to eat to stay alive.

Those final words were a whisper in my head. Imagined? Hypnos shook his head, his eyes piercing mine.

Stay alive.

My eyes were pulled toward the table mounded with food. Charlie lunged forward and fell into the dishes, slopping it up with two hands. I remained still, but my stomach hurt so badly with hunger, it didn't take much for me to give in.

"Sit!" With the queen's command, I sat and stuffed my face. Enemy food or not, it might be the only meal we'd get for a long time. The bread was crusty and buttery. The cheese, rich and salty. I'd tasted the delicious agrius beast before in the Lost Realm. I filled my stomach until it ached, washing it all down with cool water from a jug. So did Charlie.

Artemis smiled. In my delirious state, I found myself smiling back until Charlie and I were pulled up and led over to a bed in the shadows.

"Rest here, my young tasties."

I fell on plump pillows next to Charlie, thinking how strange her name for us was before sleep whisked me away on my first full night in the Arrow Realm.

We feasted again our second day. Charlie and I stumbled from the bed to the table and back to doze after we filled ourselves with delicious treats. Sweet apple pies with flaky crusts. Biscuits dripping with butter. Mashed potatoes and rich gravy. And my favorite, oh-so-good agrius beast.

At each meal, Artemis nibbled and smiled at us while Hypnos twitched along the wall, watching us with hungry eyes. Grease dripped down Charlie's chin, his eyes wild like a mad man's. I wondered why Artemis hardly touched anything on her plate and why she never invited Hypnos to eat with us. A creepy feeling filled me.

Artemis watched us.

Hmm … so delicious. Fill your youthful bellies. Young boys need their energy, and you'll be running around again soon. Trust me. So eat. Eat!

"You like agrius beast?" Artemis asked, leaning in with a smile, her sunglasses like hovering black orbs. I nodded, my stomach full, bursting at my pants. "Good.

I think they'll like you too."

I pushed my chair back and stood up, shaking off my food coma and the soothing words inside my head. "What's that mean?" I pulled Charlie off his chair as he continued to gnaw on a meaty bone.

"I hope you enjoyed your last meal, Reekers."

Hypnos shrank back against the wall, easing toward the door, but squealed when a guard blocked his path. Artemis kept smiling as Charlie and I fumbled backward. I ripped the bone he still ate from his hand and threw it on the table.

"*Attendez*! Why'd you do that?" he cried, reaching for more food but I shoved him back.

"Hypnos, take them to the pit." Artemis stood and swept her hand at us. The fire shrieked. A cinder shot out. Hypnos beat his fists on the wall, shaking his head. "Now, Hypnos! You need reminding of how your people will suffer if you do not obey me."

I clung to Charlie in my wooziness as Artemis tilted in my vision. The guards pulled us out the door, led by a whimpering Hypnos. My vision cleared, and I struggled but was no match for the stocky soldiers. Charlie kept begging for food.

"Your soul may not be taken here, but there is no immunity in the Wild Lands even if you survive. You are no match now for the beasts and Black Hearted one," Artemis said.

"Why?" I rasped out, scraping my feet on the floor as the soldiers pulled us away.

"Because you've been fattened up for the hunt."

Her words and smile froze my gut as we left behind the throne room.

There'd be more than death handed to us—there'd also be pain.

We were pushed and shoved down winding hallways. The digging grip of my captor tightened as I fought against him, the forbidding *thunk* of his boots leading me toward my end. Monster shadows from the quaking torches clawed at us from glistening rock walls. Disoriented by the dark and unsure of my footing, I staggered along

"Let us go!" I yelled in a hoarse voice but the soldiers merely grunted as Hypnos led the way. He turned back once to eye me, then hunched over and shuffled faster. Charlie lurched along beside me spitting out French curses in between sniffs.

Sobs and cries for help jolted me as eyes popped out from behind barred cell windows. Dirty fingers clutched at us as we passed. "I want my mom!" "Let me out, please!" "I wanna go home." Others spoke in strange languages but their fear was the same.

I wanted to wrench open each door and set them free, but I was a prisoner like them. The cries haunted me as we were pushed farther along after Hypnos.

Down another hallway, we were jerked to a stop and tossed onto chipped stone. A creak. A clang. The door to our new cell bolted us in. One torch lit our prison. My eyes adjusted to the gloom and rough rock that made up our tiny room.

"Charlie, you okay?"

He rubbed his leg where he'd slammed into the stone floor and wiped his face. "*Oui*," he mumbled, picking up a chipped piece of stone. He fingered it, then used it to scratch *Charlie was here* on the wall. He handed the rock to me and without hesitating, I scratched *Joshua was here* under it. His nostrils flared as we probably shared the same thought: no one would find our message this time. No one would find us.

"Thanks for not letting me give in to Artemis," I said.

"Thank me later when we're back in your kitchen eating pancakes—*real* pancakes."

"I wouldn't have given her my powers ... even if I had them ... or if I knew how."

"I knew that. But I also think ... you're this Oracle they keep calling you."

I touched the words on the wall, my fingers smudging the dust. "The only thing I know right now is that I'm full."

"*Mon Dieu*! Me too." Charlie pulled on his bangs. "Some spell drove me to eat and eat. At least I'm not hungry anymore."

"Neither will the beasts be when they're done with the food of ye." A window to our door slid open and Hypnos peered in.

I ran over. "Are they auctioning us off?"

"You are to enter the Wild Lands zone. Make haste with your heart and bone," Hypnos said, his eyes growing bigger. "The great beasts will chase you to the Black Heart Tree ground."

"What happens there?" I said.

"You will be bewitched, and your powers got. I hopefully pray not. You resisted my mind meld. Great strength you carry and wield."

"*Zut*!" Charlie put his hands to his head. "Stop talking like that!"

"Why are you trying to hurt us?" I clenched the bars on the window, staring into the chubby man's face.

Hypnos shook his head and pulled on his bits of hair. "Not me. If I obey not. She kill my family. Shot. Shot. Shot! Like you killed hers."

"I never killed her family!"

He opened the door and threw Leandro's bow and

a sheath of arrows at me. Charlie rushed the door but it slammed shut.

The whimpers of the other prisoners faded, their hope of rescue gone. Hope and loss tugged at me in a painful mix as I held the one thing of Leandro's that renewed my faith in getting out of here and getting home. "How did you—"

"Mindbend a guard. Not so hard." Hypnos grinned, his cheeks bursting like a chipmunk's stuffed with nuts. "He hid them for me here, oh great seer."

I had no idea what a seer was, but it was soon forgotten when he pushed his fat face up against the window's bars, reached in his arms, and pinched my hands in a knotted hold, his moldy breath heavy on my face. I tried to pull away but he grasped me tight and whispered, "To the Wild Childs you must get. And you'll be set. Past the Grand Tree they're found. First, you must pass through terrifying ground. Watch out for the Black Hearted one. If not, you'll be done."

Metal jarred against our rock cage and wind rushed in the room, driving the smell of wet earth with it. Hypnos pushed me away and stepped back.

"Joshua, there's a new doorway!" Charlie tugged at my sleeve. I jerked around. An opening in the rock now faced us. In the dim light, a tunnel stretched beyond it.

I twisted back to the cell bars. "Help us, Hypnos!"

"So sorry am I. Goodbye!" His face disappeared.

"Wait! Tell us what to do!" I begged him to come back.

His terror-stricken face popped into view again. He pulled on his cheeks with fat fingers, sucking them in with great gasps. "Dang and blast! Run. Run very fast!"

Then he disappeared. And I knew.

This pit was no auction to be sold as bait. This was the food pit and Charlie and I were dinner.

Chapter Twelve

The opening led out of our room. A way out and a trap at the same time.

A howl zipped through the tunnel on the wind, mournful and needy. A beastly rumble answered back. We had no choice but to face our stalkers.

"Come on!" I ran into the ragged hole as I swung the bow over my shoulders and snapped the quiver onto my belt loop. Charlie didn't follow. He stood in our cell, the torchlight blowing smoke across his thin face. He stared at me with wide eyes. "Charlie!"

"*Non.* If we don't go out there, they can't get us."

"They'll come in here and get us. There's nowhere to go in here!"

He shook his head. "Men with swords are bad enough but to get eaten? Ugh."

"Out there we can fight," I pleaded with him, drawing an arrow out. "We can figure a way out, for Apollo and us. Climb trees to safety. Something! Don't you get it?"

"And Leandro?"

"Yeah." I hadn't wanted to think about him being imprisoned too. I wanted to think of him busting his way out and finding us.

Charlie still didn't move.

"Artemis tried to hypnotize me and get whatever powers I have, but she couldn't! That's a good sign, right?"

"But she took your orb."

"Maybe I don't need it." I dared it to be true. "Maybe I am what they say."

His eyes grew wider. "But we're bait out there."

"We're meat in here. Bait has a chance."

He blinked and nodded. Then we were running together through the dark tunnel with urgent gusts pushing us along. We ran in darkness, our racing breaths and footsteps striking the air in tune with the whistling wind. We soon burst out of the passage and stopped fast. Leaves flapped down and blew through an army of giant trunks spattered with moonlight.

"What is this place?" Charlie whispered. I didn't answer back.

We'd entered the Wild Lands.

The damp castle dungeon was a comfort. Out here, the wind clawed at me as howls and shrieks stabbed the air. A giant thorny hedge thrust up from the ground as tall as the castle. It grew around the tunnel we'd escaped and raced along either side of us, obscuring the castle and all beyond it.

Whatever stalked us in here was trapped. Like us.

We huddled by the hedge as I readied my bow—Leandro's bow—with shaky hands and set an arrow in place.

"Hypnos said if we get to the Wild Childs, we're set," I whispered.

"How?"

I tried to forget Hypnos's other words. First, we must pass through terrifying ground. "We have to find this Grand Tree. Hypnos said the Wild Childs are near it."

A growl clobbered the air, and Charlie jumped around with me. Thunder clapped and lightning flashed. Dark shapes moved in the shadows. The trees trembled, shaking off their leaves, and twigs were tossed up in mini tornadoes.

"Dang and blast! Run fast!" I echoed Hypnos's words.

We ran low to the ground, dodging gnarly trees. Squirrel creatures scurried along branches, flying from tree to tree as if following us along—or leading a hungry hoard to dinner.

Snarls cut through the wind and we ran faster. On and on the woods stretched. Thorns ripped my clothes and skin. I held Leandro's bow tight, ready to aim and shoot at anything that came at me—being or beast. Branches snapped beneath our feet as we flew over rocks and roots.

White jags of lightning shot the earth, and the sky cracked open like a great ax to a door. A flash dazzled me, branding the inside of my eyelids. Charlie yanked my shirt and we both fell down. Flames shot up where lightning struck, and the screams of a wild animal in pain filled the air. In the soaring flames, a hairy beast slammed to the ground with a great cry. Hulking shapes crept out of the shadows and pounced on the dead creature, ripping and chewing.

Charlie and I kept running. My legs ached as I pumped them.

"There they are!" Artemis's voice rang through the woods. "*El-el-eu!* Victor I am!"

Hairy beasts loped after us and men tore up on horseback behind them. An arrow whizzed past my ear. I dared a look behind me. Lightning lit up the man who'd fired the arrow. He led the charge, riding his horse hell bent around the trees, moving in and out like a dark ghost. A hood covered the top half of his face. He nocked another arrow at me and threw back his hood.

It was Leandro! He'd found us all right. His scowl stung me with fury.

"Joshua, use your powers!" Charlie yelled in between breaths.

If I had powers, how to command them? How could I hurt Leandro with them? It didn't seem like he was playing a trick to save me this time. The hate on his face was real.

Leandro wanted me dead. Why?

As if I wished it, lightning struck, torching the beasts behind us. The horses behind them screeched, throwing their riders in the air.

"Get up!" Artemis stomped her horse around the tangled mess of soldiers. "Round up more beasts and drive the Reekers to the Black Heart Tree!"

Rain streamed down and the wind whipped at me, driving the stinging pellets. Charlie and I ran on, leaving our enemy behind in this terrifying game. We held each other up as we staggered through the storm.

"Joshua, stop! Can't. Go. On." Charlie gasped out the words as he dragged me back.

I tugged his shirt, ripping it. "We've got to!"

Oh, where was this Grand Tree and could these Wild Childs even help us?

When my lungs threatened to explode, a howl behind us pushed my aching legs to full throttle. Claws swiped at us and a blast of rotten meat stench hit me. Anger at this world choked me into a fury. For sucking me up into its danger and death again. For turning my friend against me. For having to run for my life again. For wanting me to be their hero.

I skidded to a stop, riding wet leaves. Charlie's eyes blinked with surprise as I shoved him aside and turned to face the unleashed creature. It flew over my head—an exploding mountain of fur and legs and tail—and slammed onto the ground. It turned to face me, panting. Pacing back and forth, its massive paws glinted with curved nails as it smashed the mud. Steam bellowed from its giant nostrils and horns protruded from a head covered in a shaggy brown mane. Tinted burnt orange, the beast raged part lion, part bull. I backed away from the monster, hauling Charlie with me.

"What now?" Charlie stuttered.

I carefully nocked an arrow to my bow, keeping my eyes on the beast as it snorted and pawed the ground, spewing up clomps of dirt. The rain spiked harder.

"Let us go," I said.

The beast churned up the ground and shook its giant mane, groaning low in its throat. "Hungrrrry." I must've imagined him speaking. Without my lightning orb, I didn't have powers to understand animals on Nostos.

Charlie pulled me back. "What did it say?"

"I don't know," I said.

"Well, I think it said 'time to eat.' "

He had no idea how right he was.

With each step the beast inched toward us, we took one back. I pulled back my arrow, the tension scorching my arm. The lion-bull shuddered; loose skin flapping against its gigantic, bony frame. Its swollen tongue hung from its mouth, and its ribs outlined sharp against its skin with each desperate pant. Red-rimmed eyes burned into mine.

"It's starving, Charlie," I whispered.

"And we're dinner!"

"Artemis starves them, fattens them up with us, and hunts them for food! Don't you get it?"

The beast snorted and rolled its head. "Fooood. Hungrrrry."

Its words filled my ears clearly now, not imagined. Stunned, I recovered, lowering my bow. "Come with us," I said to the creature. "We'll find you food. We'll find freedom."

The beast moaned with a great shake of its head, ragged teeth dripping with saliva. It *whomped* its tail, panting faster. "Cretans never be freeee."

"You're making it madder," Charlie whispered. "Let's run."

"We'll never make it," I whispered in return.

The beast matched our steps as we inched back. Rain dripped from every part of me. I wiped it from my eyes and Charlie tore away from me.

"Charlie, no!"

The beast roared and leaped high. "Fooood!"

I lurched around. Charlie ran fast but didn't have a chance. He twisted his head back, his eyes headlights in the dark. The beast catapulted over me, and in that split second, I shot my arrow into its chest.

With a shriek, the monster thundered to the ground. I tumbled away before getting crushed.

The rain pounded down without mercy. Blood ran

fast from the beast. It wailed in pain and chuffed softly, paws twitching. "Cretan ... freeee."

Its chest heaved in and out, then stopped. I bent down and pulled the arrow from its rough bloodied fur, my tears mixing with the rain. Its face sagged in its stillness. Charlie stood next me once again.

"You were a prisoner like us," I said, stroking the fur. "I didn't want to hurt you ... cretan."

Charlie touched my shoulder. "You understood it even without the orb."

I didn't answer but wiped the bloody arrow on the ground, and slid it back in my quiver.

Charlie cleared his throat. "Sorry I ran off. I thought we were dead. But you saved us. I didn't think we'd survive." He wouldn't look at me. He hadn't trusted me.

Shouts in the distance alerted us to Artemis and her men heading our way again.

Charlie and I ran on through the woods. I glanced back once at the dead creature. What new terrible deed would I have to commit?

Chapter Thirteen

Cramps bit into my lungs and legs from running, but there was no time for ache cakes to help the pain. Fear wouldn't keep us going much longer. We needed to rest.

The rain let up and shouts grew closer. I tugged Charlie's arm. "Can you climb?"

He nodded at me with wild eyes and, with a final surge of adrenaline, we pulled ourselves up to hide amongst the leaves. Rough bark, slick with the slowing rain, cut into my palms. Blood welled but I didn't stop climbing. Getting eaten would be way worse.

We moved higher, camouflaged by leaves. The rain finally stopped, and the purple night hung like a tent over the treetops. A stampede of hooves barreled below. Charlie and I froze. Leandro led Artemis's soldiers. His long hair streamed like dark flames behind him.

I'd have followed him anywhere once—died for him.

Not now. I raised my bow fashioned by his hands.

Leandro passed so close I saw the scar that cut down his face given to him by a Child Collector—when he was a hero, not a villain. Why did Leandro have Ash bring us here? Was his getting "thrown" in the pit with us a lie?

"The first man that gets the Reekers gets a month's supply of agrius beast for dinner!" he called out with a fist in the air.

The army cheered as they raced behind him, mud flying up in big clops.

Artemis followed up the charge. Her purple hooded cloak sparkled like rich wine. She trotted under our tree as Charlie's foot slipped on the trunk he sat on. A branch snapped and fell. And another. They landed in pieces on the ground, arranging themselves in letters. Not letters but words! GET … TO … TOP … . I blinked but the words remained. Another branch fell on Artemis's saddle and she pulled her horse to a stop, grasping a falling twig shaped like the letter J. For Joshua? My brain squeezed in and out trying to understand this mystery.

Artemis turned the twig in her hand as her horse nickered, trampling the words formed on the forest floor. They were soon erased. Artemis looked up, her hood falling back. My heart fluttered with her stare, begging for the leaves to hide us. She tossed the twig away, kicked her heels into her horse, and sped off after her army. They were soon gone but Charlie and I sat for a long while to be sure they weren't coming back. The J still called to me from below, a mystic symbol of hope.

Signs.

Like the signs I'd drawn in the Lost Realm with the hope someone would follow our trail. Now we had signs to follow. Someone—or something—was trying to help us.

Branches cracked below, and a head peeked out from between the trees. I let go of my branch in surprise and nearly fell.

"She's gone," the face said.

"Ash?" I whispered, looking closer.

"Why are you here?" Charlie said, shaking his branch.

She shook her head and whistled low, waving at us to come down. Charlie shook his head back.

"We need a friend," I said to Charlie.

He grunted. "You need help picking friends, Joshua."

"I picked you."

He grunted again, and we climbed down to face the girl who'd forced us to the Arrow Realm.

With her animal skin clothes, she fit in here much better than my kitchen. Her earthy smell sprung up and blended with the woods. Her pale face stood out against the dim shadows. She now wore a bow clasped to her back and a quiver of arrows across her chest.

Ash pressed her thin fingers into mine, her bright green eyes darting around, and pointed up. "Got to scram to the tree house."

"Your camp?"

She nodded fast, jerking me to come.

Charlie crinkled his eyes. "Lions can't climb, right?"

I shrugged and followed her around a boulder, coming face to face with a giant black beast bearing a bear's body and a wolf's snout. Charlie and I scrambled backward. The beast hung its head and she pet it. "My Agri." She climbed up the rock and vaulted onto its back, urging us to do the same.

"*Mon Dieu*! An agrius beast for a pet?" Charlie said with a groan. "Why not a nice pony?"

"Better than being eaten by that lion-bull beast," I

said, pulling myself up on the rock.

"You met a cretan?" Ash said, whipping her head around.

I nodded.

"Not many survive those. You're either very lucky or very smart."

"This whole place is unlucky," Charlie said.

"Maybe you carry more than luck," Ash said.

"Maybe," Charlie said squinting at me.

Luck seemed to be all we carried for the moment. I jumped on the back of the creature behind Ash, sinking into its thick fur. She urged Charlie on who stood frozen, mesmerized by the beast's boulder-sized, shaggy head. Its pointed ears and snout twitched as it trembled, eager to be on the run.

"Come on, Charlie! The army might come back."

That did it. He scrambled up the rock and jumped. I grabbed him as he slid sideways and, with a leap, the agrius beast sprung away. Raindrops doused us from trees as their leaves shook in the wind.

"It's like the forest in France behind my home," Charlie said. "Well, what used to be home ... where my mother and brother live."

"I'd like to see it someday when we get back."

"If we get back—"

"We will," I said, wanting to believe. "We did before."

"I miss walking my brother to school. I even miss reading him the same dumb stories over and over." He looked at the forest floor leaping below us. "If I don't get back, he'll think I've left him again. I think it's one of the reasons my mom sent me to America with my dad."

"What do you mean?"

"As punishment. They didn't trust me to watch my

brother. Last time I watched him, I disappeared ... with you."

"You never told them what happened?"

Charlie laughed with a gulp. "How could I have explained that?"

I had no answer. He was right. Bo Chez was part of this world and we had both experienced our last adventure. Charlie had been alone with no family in it.

"Even if I do get home, it doesn't matter," he said. "I don't have a home."

"You do with your dad and it'll feel like home soon." I'd spent enough time in new homes to recognize the lie but it sounded good.

"Not like you and Bo Chez. You're like ... a forever kind of family. Nothing can split you up."

Doubt spun through me with his words.

"It's like you're my brother now." I didn't know what to say so I remained quiet. So did Ash, who'd been silent as we rode along.

"Where's the Grand Tree?" I said to her, hoping we were close.

"On the move," Ash said. "Leandro says it travels from realm to realm and takes root where it's needed most to help those in peril. It's fought many battles and its scars tell those stories. Leandro calls it a lighthouse of hope in the darkness of this world. The Grand Tree claims its home here—a symbol of righteousness. We claim it as our great protector. It's part of the reason Artemis leaves us alone. Long ago, another Queen Artemis fought and lost against it—with her life."

It was the longest speech she'd given since we met her, but I didn't have the energy to respond to her story or tell her the Leandro we knew was gone. Exhaustion engulfed me, but a screech of some strange bird kept snapping me to attention. Finally, the agrius beast slowed, its paws padding the forest floor with a soft *thoomp thoomp* rhythm. Just as I wondered where we were going, the beast lumbered through a bush. Branches whacked us on all sides.

"*Zut!*" Charlie muttered, swinging his long arms at the bush.

"*Zut* to you, boy," the agrius beast muttered and I choked down a laugh.

We followed Ash up a tree with only the moonlight as a guide, leaving the ground and beast behind. A platform loomed above us. A tree house.

Was anywhere safe here? Hypnos said we'd be set with the Wild Childs.

Could we trust him—or Ash?

My trust was running on empty.

Chapter Fourteen

We climbed through a hatch door into the tree house that Ash had said was their base camp. I crashed on the floor, every limb aching—and my heart, now that Leandro was our enemy. Ash found a clear tube on a shelf and broke it in two. Little bugs ran around the inside, keeping it lit. Nature's glow stick.

"How can you help us rescue Apollo and get home?" I said while Ash peered out the one window.

"*Oui*," Charlie said with a tired sigh. "You drag us here to free Apollo and served us up to some guard dog and now bring us here."

"And now Leandro's turned against us," I added.

"I know," Ash said flatly. "We see much from up here."

She pulled a book from a hidden cabinet. "But we also don't believe all we see."

"Thanks for saving us but we need a plan, not a

book," I said.

"A plan is right," Charlie said, popping a finger to his cheek.

"This may help," she said, urging me to take the small but heavy book covered in worn leather. "He gave it to me for you."

Light shone across it from the glow stick. Leandro's journal. I'd once sneaked it out of his bag in the Lost Realm. I didn't get far reading it before he caught me.

Ash placed a hand on my arm. "Take knowledge to face adversity. Find courage to go where you dare not go. If not, the pain of where you stay will far outweigh the pain of the unknown."

"What kind of words are those?" Charlie said, peering at the book.

"The lionheart once told me them," Ash said. "I'll never forget it."

"Lionheart?" I fingered the smooth cover.

"Leandro."

It did fit him. The old him.

I opened the journal to the first entry I'd read in the Lost Realm.

History of Our People
By Leandro of the Arrow Realm,
as told to me by my father,
Mortimer the Steel Twister

Long ago, the Greek gods fell from power. They were real and mighty until the rise of other people questioned their rule—the Romans and then the Christians. And so, Zeus, the king of the gods, commanded his family to leave Mount Olympus and conquer a new world before their powers drained completely. They called our new world Nostos and took over rule of the primitive folk that dwelled here. On Nostos, the twelve Olympians would each rule a land with Zeus leading as their great king. Zeus ensured they would have a way to plunder Earth for their own use. With his dying thunderbolt, he created a Lightning Gate for each realm and a Lightning Road to connect our new world to Earth. And so, the Greek gods left their home, never to return or be immortal again. Or so we thought.

The Greek god's super powers faded forever. Over the years, the powerless heirs of the twelve Olympians squabbled while the lesser Greek gods blended in with the conquered people. All became lost in our new culture on Nostos. A select few of mixed blood held ancient powers and immortality and were forced to serve the heirs in any capacity. Many of these few came to hide their powers to remain free from enslavement. Chaos soon reigned across Nostos. Our land was plunged into the darkest of ages, leaving thousands starving and dead. The Olympian heirs believed their time had come to an end when one discovered that mortal children of Earth possessed powers to fuel their world. And so began the stealing of children. In time, a deep hatred of these mortals grew inside the Olympian heirs, for these Earth beings held power they needed to survive.

The Ancient Ones foresaw what would become of the Olympians. Angered by the corruption their people would embrace, the Ancient Ones prophesied that an Oracle would arise to save their world. Today, the Secret Order of the Ancient Ones hides on Nostos, watching and waiting for the Oracle to come forth and redeem their people. They will protect him at any cost, if an immortal Ancient Evil One does not kill him first.

Each Oracle will have the ability to restore full powers to the heirs of the once-great Olympians if they prove themselves worthy. Once restored, then so shall the Lightning Road to Earth be broken forever … if the Oracle survives.

I slammed the book shut, dust flying, twisting with emotion about being the Oracle—and not surviving. About Leandro being a real traitor this time and wishing my feelings for him would go away so my heart didn't hurt so bad.

"*Zut!* Why'd you do that?" Charlie asked, tugging the book from me but I held it shut. "What did it say?"

"It doesn't matter, Charlie."

Ash looked at me knowingly with her bright green eyes. How did she fit into all this?

"We came here to free Apollo," I told her. "Hypnos said we'd be set once we got here."

"*Oui*!" Charlie stood taller but bumped his head on the ceiling. "And while you're at it, Tree Girl, tell us how to blow up the Lightning Road for good so we can go home and never come back."

Ash took the book from me and opened it to a new page.

> The Oracle wins the fight alone, but he cannot succeed alone. He must seek out a candle in the dark to find the new road.

"What does that mean?" Charlie asked, reading over my shoulder.

"It means if we look for help, we'll find it, right, Ash?" I said.

"That's what Leandro told me."

My mind buzzed with this Oracle business. My life had changed with my first dangerous adventure in this world full of questions and no answers. I wasn't sure if I was ready to get answers now.

I flipped through the book some more with Charlie and stopped at one passage.

My Homeland
Journal Entry 25 on Nostos
By Leandro of the Arrow Realm

> I have returned to Artemis a pardoned man. It is a feeling of strange amazement. I handed King Apollo's letter to Queen

Artemis, requesting she place me in a higher leadership position than work camp guard, and she accepted me without hesitation. Maybe she admires those who evade her hunt, as I have evaded capture as a guard deserter. She may also have forgiven me for deserting her when we were younglings.

But she is compelled to punish me in some capacity for deserting, as a guard or a friend—perhaps both—I do not know. I am reduced to training her new work camp guards, barely out of baby breeches, and forced to share their eating and living quarters. I have faith I will gain her good graces soon. I must. Being back in the work camp brands me with the memories of my wife and son. I see them down every alleyway, hoping my son is growing well into his manhood somewhere on this world.

Meanwhile, I await my queen's orders to speak privately about a matter that the late King Apollo presented to me upon his deathbed: a new mission for the Arrow Realm to stop using mortal children as bait to hunt the great beasts. It will be hard to stand up to the laws of Zeus. We must face each realm's resistance one at a time.

Where does the boy fit into all this?

I must prevail on my queen's compassion now.

However, I find it wise to keep our
secret time spent together as youth to
myself.

I slid the slim book inside my deep coat pocket. It fit perfectly. It was Leandro who didn't fit anymore. He wanted me dead. My chest tightened with that painful fact.

"Leandro trusts you," Ash said. She placed a pale hand on my chest, her warmth pulsing into me. "You must trust you."

"I will," I said with more confidence than I felt. How could I trust myself if I couldn't trust the man who once sacrificed everything to save me?

"He believes you may be the one."

The one.

"Not anymore."

"Maybe. But whatever he is now, you can't change the truth of his old words."

A great weight bore down on me with the journal of my former friend pressing into my side—and the idea I was the key to saving Nostos.

Ash lifted a latch, stepping through a door out on the platform surrounding the little house.

We followed her into the wild beyond to find the help we desperately needed.

Maybe the answers would come.

Chapter Fifteen

We'd started climbing again, only to hear a sharp cry and a great crashing noise heading our way on the forest floor.

"A hunt is on," Ash whispered. "One for the many."

She jumped to another tree and scrambled past the platform and tree house.

"What are you doing?" I called, hanging on to the trunk next to Charlie who bounced on a limb.

She jumped farther down. "It's feeding time."

She disappeared through the leaves.

"*Mon Dieu*! I'm not getting eaten today!" Charlie said, hugging the tree.

"But someone else will." I jumped down to Ash's tree. "*Zut! Double zut!*"

The tree shook and he was right behind me. A hungry roar close by had me gripping the trunk, but adrenaline pushed me to tumble faster after Ash. She'd reached the bottom branch below us, a dozen feet from the ground, and nocked an arrow to her bow.

Bash. Bash.

The beast's howl grew closer. The oak and pine trees swayed, shaking their limbs as if wanting to help but not sure how.

The heavy crunching of wood and brush mixed with the light footfalls of a runner determined to make it. Through the shadows and shafts of moonlight, a slash of purple and gold flew in and out. A pale face painted with fright burst in a clearing. Apollo! He was running for his life.

A cretan burst over the bushes not far behind him. Its massive jaws with hungry teeth stretched wide open. I yanked at the closest vine and tugged hard. It stayed. "Charlie, hold on to this!" He wrapped it around a limb as I clambered down to Ash's branch, holding tight to the vine with my heart threatening to lunge through my chest.

Ash nodded next to me, aiming her arrow. "He'll have one chance to get it."

"And we'll have one chance to pull him up."

Apollo leaped over a bush, heading right for us. His eyes widened when he saw me. His steps faltered, and the beast almost caught him!

"Grab it, Apollo!" I swung the vine toward him. My foot slipped on the branch, and for one terror-filled second, I thought I'd land headfirst. If that didn't kill me, the beast would.

Apollo sucked in his cheeks and pumped his arms faster. With a final jump, he threw himself on the vine and started climbing. I strained with Charlie above, and we drew our friend up, my arms screaming with the effort. The cretan soared over the bush with a mighty roar. Ash's arrow flew, striking the beast in the chest. *Snap!* Its jaws missed Apollo by an inch, and the shrieking animal slammed onto the ground, writhing in agony as blood seeped through its yellow fur.

Then Apollo was on the branch beside us, clinging to me with great gasps.

Ash darted up, heading to the tree house again and we followed. I shook all over as fear rushed from my body and relief surged in its place. Apollo was alive.

With no energy to talk, we climbed above the tree house until Ash signaled us to stop. Grateful for a break, I clung to the tree and smiled at Apollo on the limb across from me, as Charlie braced himself on a branch below.

"Thank you," Apollo said, closing his eyes for a long moment.

Before I could find out how he got to the Wild Lands, Ash whistled long and low into the hollow of a tree trunk. A clunk made me jump as a wooden rope ladder was tossed down. Ash started up it with me fast after her.

"Where are we headed?" Charlie pulled me back down. "We don't know where she's taking us."

"Anywhere is better than the ground," I said, clinging to the ladder.

"She saved my life along with yours," Apollo said. "She's on our side. Although once her friends see my royal clothes, that may change."

Ash frowned at our gathering and urged us to keep moving. Charlie broke off a twig and started chewing on it. "*Oui*, but she's also got an agrius beast for a friend and left us with that evil hound. Let's make it across these trees on our own and get back to the Lightning Gate and go home. We've got Apollo now, which is why we came here in the first place. He can come home with us, right?" He looked at Apollo. "We could help you find your mother, King-man, like you wanted to before."

We'd been brought to rescue Apollo, but now things were much more complicated than the original mission. One thing remained steady: all the Arrow Realm slaves needed to be rescued like the ones we'd saved in the Lost Realm.

"We need to find help," I said, peering above, eager to get to Ash who called to us to scram and cram.

"Those were Leandro's old words," Charlie said.

"No matter what Leandro's become, his old words are to be trusted," Apollo said, echoing what Ash had told us earlier.

"People say a lot of things and then they change." Charlie chewed on his bottom lip, darting his eyes from me to Apollo.

"I haven't changed," I said. "And the trees have to be safer than the ground, right?"

"*D'accord*," Charlie said. He tossed his twig away, and I let him pull himself up on the rungs ahead of me.

As I climbed, the trees groaned and the night seemed to go on forever. My legs grew heavier with each step. The forest floor disappeared. We floated in a shadowy sea of wood on the longest ladder ever. Higher we went amongst these sky-highs when a faint whistle cut the quiet.

Hushed voices called down, but there was nothing above but a wave of leaves between splotches of purple sky. Big, dark squares littered my view above like rescue rafts on an ocean. Confused, I focused on Charlie to keep climbing higher. My hands grew slimy from grasping the moss-covered rungs, and my arms ached with pulling up my weight. The squares grew walls, and the walls became shacks with eyes peering out windows. More and more eyes lit up the tree branches, following our every step.

Then Charlie cried out. His feet disappeared in the canopy gloom.

Chapter Sixteen

I found myself snatched up through a wooden hole onto a platform after Charlie, Apollo following behind. Light spilled from a gourd lantern swinging from a beamed ceiling. We were in a giant log tree house and a serious group of kids encircled us. The room stretched as long as my house back home. Vines crawled through one window and out another. Trees exploded from the floor in several spots and thrust their deformed trunks through the ceiling, waving sawed-off limbs. Over the one door leading out, etched words read:

Wild Child Rules
1. Stick 'em before you get stuck
2. Keep on the runabout
3. Scram and cram
4. Don't get grounded
5. One for the many

Ash stepped forward, the oldest and tallest of the kids. "Is he awake?"

A girl my age shook her head with solemn eyes, but I didn't know or care who "he" was right now as my knee gave out from exhaustion. Ash steadied me but Charlie pulled me close. She raised her eyebrows and let go. A dozen rough knives of all shapes jabbed our way and my bow was ripped from me.

"He's a royal one!" a skinny kid with bad acne said, poking a fist in Apollo's face. "Let's stick him!" Others started jabbering too, some in a language I didn't understand.

Ash held up her hand. "No stick," she said, clearly in charge, and motioned the thief to hand my bow back. "He's a friend. They all are. Artemis threw this royal in the dungeon and fed him to the beasts. And we help the hunted, don't we?"

The knives fell but not the nasty stares aimed our way, making me want to jump back down the hole I'd been pulled from.

Ash pointed at me and spread her hands out to the kid army. "Leandro's Joshua."

They stepped back, as if my name carried meaning for them. Good or bad?

Ash ordered a group of kids to butcher the cretan below for mash.

Without speaking, they took sacks from hooks and disappeared through the hole we'd come from. Branches screeched across the side of the tree house and the floorboards creaked beneath us. My breath squeezed tight in my chest as I tried not to peer through the open hatch in the floor that dropped hundreds of feet below.

"I expected someone taller," a short kid said, looking at me.

"Us too," Charlie spouted back.

Knives shot up again, but Ash tipped her head back and laughed. "Is that so?" Her smile faded. "We have a gift for you."

The kids parted their circle, and at the end of the tree house, a dark figure tied to a trunk shooting up from the floor slumped in a chair, a cloth sack over his head. That cloak, that shape …

"Leandro!" I ran toward him then stopped in my tracks.

Ash thrust a hand to my chest, her eyes scrunched up. "We did as he asked and faked his kidnapping to bring him here so he could lead you out safely and raise an army against Artemis. But he's not the Leandro we know. He was our friend until today. It seems now he's joined forces with Artemis. We're all in trouble now. He fought us taking him and we knocked him out. This was *not* part of the original plan, or killing a soldier to do it." She paused, then said in a subdued tone, "We'll have to toss him back or we'll all be in trouble, even with the queen's soft spot for us."

Leandro twitched awake in his seat, garbled words bursting from under the sack. Charlie tightened his fingers on my arm.

Ash pulled off the head cover, and Leandro glared at us as he strained against the ropes tying him to the chair. "Let me go, you filthy Reekers! You ignorant Barbaros!"

He twisted about to get at her and she sucked in her breath.

"Go on and cry." Leandro laughed at her. "The queen plans to clean out these Wild Lands and all of you once she gets the Oracle and rules Nostos with lost Olympian powers."

A wave of scared chatter rose from the kids.

"Why'd you turn on us?" I asked Leandro, stepping closer to him. The noise died down.

"I came to my senses. You Reekers are doomed. I'm a fighter. I grew tired of fighting on the losing side."

"We're the winning side."

"You're nothing but ash in the air. We can be immortal. The queen has promised me." He shook in his chair, trying to bust free, and glowered at me.

"Don't you remember me and the Lost Realm—how we freed all the kid slaves? You. Me. Charlie. Apollo. Finn. Bo Chez. We took down Hekate and her brother, Cronag, the Child Collector! And—"

He shook his head. "It's history."

"It's *all* history and you wanted to change it. Don't you now?" I pulled out his journal. "This could help you remember."

He lurched to get at it but I stepped back.

"Hand it over! That Wild Child gave it to you. She stole it from me!"

I looked at Ash, who stood with her arms folded. "She said you gave it to her."

"You speak untruths, Reeker," Leandro said to her.

"So do you," Ash said.

"You'll all be dead. Very soon! The queen will see to it." I searched his face for any sign of my old friend inside this new enemy. There was none.

"Artemis may hunt us kids, but she lets the survivors live," Ash said. "She won't stick us even if we help these three escape. She'll get them either way, in the Wild Lands by hunt or in the WC by slave."

Leandro smirked at Ash. "Now you speak more untruths. You'll see soon enough."

Hoarse shouts traveled up through the trees. Artemis and her men were after us. Their calls grew faint as they moved off in another direction.

Any remaining good feelings for Leandro crawled from my heart and died in the pit of my stomach. He *had* turned on us. There was no need for him to pretend here. "Why'd you have Ash bring us here?"

"Because my queen asked me to. She wanted to hunt you down before she used you. And so did I."

"So you acted all nice and got Ash to bring us here to rescue Apollo?"

"A ruse, yes, Reeker. I even had the queen toss me in the dungeon with you to see if you could be hypnotized so she could gain your powers." Leandro tossed his long ropes of hair behind him. "I'll help the new Queen Artemis rule Nostos as her head soldier. We will have Olympian powers once more and lead our world into greatness again, ruling Earth as well!"

"You'll never rule Nostos *or* Earth," Apollo said fiercely, standing tall like the royal he was born to be. "Artemis may seem like a new queen, but something else is at force here. We will find out."

"Who are you to talk, King?" Leandro spat out. "You couldn't rule your own land, and even your family doesn't believe you're the rightful king. You probably killed your own father like they say. Ha!"

"You know it's a lie!" Apollo stepped toward Leandro with his hands fisted. "You were there when he died on the battlefield fighting Hekate." He spread a hand out toward Charlie and me. "We all were."

"Doesn't matter. No one has faith in you," Leandro said with a sneer.

Apollo inhaled deeply, turning his father's ring

around in Leandro's face. "My father did."

"You can't stop us." Leandro cocked his head. "My queen will get the Oracle's powers, one way or another—in life or death. You shall see."

Charlie punched at Leandro but I held him back. "What about finding your family?" I asked Leandro. "You're giving up on them too?"

He looked away. "They're dead. I'm loyal to Artemis now."

"Cram it," Ash stepped forward and drew her knife. "We must do something with you now."

"Don't hurt him," I pleaded.

Leandro nodded at me with a raised eyebrow, as if we were on the same team. "Listen to the boy if you want to live."

"You don't tell us what to do," Ash said in a calm voice. "Your people lost that right long ago. We live by our own rules now." She waved at the words over the doorway. "We thought you were our friend. Now you're nothing."

Leandro stomped his chair legs and the tree house floor shook.

I slid Leandro's journal back in my coat pocket. "Let him go, Ash. He can't help us anymore. We've got Apollo. We'll get him home and convince his people to fight Artemis and all of Nostos. We can find a way to free the kid slaves and shut down the Lightning Road."

"Like Leandro and I were to do … but failed," Apollo said with a pitiful look at Leandro then he leaned in to me and whispered, "maybe there's still a way to succeed. Poseidon was secretly in my court. If I bring him the Oracle, he'll listen. Maybe my people too."

"Meaning me," I could barely whisper back. He

nodded and I looked at the Wild Childs, who watched and waited. I'd come to save one but now must save them all. "One for the many," I finally said.

"One for the many," the Wild Childs thundered back.

Ash spoke up. "I'll release him, but he'll face the great beasts like all kids released in the Wild Lands. If he can survive and get over the border wall, he'll live. If not ... he'll be grounded, for flippin' good."

I didn't know how to prove I was the Oracle, but my destiny was knocking. It was time to open the door.

"It'll also buy us time to figure out a new plan for the three of you boys," Ash said. "You can't stay here."

We all agreed with that. Ash cut Leandro's ropes and pushed a knife against his throat. "Now climb down and head back to the evil you work for."

Leandro jerked his chin up. "You've all set your death sentence. And you'll be the first to die, Oracle." In a flash, he pulled the knife from his boot. Charlie pushed me out of the way as silver spun through the air toward my head before crashing into the wall.

"It's your turn to die today, traitor, and I'll stick you myself if I have to," Ash said in a steady voice, yanking Leandro from his chair and shoving him toward the trap door. "Now get down there!"

Leandro did as she said. He had no choice with every knife in the place pointed at him. Ash picked up Leandro's knife and handed it to me. "Yours now. Don't live by anyone else's rules."

The tree house closed in on me as I held the knife in my hand. The lines were drawn and Leandro had crossed them. Would he come back? Or were we sending him to his death?

I handed the tiny knife to Charlie. "Thanks for watching out for me."

He folded it shut and slid it into his pocket as Ash blindfolded Leandro again. "Good luck on a blind runabout," she said, tying his hands in front. "This is for trying that little knife stunt."

"He'll die out there if he can't see or use his hands," I said.

"Maybe. Maybe not. Fate will tell," Ash said. "He's a soldier and fit to survive on his wits and instincts. We gave him a second chance to live. Let's see how he uses it."

She was the toughest girl I'd ever met. Good thing she picked our side.

"I'll survive all right and hunt you down," Leandro said with a smile.

We all watched him feel his way as he climbed through the hatch door. He peered up one last time. His blindfold mocked us. "See you soon."

"Only in death," Ash said quietly.

Leandro's grin fell and then he disappeared through the hole. The kids rushed forward to watch him descend. Beasts bawled from somewhere in the forest—on the hunt.

I hoped it wouldn't be Leandro they caught.

Chapter Seventeen

After Leandro dropped away, the Wild Childs gathered up the bows and arrows hanging on the walls and sneaked through the tree house door and windows.

"One for the many," they each said with a nod to Ash as they left.

Ash directed us to leave with her when they were all gone, and we stepped outside onto the tree house platform. Purple night deepened and long shadows softened the craggy world. We stood on a plank road with a roped netting rail that zigzagged from house to house and floated under the forest's canopy in a sea of darkness. Green lights glowed softly through lopsided windows, and branch shadows wrapped the tiny shacks in prickly fingers. Leaves battered the houses in the sharp wind as the Wild Childs skulked amongst the trees.

Ash waited impatiently on the platform's edge as we got our bearings. "Follow me!"

And we did, the three of us hanging on to the railing the entire way, bouncing down the plank path. She set us up in a vacated tree house (I didn't ask why it was empty), and a Wild Child brought us a dinner of squirrel stew and ache cakes. "You all need sleep first," Ash said, throwing animal hides on wooden slatted cots. "Tomorrow, we'll get you to the Perimeter Lands."

"Thanks," I said. She nodded and left as the moonlight struck her in its crosshairs.

Too tired to talk, sleep claimed us quickly our second full night here. It seemed my head barely hit the floor when Ash lugged me up, a lantern shedding a dim green glow swinging from her hand.

"You've slept for hours. It's still dark out but sunrise comes soon," Ash whispered. "A good time to go runabout." She pulled an animal skin coat and pants from a chest and shoved it at Apollo. "Wear these. They may save your life."

Once his royal clothes were covered up, Apollo was a Wild Child. He'd lost his slumped dungeon pose and, along with the kingly jut of his chin, revealed he was much more than a fugitive of the woods. I hoped others wouldn't see the king inside that I did.

"I wish you could stay, but I have to protect the kids and the dark will provide cover."

A Wild Child walked past our house and peered in to make sure all was okay. Ash nodded and the kid moved along.

"Where are they all from?" I asked her.

"Sweden. Italy. Canada. Those places are where the Arrow Realm steals them. Some get traded to other realms. Doesn't matter where we've lived before. We're all the same now and we're all we have—that and our freedom."

"Free? Here in the trees?" Charlie said with questioning eyebrows.

"Free," Ash repeated, her lips in a tight line. "If we survive the hunt, Artemis leaves us alone. I hope she keeps the deal even with us sticking one of her men."

"She leaves you alone forever?" I said.

"Until we're eighteen," Ash said. "Then we're Goners on our Leaving Day."

Charlie shook his head. "Then you die?"

"Not the lucky ones." Ash pulled out her knife and twirled it expertly in her hand. It flashed in the lantern light, spinning like a bullet. "We raid the WC—the work camp—for weapons and extra mash. It's easy for us to get in and out. We're protected in our tree community, unlike anywhere else on Nostos. As Wild Childs, we stay alive for a reason. We're stolen children once used as bait to hunt the great beasts—and we survived. Queen Artemis respects this, as did her ancestors. When the first group of Wild Childs started growing up, Queen Artemis of long ago sent an army to round us up. She got most of us, but not all. Those caught were sent to their death on a great hunt. Those that didn't get stuck were sent to the WC. So, the Wild Child leader in charge went to her and made a deal to save us. If we turn out our own to the ground for the WC on their Leaving Day, then the queen lets us all live. Payment for being left alone. There's no other place safer on Nostos for Earth kids. The Goners either get to the WC safe and work there … or they don't."

"They get stuck and grounded as in—"

"Shot and dead." Ash lowered her head. "The queen gets them either way—by hunt or by slave. Life in the WC is still imprisonment, but it's a life."

"Not all the queens have honored this deal," Apollo said. "My grandfather told me hunting stories about it from when he visited here as a young man." He bent his head. "He loved the hunt."

"Well, Leandro doesn't … or didn't," I said. "In the Lost Realm, he told me he got in trouble for refusing to hunt kids. It's how he got his broken arrow scar—the queen branded him a failure."

Ash handed me a wrap from a trunk filled with squirrel mash and ache cakes, bringing me back to this realm's unpleasant reality. "Time to leave."

First, I needed more from her. "Why'd the old queen make that deal to save you?"

She sighed and talked fast, filling us in. "Hundreds of years ago, the son of that ancient Queen Artemis wanted to become a Wild Child. He hated how his people stole kids from Earth, and he went runabout to join ranks with the Wild Childs. His mother sent in her soldiers to bring him back, but there was a fight and the son was accidentally wounded by a soldier's arrow. The prince nearly died but the Wild Childs healed him and the queen agreed to let her son live a double life as prince and Wild Child. Now every Queen Artemis—with some exceptions—carries on the tradition of letting the Wild Childs live."

"First they have to escape the hunt and live to become a Wild Child," Charlie said.

"Yeah, until their Leaving Day. Then the hunt restarts," I said, my voice rising. "You're no different from this world, Ash. You throw your friends to the wild beasts, and if they don't get *stuck,* they get to live as slaves in the WC?"

"They live, blockhead," Ash said in a clipped voice

with flared eyes. "One Goner at a time saves us all. One for the many. You better be a Goner now too or we'll all be. Three for the many."

"I'd rather be a Wild Child," Apollo said quietly, fiddling with his square buttons. "Better to be imprisoned on your own terms than by someone else's."

"That's flippin' right," Ash said, punching fists to her waist.

Apollo rubbed the fur of his new coat and stared into the morning light spilling from the window. "Zeus will never let Artemis win. Once he finds out her plan—and he will—he'll swarm this realm. He'll have no tolerance either for the Wild Child community." He turned back to Ash. "Then you'll all be Goners, for real."

"We can hide from Zeus," Ash said. "We can live in the Perimeter Lands."

"He empties them out once a year and tosses people off The Edge. Do you want to float to death in the Great Beyond?"

"We'll cross into another realm then; keep moving if we have to. We can hide in the red desert canyons of the Dred Realm or in the Argos Realm where it never snows." She threw her hands out to Apollo. "We built all this. We can build it again."

"You'll still be living under Zeus's rules for Nostos wherever you go," Apollo said. "We all will. And he wants the Oracle as badly as Artemis," he shot me a look, "and for similar reasons: to control the Oracle. Zeus rules all of Nostos with a heavy hand, but if someone with the power of the original Olympians were to rise, they'd be a threat to him. Some Nostos rulers want Olympian powers and some want things to stay the same." He lowered his voice. "We are a world divided."

"Zeus didn't stop Hekate in the Lost Realm when she took over King Apollo," I said. "Why now?"

"He doesn't care about the realms fighting each other," Apollo said. "But if he finds out the Oracle is here and someone else is after him, he'll hunt them both down."

He let these words hang in the air. I scrunched my shoulders in with them all looking at me as if I was the answer.

"Then Zeus will do what?" I said to Apollo.

His black eyes fired into mine, his jaw twitching. "Kill them."

Ash bent her head, her long hair hiding her face. "My Leaving Day is coming. Someone else will lead the Wild Childs soon."

"Why don't you escape on Leaving Day and head into the Perimeter Lands? Bribe someone to help you get to Earth," I said. "My grandfather did. My mother did."

She crossed her arms. "If we don't honor our deal, the queen rounds us all up for the hunt. It's happened once before. No member since has put our people in such danger. One group of Wild Childs tried to escape all at once. Too many died and the survivors returned to their home here."

"It's been the way of the Wild Childs for hundreds of years, Joshua," Apollo said matter-of-factly. "It's how our world works."

"Your world stinks, King-man," Charlie said.

Agreed.

"Ash, what about Leandro?" It hurt to say his name.

"He won't get grounded." Ash shook her head. "He knows how to stick the beasts good. Some animals may fear him, and Artemis has a weakness for him too. After all, her daughter was fathered by a Wild Child."

"What happened to them?"

"The father got grounded on his Leaving Day. The beasts got him before he reached the WC. Artemis found his torn apart body in the woods. Her daughter died years later in a hunting accident."

"How do you know all this?" I said.

She waved a hand. "We see a lot from these treetops ... I see a lot. Like Artemis visiting the Black Heart Tree and sharing secrets with that evil tree monster."

She shook her head as if tossing those thoughts away. "Enough gossip. You've overstayed your welcome."

She turned to leave when shouts burst from nearby.

Artemis and her men were back!

Chapter Eighteen

"Scram and cram!" Ash pulled at me. "We have to get you out of the Wild Lands." She ripped open the door, and we peered down over the platform that wrapped around the tree house. The lurid light of lanterns far below fought to find us through the thick of the trees.

"We'll get you to the Perimeter Lands and then you're on your own." Ash dashed through the door to the platform outside. I slid along the tree house, wincing as I scraped against rough bark, splinters skewering my palms. Charlie cried out with pain behind me as a low hanging limb whipped him.

Ash urged us on with a grim face. "If you are the Oracle, Joshua, I'm sure you can come up with a new plan to survive."

"I have no idea what that is."

"Then you better flippin' plan fast."

Charlie, Apollo, and I bolted after her on the plank

path. We ran across the top of the forest, dashing from one tree house to another. They were connected like roads through a hidden village. Wild Childs were positioned at windows with bows and arrows in hand.

"Nearly there?" Charlie asked between breaths.

Ash put up her hand to quiet him. The muffled calls of Artemis and her men echoed in the distance. It was hard to tell which direction they came from. They faded in and out.

"I'd hoped to scram to the Perimeter Lands, but it's too far and there's no time," Ash said.

"Where are we?" I said, clutching a branch. Clouds flew across the fading moon, and wood smoke wafted up. Ash spread the branches apart, and a city of thatched roofs sprawled before us beyond the giant hedge fence that imprisoned the Wild Lands. Blackened chimneys puffed angrily with work in the early morning hours, and muddy paths wound between the mishmash of crooked buildings, their wooden features sagging with rot and age. Torches flickering on shack doors revealed rats running along the dirt ruts in the road.

"The WC," Ash announced.

"Where they send grown-ups?" Charlie whispered. "I don't want to go there."

"They'll be climbing up to us soon to look for you. Artemis thrives on the hunt and the WC is the last place they'll check," Ash said, scanning the woods. Artemis and her men moved off in the distance, their calls growing faint.

"She's right," Apollo said. "And I've got coins in my boot. We can bribe a guard to get out and make it to the Sea Realm. Poseidon may be my one ally left. Let's hope he hasn't turned on me like Artemis."

"What if we try heading for the Perimeter Lands?"

Our choices were slim. "If we can avoid Artemis, we can find help there—maybe from other escaped people."

Charlie shook his head. "Remember those Takers we ran into in the Lost Realm? They thought we were the bad guys and wanted to kill us, and they were from our own world!"

"Sometimes the people you think are on your side betray you," Apollo said.

"Yea, and sometimes people who betray you really are on your side," I said.

"True," Apollo said in a low voice. "We need more of those right now."

"The one I trusted is a Goner; he may be in there," Ash thrust her hand to the decrepit city. "We call him Oak. He's tall with red hair. A friend from my country, Canada. If you meet the blockhead, say this spudhead Ash sent you to him for help."

The dawn of our third day approached. The sky grew light lavender. The hint of a blue sunrise glowed on the horizon. A guard marched along one side of the wall, pacing the length.

"If you don't meet Oak, there are others," Ash whispered. "An underground group has taken root in the WC. They may have ways to help you."

"How do you know this guy Oak?" I said, wanting to keep the conversation going—wanting to stay right here on this branch and not head down into that sprawling darkness of muck and danger.

"I cured him from an injury and helped save his wife. In return, he risked coming here to give me news of what's going on in Nostos. I grew up in an orphanage on Earth and he … well, he became like a father I never knew. After my Leaving Day, I'll join him in the WC."

If you don't become a dead Goner first.

Ash handed us each a vine.

"*Mon Dieu!* What am I supposed to do with this? Fly back to Earth?" Charlie said.

Ash didn't crack a smile. "No. Fly over the wall when the watch turns the corner."

We all gripped our lifelines and stared down at the new world waiting to consume us.

Ash scanned above. "There's no other way. I'll watch for the korax. They answer to Artemis and hide in the trees waiting for us to escape. I've seen kids snatched up by them and thrown to the beasts."

I imagined this new horror as tails flicked through the trees and grunts called up to us. "Ash is right, Charlie," I said. "If we go down to the ground and try to cross the wall, we'll be eaten before we get out of here."

"*Zut!*" Charlie shook his vine. "Death by flight it is."

Building up the crazy courage to fly off the tree I asked, "Why save us, Ash?"

Her green eyes creased. "If the Oracle is real then Earth people can be freed. There'd be no more Wild Childs. The ones who grew up and are Goners out there," she swung her arm toward the WC, "can go home or choose to stay. I can find my friend, Oak. We can be a family." Ash hooked a hand to my shirt, her eyes boring into mine. "Are you him?"

"Him—who?"

"The one. The Oracle."

I tried to back up but slipped on a branch. My foot slid. Twigs cracked and I clung to Ash. "I—I don't know. I could be."

Saying those last three words sent an electric twang through my body.

I. Could. Be. The. Oracle.

The hunger snarls below grew louder. Ash pulled me closer, her leaf and earth smell washing over me. "I hope you are."

"If he is, I swear to be the king he wants me to be," Apollo said in a commanding voice I hadn't heard in a long time.

"You can do that anyway, King-man," Charlie said, patting him on the shoulder.

Ash pointed to a darker spot in the corner of an alley. "Swing wide and aim for there. Today's market day where all realms come to barter for goods the slaves make. Most of the money lines the pockets of Zeus who watches over it all." She spit out those last words. "If you're lucky, you'll find someone in the crowd to keep you safe."

"If not?" I asked.

"If not, you may get turned in for a reward."

"We better pick the right someone," Charlie said.

She started to say more when the guard below turned the corner. "Go!" she urged. "Don't get stuck or grounded for good!"

Great advice. "I'll make mash of them first."

She shot me a tight-lipped smile as I clenched my vine. It bit into my palm and fingers, but I held on harder. Its pain would keep me alive.

Charlie, Apollo, and I darted looks at each other and—sucking in a breath—we jumped.

Chapter Nineteen

We landed with a hard whump on crusted mud, tumbling into each other. I bit my lip to stop from crying out. Charlie's faint oomph and Apollo's gasp told me they were both okay. Charlie's long legs stuck out in the moonlight, and I dragged him and Apollo into a dim corner. The vines we'd swung from curled back into the treetops. Far up, Ash waved and was gone.

Torchlight glinted on the rut-filled streets and written in the mud sprawled the words GET ... UNDERGROUND.

How? There was no time to wonder where the message came from or how to follow its command as the determined smack of boots headed our way. We shrunk farther into the shadows.

The road between the shacks spread too narrow to hide us and the doorways offered no cover. I considered climbing to the rooftops but they didn't appear too sturdy.

Caving in to someone's bed didn't sound appealing.

Smack-smack.

The guard grew closer. We'd be destined for the hunt again—or worse.

"Runabout!" I pulled my friends up and we ran in the opposite direction of the watch. It was dangerous muck to run in, and we twisted our ankles several times as we dashed past tilted buildings. Light bled through the cracks of boarded up windows here and there as the shantytown came awake for market day.

Beyond the thatched roofs, the menacing hedge loomed as far as I could see around the Wild Lands, a constant reminder this WC was a prison. Smoke blew down from chipped chimneys, stinging my eyes, and I slipped in rotten slop flung from doorways, its stench making my stomach curl as flies buzzed our heads. With each step, terror chased at me with the thought of running into another guard or people in the streets calling out the alarm. Would they take us in or turn us in?

Voices murmured through thin walls of the huts as people started their day. Every door we passed had a hanging sign with an image painted on it: a hammer, a loaf of bread, a shirt, a boot. Things the grown-up slaves produced? I darted my eyes about the streets for any place to hide when a door flew open and a heavy-set man stepped out. He wiped his hands on a blood-splotched apron.

We all froze for a second before lurching forward again, but the man saw us and yelled out, "Hey, you kids, stop!"

Charlie and Apollo looked at me with faces like terrified wooden puppets. We ran faster, turning a corner when two skinny dogs with bared teeth raced toward us.

A shadow loomed and a tall man stepped in front of us from a doorway. We slammed into him. With a grunt, he clutched us by our clothes and kicked at the vicious dogs. They yelped and ran off.

There was no shaking off the man's hold. He gripped us tighter, glaring down with thick eyebrows and black boulders of hair that framed his face.

"Kids in camp!" A woman yelled around the corner. At the announcement, the man whipped open a hidden door in the ground and shoved us into a dark pit. He hopped down and closed the hatch.

"Don't make a sound," he growled in a low voice. In the disorienting but safe darkness, I had no problem with being quiet; neither did Charlie, who pinched my arm or Apollo whose heavy breaths pumped on my neck. Voices rang out above our hideout.

Doors opened as people called out to one another. "Who was it?" "Wild Childs most likely." "I could use the food as a reward!" "Aww, let 'em go." "Yeah, poor dumb kids." "They'll never survive the WC."

Bing-bang. The doors shut as the grown-ups forgot us. I opened my mouth to say something when a man huffed overhead. "Runaways, Mack. We could split the reward."

"Not if the guards get 'em first."

"Hold up, I got a stitch in my side."

"We'll lose 'em! Think of all them meat and potatoes to eat up!"

"Your stomach doesn't need it. I've got a sick wife, and we can't make our food quota 'cause she can't work fast."

"You better hope it's indigestion and not a baby on the way. You know what the guards will do to it!"

"Never you mind!"

"Well, move your lazy self and let's grab 'em!"

Feet thumped away and quiet hung thick in the heavy dark.

"*Monsieur?*" Charlie whispered.

A rattle brought a green glow stick to life. It grew brighter as the man shook it. We were in a dirt tunnel not quite tall enough for the hunkered over muscled-man.

"Keep quiet and follow me," he ordered.

He'd saved us so I ran as fast as I could after him with my friends close behind.

The man stopped and pushed a hatch open. He hauled us up by our shirts into a windowless room. Quivering candles lined a side table, and a stink of onions and burned grease filled my nose. A cot sagged against one wall with a thin mattress covered in a ripped gray blanket. In the middle of the room, a patched-up wooden table sloped down on one busted leg. It held a fat candle that sputtered next to three lumpy, black-spotted potatoes.

At the table sat a man with long, red, wavy hair tied behind his neck and a full mustache that curled up on either side of his mouth. His baggy yellowed shirt emphasized his thin arms, and a chain hung from his neck across sharp collarbones. A black square pendant with braided edges and a lion etched on the front dangled from it. One bony hand fingered a huge hunk of bread, green with mold. He ripped off a chunk with his chipped teeth and swallowed it in one bite, then he picked up a small rusty knife and twirled it in his hand as if debating whether to cut open one of those nasty looking potatoes. His eyes were like shards of amber glass, gleaming luminescent in the golden candlelight. They tightened as he studied us.

The red-haired man jabbed his knife in the air and drawled in a deep voice, "So … Ratchet, do we kill 'em or sell 'em?"

The bushy-haired man who'd brought us here crushed a hand to my neck in a fierce handhold. "First, let's see if they're tasty or not."

My knees buckled and I sagged under my new captor's catch.

We'd run toward death, not away from it.

Chapter Twenty

Ratchet ripped off my bow and quiver, threw them on the table, and searched us for other weapons. He laughed when he pulled out my flute. "I'll let you keep your music, Reeker, but not this." He pulled out Charlie's knife and I groaned as he shoved us to the floor. Apollo carefully slid his ring around and cupped his other hand over the band. His animal skins covered up his royal clothes, but there was no denying the gold on his finger was not anything a Wild Child would possess.

A quick glance around offered one door as another way out besides the hole we'd been dragged from. First, we'd have to get past these two men. Further scrutiny revealed tools hanging from the walls and horse saddles spread out over a long table, their shiny leather decorated with speckled stones and painted birds and beasts. One sat on a wooden frame unfinished. Paintings were propped up on the floor. The red-haired man stood and put his hands on his waist, looking down at us. Shadows fell from his eyes and sunken cheeks, and bones poked through his shoulder blades. He was as starved as the cretan creature we'd encountered.

"The queen's spies?" Ratchet said.

"Not likely," the man said. He walked around the table and stood over us, pointing at Charlie who pushed his back into the wall. "And not good eatin'. This one's too skinny."

I scrambled up, and Apollo and Charlie stood with me. "We're not dinner! We're from Earth like you." I gulped as the two men looked back and forth at each other as if trying to decide what to do with us, so I took a chance and kept talking. "We're trying to help a friend and get back home."

"What friend would that be?" the red-haired man said.

"Apollo," I said quickly, making it up. Apollo and Charlie darted their eyes at me, then back at the men. "Artemis kidnapped him and put him in the dungeon."

The man crossed his arms, his mouth twitching. "*You* are friends with King Apollo? You and these other rag-bags?"

I forced myself not to look at Apollo, afraid I'd give him away and they'd recognize him. I jumped as the man's laughter boomed around the tiny room.

"It's a lie!" Ratchet said, clawing my shirt with his grubby hand and shoving me backward.

"*Non!*" Charlie said, waving his arms. "*C'est vrai!*"

"Say what?" Ratchet raged, shoving Charlie now.

"T-true," Charlie stuttered out. "It's true."

Apollo remained silent, eyes on the floor, then he nodded at me and mumbled, following my lead. "We got caught saving King Apollo and were tossed in the Wild Lands. We survived and got here. I found these clothes hanging from a tree." He tossed his head toward me and Charlie, then looked up at Ratchet, who poked his knife at him. "My friends are heroes. You hurt them and you'll have to answer to me."

Ratchet pushed him farther into the wall. "You lie! There's no way into the queen's castle." He turned to the red-haired man. "They're just Reekers. I hid in the shadows waiting to reel in some Wild Lands runaways for reward when I caught 'em running from the guard. I say we sell 'em for food. Tie 'em up for now. We've got to open up for market day and get these saddles out or Zeus's men will fine us, or worse."

"We've got some time … I'm curious about their story," the red-haired man said, thrusting a hand at me. "Speak fast, boy, and it better be the truth." He sat back down and began to slowly peel a potato and cut pieces from it, swallowing the slices whole as he watched us.

Charlie urged me to talk. I spewed out everything, not wanting them to change their minds and sell us— or eat us. I told them about being stolen away to the Lost Realm months ago and sold off in the Auction Pit, made to work as an energy slave in the power mill by the evil Hekate. How Charlie and I became friends in the Auction Pit. How the son of the former King Apollo, Sam, helped us escape the power mill and rescue my friend, Finn. How we were nearly killed by bandits and beasts. How my grandfather, Bo Chez, turned out to be a Storm Master from the Sky Realm and how we used his lightning orb to help us. How we freed all the kids enslaved in the Lost Realm. And finally, how we'd been brought back to Nostos to free the new King Apollo from Artemis, who planned to rule all of Nostos with the Oracle's Olympian powers.

"We couldn't have done most of it without Leandro," I finished up.

Apollo nodded but Charlie shook his head, muttering in French while tearing at a ragged nail with his teeth.

The red-haired man stopped cutting his potato, hand in the air and shared a glance with Ratchet, who twisted his face up with doubts about our story.

"You know Leandro?" the red-haired man said in a flat voice.

"Yeah, he is … *was* our friend."

"He's not our friend," Charlie burst out.

"He saved us all once," Apollo said. "He was a good man … may still be."

I fixed him with a look to shut him up, afraid he'd reveal his true identity.

I told the man how Leandro, now head guard to Artemis, had betrayed us.

"I doubt very much Leandro would do such a thing," the man said evenly with a dangerous tone and a raised eyebrow.

"You know him?" I cried out. Of course he would! He was old enough to have been a slave here when Leandro had been a guard. It struck me he might have also known my mother. I fingered Leandro's journal in my pocket, trying to believe he could still be the hero I'd fought alongside once. If I showed this man the journal, would he help us? The chance disappeared when a gong sounded. It rang three times, and I squeezed the journal between my fingers before letting go. Wheels clattered on hard mud outside the door and voices bounced around as the street came alive.

"Enough of this garbage," Ratchet said. "We've got to put up the shutter and signs. All of Nostos will be in the streets soon, and if our table isn't out, we'll lose rations! Throw 'em in the box for now, Oak."

My heart flipped at his name. "You're Oak?"

"Yes, that's my given name."

"Given to you by the Wild Childs?"

He stood so fast he knocked back his chair. In one stride, he forced his knife against my neck. "How do you know? Spy!"

The knife cut into my skin. I drew in a sharp breath at the pain. Charlie gasped.

"Not a spy," I whispered through tight lips, praying I didn't get sliced open. "The Wild Child, Ash … the spudhead … she told me … sent us to you for help … you … blockhead."

Oak flared his nostrils as his face sagged and he withdrew his knife.

"How do you know Ash?"

"She saved us in the Wild Lands. Me, Charlie, and … all of us here."

The gong cannoned again.

"Second warning," Ratchet said. "One more and we're done for!" He shook a fist at us.

Oak tugged on his thick mustache. "Get out there. I'll come before the final bell. If they ask, you're watching the stand for me as my apprentice because I've got the stomach guck. That will keep them away for a while."

Ratchet threw his hands up, weighed himself down with four saddles, and ran out the low side door. His footsteps clumped upstairs and a door opened and slammed, offering up the noisy bustle of the street as market day began.

Oak shoved aside the table and flipped up another hidden door under a worn rug. "You boys stay here for the day and don't make a sound."

"Wait—" I hollered but he shut me up as he tossed me down into a deep pit. Charlie and Apollo followed, slamming down on me in cold dirt. I rolled away in pain, massaging my leg.

"If you don't want to get dead, then get quiet—fast. We'll talk later. There's water, blankets, food, and light sticks down there. You seem resourceful, I'm sure you'll find them." Oak's stern face hung over us and was gone.

Chapter Twenty-One

The lid on our new prison shut us in total darkness. A click told me we were locked in.

"Can you find the light sticks?" I scrambled around on the dirt floor, trying not to think about creepy crawly things.

My question inspired French curses of what I imagined were the kind I'd lose TV over for spouting off in English. The idea of punishment with no TV filled me with longing for home.

Pitch black crept all around, suffocating me with the panic of being buried underground with no way out. Something slithered across my hand. I snatched up my fingers, catching my breath.

A green glow infused our cell with a shaky shadow from Charlie's hand as he ignited a glow stick. We pushed up on the hatch to no use. Trapped. After crawling around, we discovered we were also walled in. This was no tunnel—this was a grave. Resigned and exhausted, we found water, more squirrel mash, ache cakes (didn't they have any other snacks here? What I wouldn't give for some pretzels and blankets), and curled up to find a shred of warmth in the damp hole.

"Joshua, I'm scared," Charlie said quietly.

"Me too. At least we're among people like us."

"Except that mean guy who wants to sell us." Charlie puffed out his cheeks.

"Mortal kids are a big barter item for food in the WC," Apollo said. "These people are hungry. Zeus doesn't ration them enough, and he punishes them by taking their food away. That's when things can get ugly. I remember a few big riots in my father's time. Many were killed. So you can understand why people are desperate, like Ratchet. Desperation means unpredictability." He spoke with the weight of his kingdom—and world—on his shoulders.

"I don't care how hungry he is," Charlie said. "He's not selling me for food."

"Maybe we can hide here in the WC?" I offered. "Oak seems like he may help us more than his friend."

"We can't hide out forever." Charlie hid his face in his arm, followed by a heavy sigh. "We're not getting back home this time."

"Yeah, we will."

"Promise me. As a brother—for my little brother." Charlie held out a pinky. I hesitated, then hooked his pinky with mine.

"For brothers."

I bumped Apollo, who looked surprised then hung his head. "You came here for nothing."

"Not for nothing. We're all together again."

Charlie hooked Apollo's pinky with ours.

Apollo quickly let go. "I didn't uphold my end of the bargain."

"What was that?" I said.

He twisted his ring back around. The "A" glinted in the dim light, a symbol of the many King Apollo's that came before him, all the way back to the original Olympian—the one with power. "To make a difference. Work to end slavery, unite our realms, and someday confront Zeus to find a better way for our world." He scooped up a fistful of pebbles and dirt and threw it at the door in the ceiling. It rained down.

"Have faith, King Apollo," I said.

He sank back down. "I did. No one else did."

Charlie rapped Apollo's deerskin coat with his knuckles. "We did. We do. And we left our world for you, didn't we?"

"Yes, you did," Apollo said. "But is it enough? Look where we are now."

"You led us to freedom when it seemed impossible before. We believe in you," I said. "Can't you?"

Apollo pointed a finger my way. "*You* don't even believe in you, why should I?"

I had no good answer and we curled up in silence on the ground of our dirt prison.

"Joshua, promise me something," Charlie whispered.

"Okay," I said, knowing promises made here didn't count.

"If I don't make it back but you do, tell my dad to please stay."

"Stay where?"

"With my mom. Tell him they can work it out. Like they used to tell me and my brother when we'd fight."

"You said your mom and brother were coming to America soon."

He sighed and rolled over, facing me. "This move was a last chance. All they do is fight. My brother worships my dad. He can't lose me and our dad. I think my dad loves him best, but it's okay because I love my brother best." He inched closer, his breath hot on my cheek. "Promise me you'll tell my dad he has to do this."

"I will. But you can tell him yourself when we get home."

He put his head on his hands and didn't answer. I started to doze off when he said softly, "If we both don't get home, can we be brothers for real?"

I hugged myself harder in the dirt. "Sounds good."

With a sniff, he said no more and his breathing slowed. Apollo sighed and rolled over.

Escape seemed impossible. *If only Leandro were here—the real Leandro—he'd know what to do.*

Apollo soon fell asleep too, but restlessness and anxiety filled my exhausted body. I pulled out Leandro's journal and inhaled the worn paper, trying to find his smell—a rich leather scent soaked in earth and chocolate—but it just smelled musty like a lost library book. I flipped to a page and, in the light of the glow stick, read his private thoughts written in scroll-y handwriting.

My Homeland
Journal Entry 30 on Nostos
By Leandro of the Arrow Realm

My penance is over. Queen Artemis has named me head soldier to oversee the castle guards and given me quarters in the castle. My room is drafty and cold, but I suffer it better than a roomful of forty immature recruits.

I met with her alone for the first time today to discuss the late King Apollo's final command for his world and his son's promise to enforce it. I found her much different from our first meeting, as if her mind had shifted. She is no longer willing to help our cause. Her face was stone, and I surmised that stopping the baiting of mortal children and standing up to Zeus are not on her priority list.

I knelt to her then and said, "The first Artemis was a protector of children. Remember the children. All of the children." She merely stared at me as if that time was forgotten. She pulled off her sunglasses, and the hollows under her eyes revealed her sleepless nights driven by some unknown anxiety.

Truth: I must think of another way to convince her. I cannot bear to remain on this world without my family if there is no chance for change.

Truth. Its meaning changed here constantly. I was too tired to think about it more. Charlie and I'd been here for three days, mostly on the run. Sleep came for me fast, and I dozed off with Leandro's comforting words, escaping this nightmare for the world I'd left behind. But it wasn't Leandro who came to me in my dreams. It was Bo Chez.

"Be who you are destined to be," he said, offering me the lightning orb. Our hands touched as we held it together.

"Why aren't you here to show me?"

"You are not alone," he said and let go of the orb. It exploded in my hands with brilliant light, taking Bo Chez with it.

I awoke in the dark pit, and even though I shared it with my friends, loneliness wrapped around me like a gauntlet.

Chapter Twenty-Two

The hatch flew open and light stunned my eyes. The glow sticks had died out. I shook my head to wake up and moaned from a painful crick in my neck.

"Come on up, boys."

We climbed out with Oak's help. "I checked on you earlier but you were asleep all day and half the night." He waved his hand at bread and cheese on the table as he sat down. "It's fresh from the baker's wife. She has a thing for me. Not many dare to share. It all belongs to Zeus." He half-smiled as we inhaled the food, a welcome change from squirrel jerky and hard pancakes. The bread was heavy and the cheese creamy. They went down like pizza and ice cream with a jug of his honey water.

A heavy silence wound around us. "Market day?" I said with a final swallow.

"It's over. The WC is locked up for the night."

"And Ratchet?"

"He's in the apprentice lodge." The more Oak spoke, the more my fear of him lessened.

"Are you an artist?" I asked as Charlie and Apollo crouched down to the paintings stacked on the floor.

"Saddlemaker for Nostos … artist for me. Sometimes royalty orders me to do portraits. A few months ago, they sent Ratchet as an apprentice from the Fire Realm; he'd been working as a slave in the volcanic mines. He seems a bit too eager to capture and sell children for food, but he's only eighteen and needs more food than this old man." He tapped a fist to his chest. "We must all survive in our own way."

I noticed he wasn't eating. The food was for us, although he certainly could use it. I finished the delicious cheese, wanting more even as my stomach ached from eating too fast, and went to get a closer peek at the pictures by candlelight. Charlie stroked the edge of the paintings. We'd both wanted to be artists.

The pictures were familiar scenes: the Grand Canyon, Niagara Falls, the Eiffel Tower, Egyptian pyramids, the Tower of London, and more. "To remember Earth?" I asked.

Oak nodded. "It's been a long time. I was twelve when they stole me from Canada to the Sea Realm. My days were spent working Poseidon's great water wheel. I was glad to turn eighteen and come here."

Apollo traced the Statue of Liberty. "I want to go back."

I'd forgotten he'd been born on Earth when his mother escaped after displeasing his father, the late King Apollo—until a Child Collector stole him back. It dawned on me that Earth had been Apollo's first home.

"I wish this every day," Oak said with a sigh. "I don't want to forget."

"Me either," Apollo agreed.

We were all quiet and I wondered how many years had Oak been here. The thought of staying here forever picked at me. I shelved my lost life to ask Oak more questions. "Who do you make saddles for?"

"Folks from all over Nostos, especially for soldiers and royalty. Once a week, the market is open to all realms for people to buy the goods we slaves make and pay the clerk."

"You get to make money as a slave?"

"Ha!" Oak sliced the air with his knife he'd been masterfully turning between his fingers. "Zeus gets the money and disperses it as he sees fit throughout the twelve realms. His kingdom, the Sky Realm, gets most of it. He keeps a tight fist on Nostos, making sure every realm keeps in line with his rules. If they don't, he cuts them off from supplies. A kingdom can starve pretty quickly when that happens."

"What do you get then?"

Oak put his knife down, brushed his mustache with a calloused finger, and pointed it at me. "We get to live." He let those words sink in, then waved a hand at us. "And I'm still deciding what to do with you. Ratchet thinks we should haul you to the auction pit and turn you in for food."

"Instead of eat us?" I burst out. Charlie kicked me and I winced, rubbing my ankle.

Oak threw his head back with a big rumbly laugh. "That was a joke. But there are things out there that will eat you."

"*Mon Dieu*, do we know," Charlie said.

Oak laughed again, then grew solemn. "It's not only the slaves that starve here but the animals too." He paused then asked, "Is Ash okay?"

"Yeah, she's okay. She said she saved someone you knew."

Oak strode over to the paintings and drew one out from the back. "My wife." A sad looking woman with curly brown hair stared back at us. She might be pretty if she smiled. "She was dying from the guck, and I nearly died getting into the Wild Lands to find the Moria plant to cure her. I made it over the wall but couldn't run from the beasts. Ash saved me from being eaten and gave me the plant to take back to the WC from their garden. My wife lived … for a while … until our son was born."

Charlie, Apollo, and I glanced at each other. "You have a son?"

"Did." Oak was quiet and then he spoke. "He and my wife died in childbirth. I begged for a doctor but the guards laughed at me. I'd hoped to hide our son until he grew big, like you," he pointed at Apollo, "and pretend he was old enough to be my saddlemaker. They don't keep track of us here. As long as we produce goods for Nostos and don't escape or revolt, they don't care what happens to us. Except one man I knew, one guard who cared—Leandro."

Oak brushed the painted hair of his wife with his fingers as if she were real. "For one glorious moment, I dreamed of escaping the WC and finding a way to Earth to live out our days as a family in peace. Leandro was helping us find that dream, working with the WC underground. When the queen found out he had a slave wife and son she made them disappear. Leandro couldn't bear it and one day he vanished—deserted his post. He never said goodbye but I don't blame him. He has his demons to chase, as do I." He wiped the painting carefully with the tip of his leather vest, then slid it back behind the others.

He turned to us, his red hair edged with candlelight, and shook his fists in the air. "When we finish the tunnel, it'll be my turn to escape, join the Takers, and toss every single Child Collector over The Edge—one by one. No matter how long it takes and no matter if I die trying." He pulled his hair tighter in a knot at the base of his neck and flipped it away. "If only Leandro were in the WC again. He'd help us."

"Or betray us," Charlie said.

Oak strode toward Charlie and hammered him into the wall. "Don't ever say that! Leandro would never betray me. He's my friend, and if he betrayed you, it's because of something you did. Maybe you really are spies!"

He drew a dagger from a hidden sheath under his vest and held it to Charlie's throat. I pulled at Oak. "Don't hurt him!"

Oak shoved me aside, leering into Charlie, who looked like a squashed spider against the wall. "What did you do to Leandro?"

Charlie struggled against him with bulging eyes, but Oak was unbreakable.

"He didn't do anything!" I pulled at his arm. "Leandro's different. It's not him!"

Apollo put a hand on Oak's arm. "We're on the same side. Leandro was our good friend until he met up with Artemis again."

Oak put his arm down and Charlie stumbled away, gasping for air.

"A spell perhaps …?" Oak said to himself. "Artemis used to love Leandro. He told me they met in the forest as younglings. She was like a sister, but her mother sent him away. A princess and commoner can never be friends or family."

Where was this going? I didn't dare question the man who'd held a knife to Charlie's throat. He might do the same to mine.

"With Leandro pardoned for desertion and back in her realm, the queen must've found a way to put a spell on him to do her bidding," Oak went on, sliding his knife away and pacing the small room, his mission to hurt Charlie forgotten for the moment.

"Like hypnosis?" I said.

Charlie leaned on the wall and pointed a shaky finger at Oak, but it was Apollo who spoke the words. "The queen's slave, Hypnos!"

Oak stopped in his tracks. "She has a slave that hypnotizes?"

"Yes. Can we get him to un-hypnotize Leandro?" I said.

"Where is this slave kept?"

"In the castle dungeon."

Oak crossed is arms. "Not where I'd choose to conduct a rescue. You boys should know that." He scratched his mustache. "I do have a contact on the inside. And what if it isn't hypnosis, but a spell?"

Apollo spoke up. "The spellcaster must cast it out."

"Artemis!" I said.

"Perhaps," Oak said.

"I bet she did cast a spell on Leandro. She tried to hypnotize me to get my—" I shut up.

"Your what?"

I shook my head but Oak was already at my side, gripping my arms. "What's this?" He tugged on the journal poking out of my pocket.

"No!" I cried out but he ripped it away and flipped through it, then he blew out a big breath and sat down, slowly turning the pages. Charlie edged toward the escape hatch we'd arrived from. He pointed to the floor. But I wasn't leaving without Leandro's journal. It was the one good thing left of him.

Oak thumped the journal shut and tapped it on the table, staring at me in disbelief. "The myth. It's you? Your name is Joshua?"

"I'm Joshua. I'm–I—" the words wouldn't form. Charlie shrugged with his hands out in a question and Apollo stared at me. I looked at my feet to avoid Oak's unblinking amber eyes and fiery hair glinting in the candlelight.

"Just a boy … " I peered up as he stared at me in wonder and something swelled inside me, the knowledge that these people believed in me, in the idea of me. Their belief encouraged my own.

Oak stood up, his thick eyebrows flattened into one. "Do you have powers?"

"Only with my lightning orb," I lied.

"But you spoke to the animals even after Artemis stole it," said Charlie, calling me out.

"You did?" Apollo said. I didn't answer, still trying to figure it out myself.

Oak stared at me for a long moment then handed me back the journal. "From what Leandro told me of the myth, the Oracle will be half mortal, half Olympian and carry the power of his Nostos homeland. You've got a parent from the Arrow Realm?"

"I don't know who my father was, but my mother was a slave from Earth. She lived in this camp." Here came the chance to ask the question I'd been wanting to ask since we met. "Maybe you knew her?"

"I've known many people who've come ... and gone," he said flatly, still assessing this new me.

I remembered my wallet jammed in my jeans! I tugged it out—where I kept the one photo of my mother. Thank goodness it was laminated and didn't get ruined in that nasty moat. I handed it to Oak. "Her name was Diana."

He fingered it, his face twisting in a contorted expression. My heart beat faster with each second he stared at the photo, and my chest filled with a big bubble of air threatening to burst.

Oak looked at me with pinched eyes. "Yes, I knew her."

A chill zoomed from my toes to my neck.

He handed back my mother's photo. "She's Leandro's wife."

Chapter Twenty-Three

I let my breath go and shuffled back with shaking legs, nearly tipping the chair over.

"Leandro's my father?" The idea buzzed in my head like a crazed fly.

The tiny room melted away and a whole world opened up. My father was the hero I'd always imagined. We'd been brought together in a great adventure in the Lost Realm, fought alongside one another—winning our freedom, and the freedom of so many stolen children. He'd been my mentor, my friend. Now he was the father I'd longed for all my life.

It crumbled away with the knowledge that he now hunted me.

My own father.

It couldn't be true! Someone was using him. I resolved to find a way to get the Leandro I knew back.

Oak put a hand on my shoulder, warming it as

Leandro's once had, and pulled me back down from the stars in my head. "No. Sorry, son. He can't be your father."

The word "son" cracked a hole in my heart, ripping away the belief that for one moment Leandro had been my father.

Oak pushed up my sleeve and touched my forearm. "You don't bear the birthmark of Leandro's firstborn. Besides, his son would be older than you." He pulled his hand away, leaving me cold all over, and pointed to the shabby bed. "My wife helped your mother deliver his son, Evander, in this room on that cot. She and the baby disappeared a few months later then so did Leandro."

With all this exploding in my head, there was more—Leandro may not be my father but we now shared a mission: to find the lost family connecting us. Someday, if I ever got the chance, I'd have to tell him his wife was dead.

"Family means everything," Apollo said. "Especially if you lose them."

That was the truth.

"Sorry, Joshua," Charlie said, stuffing his hands in his pockets with a shrug.

"I have a brother." The words crashed out of me with the force of its reality. Those words spun through me with a strange happy-sad mix. Was he alive? Here? Or on Earth?

"Half brother," Charlie corrected.

"Half brother," I echoed and forced a smile up from the lump in my throat as if a full-blooded brother out there could stop Charlie and me from being "Earth brothers." Now both our brothers were lost to us, except I'd never met mine and he may never see his again. Charlie had a new goal now—to find a replacement brother in me. I didn't want to be anyone's replacement.

"Does he look like me?" I asked Oak.

He clutched the pendant on his chain, then opened it up like a book. "See for yourself."

Inside was a painting of my mother holding a baby. My brother. "You painted this?"

He nodded. "Your brother was only a few weeks old when he disappeared. He was born with a head of white-blond hair and a birthmark on his arm like—"

"A flame?"

His eyebrows shot up. "How did you know?"

"Leandro told me in the Lost Realm ... and I see it there." I touched the mini-portrait, not wanting to look away from the second-only picture of my mother and the first of my newly expanded family. Would it be better if I never knew? Would I become like Leandro, searching the world for years to find my lost family? It didn't seem like any kind of life. Leandro might as well be lost with them, except now he followed a new mission as the queen's henchman.

Oak closed the pendant and touched the lion etched on the front. "I had this made for your mother by our blacksmith, but I never had the chance to give it to her. She wanted the lion on the front for Leandro because—"

"He's a lionheart."

He nodded, dropping the pendant into his shirt and staring at the cot as if seeing another night in another time. "I'd always thought your mother and brother were killed when her relationship with Leandro was discovered. I never knew who turned them in ..." He scowled, crushing his hand into a fist.

"She escaped to Earth and I was born there," I said.

"My wife would've been glad to know she got to Earth and had another child. She must have found someone else …" He shook his big head. "Is she okay?"

"She died when I was two. She never even told my grandfather who my father was."

"Sorry to hear."

"A Child Collector found her and killed her right in front of me and my grandfather."

Oak's eyes widened and he slammed his fist into the table with a crack. "Monsters!" Fire reflected angrily in his eyes as a draft whipped the candle flames around the room in a frenzy.

"I killed him."

His eyes grew bigger and he shook his head as if he couldn't believe it.

"It's true," Charlie said, nudging me. "He blasted him with the lightning orb."

"And … my friend here," I pointed at Apollo, "killed Hekate with a curse."

"That witch! I've heard about her evil doing." He turned to me. "So, you're a malumpus-tongue and can talk to animals. Like Leandro. Your father must be from the Arrow Realm. I don't know how this all came about, but if you are the Oracle and the myth is true, you can free us from slavery. All of us in the WC have been waiting—hoping—for you. Leandro hoped for you to change this world so he could find his family again … now, it seems, your family too."

I was divided again, split between two worlds as Nostos pulled me further into its secrets and pushed me away from my life on Earth—and getting back home. He'd once said to me: *Home is a reflection of who you are. It defines you.* If his words were true and this was my new home, I must accept how it defines me.

"Leandro believes you're the Oracle," Oak said. He put a hand on my shoulder again. "I will too."

I swallowed hard not wanting to cry. Leandro and my family were lost to me, but help had arrived in a new friend.

Oak's forehead creased. "If you are a malumpus-tongue with ancient power to speak with animals, you may have the power to do more, according to Leandro."

My pulse raced, wanting to know … not wanting to know.

"Like get us home?" Charlie said.

"No." Oak crossed his arms and paused. "The power to transform into animals."

Charlie snapped his fingers. "Like Lore did!" Oak seemed confused and Charlie went into detail about our dungeon experience.

"No," I whispered, shaking my head to rid myself of the image of turning into a beast. "Artemis said only a rare few can do it."

"As the Oracle, there's none rarer," Oak said. "But a power this big comes with great responsibility. Not all who carry it use it wisely."

"Very true," Apollo said. "I've seen it."

"Leandro can't do that, can he?" I said.

"No, he talks to animals but only those with the rarest of malumpus-tongue powers can transform."

How to transform—and into what creature?

We all stood in silence for a long moment. There was so much more to learn … especially about my mother. And there wasn't much time. Where to start asking? Like what her life had been like here, things she said, and about her relationship with Leandro. Suddenly, the gong bashed the air in a frantic rhythm.

"A raid!" Oak blew out the candles while grabbing a glow stick and activating its green light. He threw my bow and arrows at me and shoved Charlie's knife at him, then he pulled a bag out from under his cot and fell on his knees to the floor, ripping open the hidden door to the tunnel we'd first come through. He jumped down in the hole, his head sticking out like a ghost in the garish glow. "Come on, boys!"

Charlie inched away from the tunnel, glancing at the door that led outside. He pulled me aside and whispered between the gongs, "Joshua, we can run through the street. Find another way out!"

"You'll have no chance once the WC guards get you," Apollo said.

I agreed with him. "No, we have to follow him," I said. "He knew my mother ... my brother ... Leandro."

"But Leandro wants to hurt us now!" Charlie argued.

"No! We trusted him once. We could again. We've got to trust Oak now. We won't make it here without trusting someone."

I did trust this man, Oak, even though he'd held us by knifepoint—like Leandro had when we first met. Like Leandro, Oak was living on the edge, trying to survive, searching for a better life—for himself and his people. So were we.

"I can run fast," Charlie said. "You too! *Allons*!"

"If they catch us, they'll kill us—or worse," Apollo said.

"Throw us to the animals," Charlie nodded miserably.

The floor shook as guards pounded on a nearby shack, yelling at the inhabitants to open their door.

"Enough debate!" Oak thundered, his face a light in

the dark shadows. "The time to escape is now!"

I jumped into the tunnel.

Charlie carved his hands through his hair and jumped with Apollo right behind. Oak clicked the hatch shut and led the way hunched over, his scrawny shoulders filling the tunnel. Through the dark, we ran after him and the sickly beam of a glow stick.

Oak huffed as the tunnel split. He ran left, switching his sack to the other shoulder. "We've been tunneling our way out. There are too many booby traps and guards on the wall to get out that way. Many of us have been working on this tunnel for years and generations before that."

"Where does it end?" I asked in between breaths.

"Someday it'll go under the wall and into the forest of the Perimeter Lands."

"What's out there?" Charlie asked.

Oak's face was like a ghoul in the ghastly shadows. "Freedom."

When I thought my legs couldn't carry me anymore, Oak stopped and felt around on the wall. "You'll be safe here, for now. The only ones who know of this place are the parents."

He pushed at the wall and a door opened. Light creaked through the crack. "The parents of whom?" I asked, the light burning my eyes.

We entered a cavernous room filled with lit candles along the edges of glistening walls and the smell of stale sweat—and dozens of kids staring right at us.

Oak pointed. "Them."

Chapter Twenty-Four

Oak set the sack on the floor and the kids pushed Charlie and me aside to hug him. The lines in his face softened as he smiled at them, wrapping his long, thin arms around as many as he could. They yanked on the sack but he shook his head and threw it over their heads to the side. The kids jumped on it, their long stringy hair hanging against dirt-smudged faces. One tall kid shoved the mob away, making them form a line. He started distributing food from the bag to the kids, and the crowd soon dispersed, darting off to darkened corners, hugging their meals with starved desperation. The rush of running water echoed around the sloped walls of crumbling rock along with the munching of food. I backed up into sharp stone, my feet crunching on scattered bread crusts and apple cores, and tore my hands away from the feel of slimy moss.

"Where'd they all come from?" I whispered, rubbing

my fingers on my pants and sucking in musty air. They glanced at me with curious eyes as they fed their hunger. In all this ordered chaos, not one word was spoken, as if they'd been trained to be silent in the dark earth that hid them from life and death.

"Their parents are slaves of the WC," Oak said.

"Like you," Charlie said to him in a tight voice, then looked at me. "And your mom. *C'est terrible.*"

"Terrible, yes, but wonderful because they are alive … unlike my boy," Oak said with a broken voice and red eyes.

"I've heard of the WC underground slaves," Apollo said. "These kids get a second chance."

"Second chance to what?" Charlie said, blinking fast.

"To live."

In this moment, it seemed like weeks since I was zapped to Nostos, but I'd left barely four days ago. I came to free Apollo but there were so many here to free. With these lives at stake, one absolute truth filled me: I came here to save them all. Not in one realm this time—but an entire world. Every path I'd been on led to that truth. Whether I was this Oracle or not, I had a part to play on Nostos.

Apollo left our side to go to the kids. He walked the cave, stopping at each group to talk with them. Their conversations were too faint to hear, but he worked the room like a king with his royal subjects. He touched some on the head and the shoulder.

"Stay here with the others," Oak said while watching Apollo with curiosity. "There's food and water. An underground river runs through the back of the cave but stay away from it. You'll be safe in the cave for now. Only the WC underground knows of this place. I'll come for you after the raid is done."

Oak turned away but I pulled him back. "You didn't tell me about my mother."

"There's no time." He placed a hand on mine. "I have to get back to my room. If they find me gone, they'll think I'm out after curfew—or worse, escaped—and set the beasts after me."

Charlie shuddered. "Fire-breathing mutts."

My woeful face must have softened Oak for he squeezed my fingers. "Your mother was beautiful on the inside and out. Her laughter was infectious, and it's why Leandro was drawn to her. She carried a shining hope despite the dark circumstances she suffered every day. She knew how to love well. She would've loved you very much."

I let go of his hand, filled up inside but still wanting more—it was all I'd get for now. Oak turned again, opening the door, but my instinct kicked in: we couldn't stay here.

"Wait!" I watched the kids scarfing down dinner with their fingers. "Maybe we can come up with a plan to get these kids out." It sounded too huge to comprehend as it flew out of my mouth.

Oak stepped toward me. His head grazed the ceiling and clods of dirt rained around him as he curled his long fingers around my fist. "My top mission is to keep them alive. One step at a time, Joshua."

Charlie nodded. "*Oui*, one step, but Joshua is good with coming up with plans."

The gushing water gave me an idea. "What about this river? Let's ride it out of here!"

Oak grasped my hand and bent his head to mine, blowing sour breath on my cheek. "Do. Not. Go. In. The. River."

"It's a way out." I struggled to free my hand, but Oak's boney fingers crushed mine with hidden strength.

"It's a river of death."

He saw my pained face and dropped my hand. "When we first found the subterranean river and moved the children to this cave, one desperate boy jumped in."

Charlie leaned in. "Did he get out?"

"No, he came back." Oak plucked both our shirts now, pulling us toward his stricken face. "Dead!" He flung us away from him. "Flippin' dead, I tell you!"

"It's a chance."

"No! The river loops around. He came back to us from the other direction. His head bashed in. There's no way out, except in death. Get it?" Oak twirled his mustache into vicious points.

"All rivers lead somewhere," I said, not ready to relinquish hope of a watery escape, but the wind from the river shrieked around the hollows of the cave, predicting our death if we did.

Apollo returned to our side from his cave tour. "Let me go into the river. I have a powerful alliance with Poseidon; if I can get to him, we can work together." He looked at all the kids, then back at us, flexing his muscles. "My father would've wanted it."

Oak snatched Apollo's hand and flipped his royal ring around, his mouth dropping open when suddenly the creak of the door scratched the air and a familiar voice called out. "What you been hiding down here, Oak?"

Ratchet! He strode right in with a big smirk.

Oak jumped around. "How did you find this place?"

"You've been sneaky lately so I followed you. The raid chaos gave me cover to see what you were doing and check up on my Reekers. Took a wrong turn but backtracked and found you now–and the Reekers." Ratchet's smile grew wider. "This is why you hoard your food. Like you always say Oak, one for the many, eh?"

I backed up with Apollo and Charlie, who'd flicked out his knife and held it behind his back.

"Oh, you're not going anywhere, boys," Ratchet said with a twitch of an eyebrow.

I believed him.

Chapter Twenty-Five

Oak rushed to shut the door behind Ratchet. The candle flames flew sideways casting darker shadows. "Ratchet, you can't know about this place!"

"What's he mean one for the many, Oak?" I said. How did a Wild Child rule work here?

"Never you mind," he said, his voice like gravel thrown at me.

"Why, the honorable Oak and I catch runaway kids to exchange at the auction pit for food, don't we?" He patted Oak hard on the shoulder while staring at me with slitted eyes.

I'd forgotten about this but defended Oak. "Yeah, so what? We know."

He sneered at us. "What you don't know is that he sells them for a higher price as bait for the queen's Wild Lands hunt. A bigger gold mine of food for us, right, Oak?"

Oak flung Ratchet's hand away with a stormy look

but refused to answer and wouldn't meet my eyes.

Ratchet laughed and went on. "We split the food, but now I see why he's so skinny—he gives it to these Reekers."

"You're a Reeker too," I said.

Ratchet pulled me to his side. "No, I'm a survivor."

I shoved at him but Ratchet gripped me harder. "I'm taking this one up top for reward, Oak. One for the many, right?"

"No!" I kicked at Ratchet.

He shoved me away and grabbed Charlie and his knife. "Maybe this one instead." I punched at Ratchet until the glint of the knife flashed at Charlie's throat.

The huddled kids seemed closer to us than a moment ago. I blinked and they were closer still.

"Turn me in, Ratchet, but leave them alone," Oak said.

His friend snorted. "You're not worth anything."

"I can tell you where there's more," Oak said quietly.

"You lie." Ratchet waved the knife, holding Charlie tighter by the throat, his eyes popping. "You're weak, Oak. My friends died in the volcanic mines in the Fire Realm because they were weak. That won't be me. Come to think of it, exchanging this bunch will feed me for a long time."

"No, you can't trade them!" Oak sucked in a warbled breath. "I made a promise to myself … to their parents."

Ratchet shook Charlie. "I take him now, and we trade them one by one and add to the stash—or, trade them all now, I turn you in, and your hide-n-seek game is over. Your choice."

The water dripped from the cave walls in a sullen drum.

Oak gave a heavy sigh. "One … for the many."

"Let me—" Charlie said but was silenced by the knife tip pressing deeper into his throat where his vein pulsed.

"Oak, do something!" I shook him but he stood there, limp. "How could you turn kids in as bait?"

He stooped over. "It's a cross I bear to feed them all. One traded child feeds them all for weeks. We hardly get enough rations for ourselves to live on. It was the only way." He looked up, his face a grimace of pain. "After my son died, I swore I'd never let another child die in the WC again. Not by birth. Not by murder. Not by starvation. But I found I had to sacrifice one in order to save the many."

Like the Wild Childs.

"I try to pick the weak ones who might not make it." He put his face in is hands, then looked up. A lone tear fell down his cheek. "I'm so sorry," he said to the kids. They nodded as if they understood it must work this way.

My chest tightened for the fate of the kids. They never knew what they were missing: sunshine, a comfortable bed, a family to love. Pain ricocheted through my heart with renewed thoughts of home, my friends, and my grandfather. Looking at these filthy kids growing up in the dark, I swore like Oak I'd never let another one die—I'd get them out no matter what.

"What's it going to be Oak?" Ratchet sang out, his knife hard against Charlie's throat. A drop of blood welled and trickled down. The breath of the kids pulsed in a single beat, matching Charlie's nostrils flaring in and out. Water pinged off rock walls as seconds marched by in slow motion.

Oak wiped his face and opened the door. "Go then."

Ratchet twisted around with Charlie, who dragged his feet on the ground. Oak flicked his eyes past me and threw his hand up. A warm wind rushed. A low screech swelled. A flurry of arms and legs whirled past us. Charlie was ripped away from Ratchet, who disappeared beneath a mass of angry kids. His muffled cries echoed around the cavern. I helped Charlie up, who reclaimed his knife and Ratchet's, while Oak barred the door shut and towered over the quivering, kicking mass that clawed at the traitor.

"They know you're down here!" Ratchet's words cut through the angry kids.

"Children, off!" Oak commanded. They scattered like cockroaches to hide in dark corners, their gleaming eyes watchful.

Ratchet twitched on the floor, a lump of torn clothes, then slowly stood, scowling at us with a puffy eye while blood ran down his cheek. "The soldiers are already searching the WC for the Oracle. The word on the street is he escaped the queen's hunt."

Oak's eyes flashed to me.

"It's him isn't it?" Ratchet stumbled toward me, but I moved behind Oak.

Apollo stepped forward, a fist in the air. The A on his ring glinted clear in the lantern light. "I'm King Apollo. I can help free you. If you let us go, we can raise an army, fight Artemis and Zeus, and open the WC."

Ratchet wheezed with laughter, blood bubbling at his mouth. "Think I believe you? You stole that ring, thief." He lunged at Apollo. "Give it to me!"

I cut him off, my bow readied, an arrow aimed at his chest. "I'll stick you good." My words came out strong while I shook inside.

Charlie clicked open his knife and held it against Ratchet's throat. "So will I."

Ratchet clawed at his side and moaned in pain. "You

better run, little Reekers. The WC is no place for kids."
He moaned again and swayed.

"You were one of us," I said.

"Now a traitor to your own kind," Apollo said.

The drip of water from the cave walls tick-tocked as
Ratchet threw his head back and laughed. "They'll find
the tunnels, Oak. I left the secret hatch in your room
wiiiiiide open."

"No!" Oak cried in a terrible, deep voice, seized Ratchet
by the shoulders, and dragged him to the back of the cave.

A sharp cry and a splash told us all what happened.

Oak hunched toward us from the shadows.

"What if he comes back?" Charlie said, breaking the
silence.

Oak, punched a fist to his palm. "He'll be dead—by
river or by me."

Charlie handed Ratchet's knife to him. "Then you
may need this."

Oak took it, turned it in his hand and thrust it at
Apollo. "You're no friend of mine, King."

Apollo stood taller and met his gaze. The water
dripped in time with my racing heart, hoping Oak
wouldn't kill him, but he nodded curtly and put the knife
away. "Neither is Artemis and if she kidnapped you, then
you must be against her, which makes you on my side—
along with your friends here."

"She was my ally, along with Poseidon," Apollo said.
"We were in secret negotiations to start a revolution, but
evil came in to play and put a stop to it."

"You'd better escape and work with your friends here to
succeed next time," Oak said. "We're depending on you."

Apollo bowed and clamped two fingers around his
king's ring. "My friends here believed in me when I

didn't. You can count on it."

Oak peered closer at him. "You look like your father. He came to view Poseidon's slave operation as a young king when I worked in the Sea Realm."

"What was he like?"

Oak rubbed the end of one side of his mustache. "Full of vigor and ideas. He was also kind, I remember. He spoke to some of us, touched my shoulder in passing."

"He changed after that," Apollo said in a tight voice.

"We all change," Oak said. "Good or bad. It's a choice. Unless evil breaks our will …"

The floor shook and mud clumps battered our heads.

"They're in the tunnel!" Oak said. The kids crowded in a circle, tears running down the faces of some, yet they remained silent.

"The river!" I said.

Oak shook his head wildly.

"All rivers lead out. It must split," I pleaded with him.

Oak snapped his fingers and jumped into action. "Rafts!"

He pulled down crates piled up in a hole in the wall, and we carried them toward the sound of water. Around a turn, we faced the river's roar. It raged between glowing rock walls, a mad, swirling foam.

Charlie backed up, wiping away the blood at his throat. "We'll die for sure, *mes amis*."

"Maybe not, but we will in the WC." I tried to convince him, tried to convince myself.

"It's the only way," Apollo said. "Together." He held up a pinky.

So did I. "Together," I repeated, hooking his finger with mine

"*Oui?*" Charlie said doubtfully.

"*Oui*," I said.

Oak rounded up the kids. "Follow these boys. They'll lead the way."

The kids rushed him in a hug. "It wasn't the way I'd planned. But it's no longer safe here. Pair up on your sleeping crates." He pushed them away. "Now go! Follow Joshua. He'll lead you out."

It wasn't a question.

Apollo thrust coins at him. "Take my money, Oak. It may help you. Your sacrifice won't be forgotten."

Oak nodded and shoved the coins in his pocket.

"What about you, Oak?" I said.

"I'll follow, no worries." He nabbed my shirt by the collar and pulled me close. "If you ever come upon the Leandro we know, tell him we'll meet again to fight the good fight."

I didn't want to mention the fact that Leandro might kill me if we ever met up again, so I kept silent and nodded. He drew the pendant off his neck and placed it around mine. "They go with you—always."

I clutched my lost family as he turned away from me, urging the kids to leave. "Don't let them catch you! I'll find you. Your parents will find you. I promise. Now go!"

He could keep no promise but the kids scrambled together, led by the older ones and helped by Charlie and Apollo.

Shouts burst from the cavern. Thumps echoed around the walls. Oak grasped my arm. "Save them. Save them all!"

He ran back to face off with his keepers.

With a gulp, I grabbed a crate, along with my friends, and jumped into the icy monster promising to deliver us to freedom or death.

Chapter Twenty-Six

Numbing cold slammed into me as I hurtled on my crate. We raced down a deep blue torrent more horrifying than riding the Lightning Road. The river slapped us with icy fingers in our torpedo escape. Behind me, eyes of white fire pierced the cave's gleam as the kids screamed in terror. Charlie rode a wave next to me, our crates bashing into one another. I dared another glance behind. Apollo's head bobbed far back in the cave's glow, bringing up the rear. Eddies swirled and spun into water tornadoes that threatened to swallow us, and the glistening walls rushed by in a mad streak. Stalactites stabbed down from arched ceilings. I yelled at the kids to keep down.

Our view widened ahead. "Charlie, what's that?" I shouted to him.

He craned his head. "It splits!"

"Which way?"

He shook his head, uncertain as me. If we didn't veer one way or the other, we'd crash into the center wall in a deadly pileup. If we headed the wrong way, we'd be smashed to pieces and float back dead to Oak.

I clasped my pendant. "Show me the way," I whispered and blew out hard—certain to be my death exhale—when a spot of light grew to my right. Instinct drove me to make a last-second decision for us all. I jerked my crate to the right. The crate reared up on one side and almost threw me off, but I rebalanced and steered harder.

A frenzied flap of wings burst before us as bats whizzed overhead while we raced to our new destination. The light grew brighter and the tightening in my chest released. The water churned slower, becoming flat as glass. We glided along and I sat up, my breaths slowing with the current, and looked back at the kids.

"Everyone make it?"

The kids nodded, bobbing like shipwreck survivors.

We'd ridden a river and made it out alive. By luck or by my magic? There was no way of knowing, or if Oak survived—or if he'd been caught and sentenced to death. I quickly felt for my mother's photo and Leandro's journal. Still there. The book was damp, but a quick thumb-through thankfully revealed its pages weren't soaked.

I laid my head on my crate. Starry light reflecting from the rock walls dappled the water rippling around me. Stalactites reflected like mountains on its surface. So tired. The adrenaline that coursed through me like liquid fire moments ago now drained away. I closed my eyes to escape Nostos and pretended to laze by the creek back home. There knelt my friend, Finn. We were in the creek digging up rocks to build a wall around our fort. The yellow sun shone so bright it hurt my eyes; a friendly burn warming my skin with summer happiness. The water tugged me along and I trailed a hand in its cool calm, filling Apollo's canteen that had ended up with me somewhere along the way.

I finally sat up. A glorious light glowed at the end of our tunnel. A new day dawned. It sparkled across the smooth water in a playful dance. Confusion spiraled through my foggy mind. Had the river transported us home? The fantasy fled as the sun's blue rays told me they were not from Earth.

"*Mon Dieu*! We made it!" Charlie raised a fist in the air. With his salute, we sailed into a new day under a lavender sky, the safety of the cave gone. Warm air engulfed me and I breathed in a salty tang. Sweeping willows along the river replaced the tall oak and pine trees. This was not the Arrow Realm.

"Ahh, I knew you'd take us the right way, Joshua." Charlie kissed his crate over and over, splashing water on himself.

I killed his celebration. "Charlie, we've got to get off this river. Who knows what else might get us. We're an easy target." I flung my hand at him and a giant wave from nowhere flipped his crate. With a splash and a yell, Charlie was tossed into the river. I paddled over with my hands, disoriented, scanning the water for deadly beasts but the river became smooth glass again as if nothing happened.

Sputtering, Charlie climbed back on his crate with the help of one of the kids. "*Zut!* What was that?"

"I don't know." But maybe I did.

He sniffed. "Smells like the ocean."

Poseidon's realm might have an ocean! I searched the

group of kids for Apollo to ask him about it. "Charlie, Apollo isn't here!"

He whipped his head around, searching with me. Every crate carried a kid. Except one. Its mangled wood floated toward us. Apollo's crate. He didn't make the split. He was gone.

My chest hurt so much I thought it might crack in two.

All this for what? Our purpose for coming here was gone. This place! It sucked away everything you cared about.

Charlie pulled Apollo's crate to his side. "He made it. I know he did. Back to the cave. Back to …" He slumped over, unable to finish, and turned away from me.

"He died for nothing," I said in a hoarse voice. "Nothing!"

"No one said he was dead." His bottom lip quivered and he gently pushed the crate away. It floated down the river ahead of us, turned a bend, and disappeared, as broken and lost as me.

Words from Leandro hung in my head: *Someone recently taught me that sometimes you must trust on faith.*

If I taught Leandro to trust on faith—could I?

Could I trust that he'd return to the man I knew?

That we'd find Apollo alive?

We'd stop slavery?

We'd get back home alive?

I slammed my fist on the water. A wall of water rose and raced down the river. Charlie and the kids stared at me. Shaking, I pulled my hand back and remembered more of Leandro's words from another time on another river when we'd been under attack: *Part the waters!* I couldn't then. How could I now? But I knew.

I put my hands back in the water, pushing it away, sending Charlie and the kids toward the riverbank. Charlie clung to his crate, his mouth hanging open, speechless for once. There was only one way the power to move water could live in me now: we'd crossed over into the Sea Realm and the power of Poseidon was now activated in me.

I. Must. Be. The. Oracle.

The sky and water spun around me. Grief over losing my friend, leaving my old life behind, and the scary unknown of what lay ahead filled me up. Trembling all over, I sailed toward the riverbank on the water I commanded. We all hauled our crates up under a weeping willow.

"Joshua, why didn't you tell me you could do that?" Charlie hung on to his crate and squinted at me as if he didn't know me while the kids stared at the blue sun in wonder.

"I didn't know." It was too new in my head to figure out. He nodded, wringing out his clothes, not pushing me about it.

The wind blew up and the kids whirled around, cupping hands to the air as if to catch a gift. Some held on to each other pointing at the trees. With a smile, they fingered leaves, pulling their hands away to reach out and touch them again. How strange. They'd grown up underground. They'd never seen a sun. Never touched a tree. Never felt a breeze.

Apollo may be missing and Oak captured—or worse—but these kids were counting on us now. We were in a new realm with new dangers.

"Let's keep going down the river," Charlie said.

"There's a better way," I said. "Through the Perimeter Lands."

"Bandits live here!"

"Some of those bandits are Takers from Earth. People who hunt the Child Collectors. They'd help these kids. And Poseidon may help us. Apollo said he was a friend." It hurt to say his name and I forced my grief down. "Either way, they have a chance. We have a chance to carry out Apollo's wishes and get home. So, I say we go that way." I pointed to where the sky grew brighter through the trees, "to the edge of the Great Beyond, where the Takers hang out, then you and I can figure out how to meet up with Poseidon without getting killed first."

"Sounds easy," Charlie said with a thumbs-up but his scared face gave him away.

Yeah. Not so easy with our big group. I counted the kids. Twenty-two total.

"We go that way," I ordered the kids. "We'll find people to help. Get to Poseidon. He and Apollo were—are friends."

The tallest kid signaled the kids to follow us when voices jarred our peaceful spot. Heads bobbed through the trees. We all crouched behind a row of bushes. An idea was forming in my head, but I had to think it out some more.

"Scram and cram," I whispered to the kid and pointed to the Great Beyond. He seemed puzzled. "Run and be quiet. We'll hold them off. Give you a head start."

Charlie met my eyes, probably wondering like me how we'd hold them off, then gave the kid a fierce nod.

The boy gripped my hand, his dirt-smudged face thankful. "Good. Bye."

Nothing was good about any of this but I nodded. "Watch out for The Edge. You don't want to fall off and die in space."

He nodded and ran off with the others close behind, silent as they'd been raised to survive. One by one the kids left, flashing me and Charlie grateful nods. They soon disappeared from sight. The voices grew louder. Arguing about escaped slaves.

We needed a plan B.

Now Charlie and I had only ourselves to worry about. That was scary enough.

Chapter Twenty-Seven

"We split up," a familiar voice blared, closer. "Their scent has crossed into the Sea Realm. You patrol to the north and west. I'll take the east. Move fast. Queen Artemis tires of the chase. Watch out for Poseidon's soldiers. Take them down quietly and toss them off The Edge, if you have to."

Leandro! I pulled Charlie farther behind the bush.

"Yes, sir."

"We don't go back to the queen empty-handed. Take all slaves alive. Got it?"

"Yes, sir!"

The soldiers moved away, heavy boots crunching on the forest floor. They faded into the opposite direction and were gone. Charlie and I remained still and quiet. The blood pumped through my ears in a raging drumbeat. A snap of twigs cut through the silence. Charlie looked at me for what to do. I motioned him to stay.

Please, pass by.

Leandro stalked us through the branches. I watched my old friend with a boulder in my chest. Wanting to cry out. Wanting to fight beside him for good once again. Now, he fought the evil fight against us. Because of him, Oak and Apollo might be dead.

Leandro scanned left and right but not overhead. In the sky-highs, we could travel across to the Great Beyond and find the kids—and a way home. I pointed up. "Got to get there," I whispered.

Now? Charlie mouthed. I put up my hands. *Not yet.* We inched closer to one another, our heat pulsing between us and our equally sweaty smell.

I dared a peek through the bush. Leandro stepped forward with hands on his hips and peered through the shadowy woods. He pushed the hood of his cloak farther back and blue rays sliced across his face. In one swift movement, he removed his bow slung across his chest and slid an arrow in place. We had no chance of winning against his archery skills. During this entire performance, he stared through the trees, his masterful eyes doing what they knew best—hunting.

If he moved his head to the right, he'd be staring right in my eyes. His scar blazed white against his tanned skin from hairline to chin. I breathed shallowly. In and out. My knees grew numb from kneeling but I dared not move. With the crackle of one bent twig, our freedom would end.

Snap!

Leandro took a step toward our spot. Another peek and my breath caught in one big terrifying gulp. A cadmean beast paced back and forth by his side! The giant fox's head reached Leandro's shoulders, and its horse-sized legs rippled with each step as it swished its thick tail. Charlie dragged his fingers down one cheek when he saw it, his face a mask of horror. Sweat broke out on my forehead. My dry mouth couldn't wash away the sour taste on my tongue.

A growl cut through the quiet followed by a chuff. "I smell the Reeker, master."

"Good work, boy."

Through our small view of the thick bush, a tail smashed the air and a giant ear twitched. The beast's head rammed into view and I almost fell sideways, fearful it saw us. Its heavy panting beat the air as its fat tongue pulsed in an out, dripping foamy blobs. No Tastykakes for this monster. Its grisly tongue wanted Tasty*kids*.

Charlie's eyes seemed like they'd burst from their sockets. It was agony to keep still when every bone in our bodies wanted to run. My legs and feet were now completely numb. Soon running may not be an option. The Wild Childs would have to wait. Plan B that had been nudging my brain came to me: steal back my lightning orb and steal a Lightning Gate key to get home. One person could get us both.

I stood up, stumbling on numb feet. Charlie pulled at my jeans, begging me to get down. No turning back now. I rose above the bush in full sun between the trees. "Looking for us, Leandro?"

Charlie shot up next to me, pulling at me to run but escape was futile. With my shout, Leandro focused his arrow on me. The cadmean beast stomped and snorted, lunging forward. Fire exploded from its mouth, emblazing a bush next to us. The blistering heat scorched my face and arms.

"Down, beast," Leandro said with a cold calm, his

finger poised to shoot me through the heart. He'd said we were to be taken alive—and where else would they take us but back to the castle?

"*Mon Dieu!*" Charlie moaned next to me, his hands falling away as he gave up his fight to run. The willow tree above unclenched its boughs as if it relinquished hope too, releasing yellow leaves. They spun down and burst into flame upon touching the burning bush. Flying ash coated my skin and mixed with beads of sweat that I dared not wipe off.

"We can use him to steal back the lightning orb and find a Lightning Gate key," I said to Charlie under my breath. His mouth formed an *O* but he still looked doubtful. I hadn't figured out how we'd sneak the key from Leandro's bag or get the orb from Artemis's chambers once we got back to the castle. That was plan C.

"We can't run from you," I said to Leandro, stepping out from behind the bush with Charlie right behind me. Firelight from the flaming bush streaked across Leandro's face, distorting it into two faces—one dark, one light.

He lowered his bow. "You did though. The queen wanted to have some fun hunting you. Come with me willingly and give her what she wants. If you do, she'll make your end easier, Barbaros."

She was the barbarian, not us!

"No end," Charlie pleaded, clasping his hands together with a bowed head and whispering a string of French words I hoped were prayers.

"Leandro won't let anything happen to us, will you?" I said.

He pushed his eyebrows down and raised his bow again. "It's not up to me. I follow my queen's orders and she ordered me to find you, Oracle. You escaped her hunt, Barbaros stinker. Very clever."

Clever wasn't the feeling inside me at the moment.

The cadmean beast threw its snout in the air. "One bite, master! I'll let them live. Hungrrrry."

"No, beast!" Leandro said sharply and thrust his bow at us. "On your knees, Reekers. We'll drive the Barbaros right out of you."

We did as he said while he threw his bow across his chest and pulled his fire belt from under his cloak, snapping it like a whip. It grew long enough with magic to tie us together.

Leandro first tied Charlie's hands in front. When it was my turn, Leandro's hair fell across my cheek. His burnt chocolate smell of earth and leather whisked past me and my longing for him to be what he once was tore through me in a raw ache.

"Don't do this, Leandro," I choked out as he finished my knots, but he pulled the rope tighter and hauled us up.

The quiet surge of the nearby river we'd escaped on called our freedom but no chance of that as the cadmean beast trotted back and forth. With each head toss, the beast's slimy slobber sprayed the air. The willow trees drooped lower as if the forest held its breath waiting for our fate to unfold.

Bits of ash floated in the air, landing on my tongue with an acrid taste. Cold crept into my toes from my muddy boots sinking in sandy soil, and my thighs and arms chafed from sweat. Smoke from the bush blinded me for a moment, and through my tears, Leandro blurred to faceless black. The bush leaped in a final fiery dance and died, leaving behind pitiful, charred stick fingers. My vision cleared but not my chest, as it rose with shudders I pushed back down.

Leandro pulled the arrows from my quiver and tossed them in his own. "As if you could ever be worthy enough to fight me. Keep your bow, boy. It has no power against me."

"Who's making you do this?"

He didn't answer as he shoved us along in front of him.

"Ahh, forget it, Joshua," Charlie said with a sniff. "At least we'll die together, as brothers."

"Nobody's brother is dying today." I struggled to loosen my ropes. One reach in my pocket and the journal would prove to Leandro we were in this together—if he remembered his old life and the people he once loved. I could show him the pendant too, but he may think I stole it. He yanked my belt rope, razoring it deep into my wrists. "We're connected, Leandro. I can show you how."

"I'm connected to no one, least of all a Reeker."

The cadmean beast snorted in agreement.

"Your wife, Dee Dee, I knew her."

The tension on our rope slackened for a moment and pulled tight again. "You could not."

"I did. On Earth."

Leandro yanked both our belt ropes, sending Charlie to bang painfully into my shoulder. "You lie!"

"She escaped from here. Please remember."

The belt rope let loose and Leandro spun me to face him, taking Charlie along for the ride. His eyes dug deep into mine as he pressed his face to me, his hair falling on either side like a shroud covering me in his darkness. "My wife is dead. My son is dead. You know nothing of this."

I feared saying all I knew might send him over the edge, but if he saw my mother's picture, maybe he'd believe and come back to me.

"I know you, Leandro. Don't you know me?"

Charlie's sniffs turned to full blown sobs now.

"Let my hands free and I'll show you," I begged.

Leandro pinched my arms, his eyes blazing, but there was no stopping now. I went on. "You helped us set all the kids free in the Lost Realm. We fought against Hekate alongside King Apollo and my grandfather. You swore to appeal to Artemis to make Nostos a better place. You saved my life, and I saved yours. How could you forget?"

His grip lessened on me and I went on, mesmerized by his fierce gaze. "You're Leandro of the Arrow Realm. You deserted your post to seek your lost family. You risked your own life to help others. You never give up. Don't give up now. We need you. *I* need you."

Leandro's hold relaxed, his forehead creased.

"You're not a broken arrow," I whispered.

His face drooped, the anger fleeing, and he caressed the branded scar on his arm.

The cadmean beast pawed the ground, breaking through our moment. "Master, stop listening to this Barbaros stinker. He is nothing!"

Leandro's arms fell to his side and he stepped back, our space broken. "I am nothing."

He said it so softly it took a moment for me to register what he said. He gazed off into the woods as if answers hid there to awaken him from a spell. Was there no way to break through to him and no one on our side? Maybe the words of his world could work.

"For the love of Olympus! Help us, Leandro!"

Charlie tugged at me but what did we have to lose? The queen wanted us alive.

"By the gods," I shouted.

"By the gods yourself, Joshua," Charlie pleaded. "Just stop!"

Leandro's head snapped to attention and the cadmean beast growled low in his throat. "Master, it's time to deliver these Reekers."

Leandro's face rearranged back to a dark veil, and he shoved us on our journey again, but I couldn't give up on unleashing the man hidden inside.

"By the arrow of Artemis, wake up!"

"Enough!" he bellowed at me.

The beast leaped to my side, silencing my quest. Putrid breath pulsed on my cheek. Hot foam splattered my shoulder. I dared not look it in the eye but kept moving forward as it kept pace with me.

"Fine," I said. "Take us to the castle. I'll prove it there. Maybe you'll change back to who you are."

"We're not headed to the castle," he said in an even tone.

The cadmean beast howled as if Leandro cracked a joke and Charlie flinched, shooting me a worried glance as he bounced from foot to foot. The violet sky darkened with building clouds as we kept up with our captor. It seemed an hour passed. The willow trees became oak and pine again, the loamy sand turned to hard dirt, and the warm salt air changed to a cool, dry breeze. Back in the Arrow Realm.

The wind picked up harder, tossing twigs down as branches sawed back and forth. Beyond us, a limb crashed to the ground, echoing across the forest. Charlie and I both jumped.

"Where are we going?" I said to Leandro, after trekking in silence forever.

"Between Artemis's castle and the Wild Lands. Not far from the bog. Two clicks that way." He nodded in the direction.

"What's there?"

He paused as if considering whether to tell me. "The Black Heart Tree. There you'll do my queen's bidding."

"I won't! Not ever!"

He pressed my shoulder hard. Where once his warm hand radiated courage and hope, it now cut me with a chill that shivered to my toes.

What had I done?

"You'll have no choice. Powers are at force here. Soon your powers—and your body—will be taken; there'll be no more use for you." He spoke flat, monotonous. Someone else's voice. Someone else's words.

Dread filled my veins with ice and the cadmean beast howled louder, its cries bouncing off the trees like shards of glass in my ears.

"Charlie, I'm sorry," I whispered.

He didn't answer. He hung his head and stared at his shuffling feet, trapped in his own world of lost hope.

Chapter Twenty-Eight

We slogged along in silence as the cadmean beast snapped its jaws at our heads whenever we slowed. On and on, we stepped through the lifeless woods, its creatures in hiding. Once, something rustled underfoot in the leaves but slithered off, as if it knew to stay far away. The sun peaked high in the sky. Our fourth day on Nostos.

After some time, Charlie managed to wriggle his fingers into his front pocket and slip out his knife. He twirled to thrust it at Leandro but I shoved him off. In a flash, the knife was back in Leandro's hand. He smiled. "Nice to have this back."

Charlie groaned and I quivered inside with relief and despair. No matter who Leandro was now, I didn't want him hurt.

I stretched my fingers into my front jeans pocket, where I'd moved Apollo's flute. Was there a chance the flute could call the korax again, like when we first arrived?

I slid it out, bent over, and blew hard. Urgent chimes filled the air.

"What are you doing?" Leandro jolted me to stop and I blew harder again and again.

Shrieks burst from above us. The korax! Our one chance. They'd helped us in the Lost Realm. Would they now?

"Korax! Your family helped us escape from the Lost Realm. Apollo set them free!" I yelled up in a race of words before Leandro stopped me. "Help us!"

Leandro reached for my flute. "Silence!"

I twisted out of his hands just in time, and the cadmean beast roared with fire. I jumped back with Charlie. We missed getting singed by a hair.

To my surprise, Leandro laughed and let go of the fire belt that led us along. "See how far you get, malumpus-tongue. The great birds work for Artemis."

We stumbled back with our freedom. Charlie shoved me to run but I held him back. A dark shadow blocked out the blue sun.

"Light bringers," a hiss screeched in my ears.

Leandro commanded them. "Take these Reekers to Artemis!"

"We're friends of King Apollo," I blew the flute again. "This is his flute! He helped your Lost Realm family, but Artemis kidnapped Apollo and he died because of her!"

The birds hovered as if debating which side to follow.

"Why do you hesitate, korax?" Leandro yelled with a furrowed brow, raising his bow. Charlie tugged me along now, begging me to run. "You answer to Artemis. I've taken your brothers down. I'll take you down!"

Black wings flapped in slow motion as the two birds hung over us for what seemed an eternity.

"Trust light bringers." The words flew around us like flames from a great blaze. A rush of wind flattened me and Charlie into a tree as the giant black ravens zoomed toward us. Leandro gripped his dagger, his smirk gone. Talons of curved bone slashed the air. Fat snake tongues pulsed from beaks. Beady electric green eyes zeroed in on me.

"The Oracle is here!" I screamed with emphasis. The korax tucked their black wings in and shot between the trees.

The leader reached us first with a loud *caw* to its partner behind him. "Save Oracle."

Leandro backed up, puzzlement on his face turning to anger. He nocked an arrow to his bow and fired. Charlie and I dropped to the ground as the arrow zinged into the trunk where my head had been moments ago. Wind, propelled by the giant birds, cut through the air, plowing over us toward Leandro. His fingers flew. Arrow after arrow shot past us. The birds dodged left and right between trees, just missing the arrows and the cadmean beast's fiery breath.

Then our captors were gone. Beaks snatched them up and carried them off. A howl and a shout charged the air. I watched Leandro's legs dangle next to the kicking cadmean beast who continued to shoot flames, catching the treetops on fire.

"Hold the key!" Leandro yelled and threw his knife down. A road of flames followed them and the black mass of wings disappeared. The woods fell silent. Charlie picked up the knife and we both stared at the sky.

"What did Leandro mean when he said 'hold the key'?" I said.

Charlie didn't answer. He popped open the knife and stared at me with a face I'd never seen before—a face full of hate.

Chapter Twenty-Nine

"Charlie, help get my belt off!"

He sawed through the end of his belt rope first to free himself.

"Do mine."

Instead, he grabbed the fire belt and tied me to a tree before I knew what happened. I struggled to get loose, but it grew longer with Nostos magic as Charlie stretched it tighter, knotting it in place.

"Stop it!"

Charlie stepped back and thrust the knife in my face. "I don't want to hurt you."

"Let me go!"

I threw myself against the tree to free myself but all it did was tighten my trap. I slumped over, my brain muddled with what was going on. How on Earth could I stop it? Except this *wasn't* Earth.

Charlie moved closer. The knife sparkled like a silver

fish as he tossed it from hand to hand, flipping in the air amongst the sun's motes. "Don't worry. She wants you alive."

"Artemis."

"Of course," Charlie snorted. "She's my family now and all her people. You were a sad excuse for a brother. Always getting me into danger. What kind of brother does that?"

"Who *are* you?"

He spun the knife in my face. "We were supposed to have fun." He yanked the flute out of my hand and stomped on it, smashing it apart like our friendship. "Instead, you drag me back here to follow you around once again. I'm sick of following you. Who put you in charge? Artemis promised I could be a leader! People will follow me now."

"Can't you see she's put a spell on you!"

First Leandro, now Charlie. Artemis was taking down all my friends with her evil.

Breathe deeply. Find the calm.

I did and backtracked through the events before Crazy Charlie became enemy number one. It happened right after Leandro was snatched by the korax. He'd said, "hold the key."

It started to fall in place.

I'd seen enough spy movies where the bad guys hypnotize their victims and use trigger words to set them on a mission. When did Artemis have a chance to hypnotize Charlie? He wasn't alone with her and her slave, Hypnos. Wait … he was! When we were separated while getting hosed down in the dungeon. Was this *her* plan B?

Charlie paced around the tree, mumbling to himself. "I'm in charge. Hold the key. Yes. Yes. He's held. Must wait. Artemis and her men will find us. I'll get all the glory! No more Reeker for me."

Each time Charlie passed behind the tree, I rubbed the belt against the rough bark, hoping to saw it in half. He caught me on one round and jabbed the knife at me as he continued his endless journey, making me dizzy as he circled. The sun blazed lower in the sky, and sweat trickled down the crook of my back. I closed my eyes to mere slits but kept them open enough to watch the knife passing by my throat.

If only I had the lightning orb! But I had nothing. Just me. No orb. No Lightning Gate key. No way home. Some hero to this world I turned out to be. I get taken off guard and captured by my own friend. I began to feel sorry for myself when those last thoughts gave me an idea.

Taken off guard.

Take Charlie off guard! If someone can be hypnotized with trigger words then maybe they can be un-hypnotized with trigger words. What were they? The clock was ticking. Artemis and her men would find us soon and I'd be in real trouble.

Think, Joshua, think!

"Charlie, I'm sorry I got you in this trouble. I tried to stop you from following me here, remember? We can get home again, but you've got to let me go."

"I can't let you go. Your powers belong to Artemis now. She's going to steal them."

"Then what?"

He stopped pacing. "Then you die."

My knees shook and I sagged against the belt.

"Why'd you come with me, Charlie?"

He turned to stare at me. "I didn't want to be left again. Lose a brother again."

"Then don't lose me now. We can still be brothers."

"Why should I? My parents gave me no choice. My

mom won't come to America with my brother even if we do get back to Earth."

"But you have a choice here, Charlie. Choose me and I'll help you get home to your brother."

He stepped closer. His sweaty heat pouring over me. "No you won't. You'd go find your new brother and forget about me." He shook his head. "No! Must hold the key." His eyes pierced mine yet there seemed no reaching my friend Charlie.

"We're all we've got right now."

His eyes froze in an unblinking stare. He flicked the knife and cold steel pressed sharply to my throat. I sank into the tree that offered no escape. Was this how my life would end? Bound to a tree by a friend on another world?

"Could you kill the friend you once saved?"

He didn't answer but pushed the knife deeper into my skin. He tilted his head, inspecting my throat as if deciding whether to stab me or not. Wetness trickled down my neck. Shallow breaths. In and out. In and out. The world began to spin. *Don't faint!*

"Must. Hold. Key."

"I'd rather die than be held," I whispered. The Charlie I knew wouldn't kill his best friend. I needed to trust in him—trust the good Charlie that still lived deep inside.

His hand shook. The knife bit harder. His eyebrows rippled with doubt and his mouth twitched in trembling waves. The blade ripped into me with each shake of his hand. "Hold the key. Not destroy the key."

"Release ... the ... key," I wheezed out.

Blackness filled the corners of my mind. A buzzing grew in my ears until it thundered through me.

Right before I passed out, Charlie's eyes sprung wide with panic.

Chapter Thirty

The black mist in my mind faded. I opened my lids. So heavy. Dim light poured in. Was this heaven? The roughness of leaves and sticks beneath me told me no. Somehow I'd gotten free of the fire belt and lay on the ground. The branches overhead nodded, welcoming me back. Dusk was here. I must've been unconscious for a while. I sat. Dizziness squeegeed my brain. When my head cleared, I saw Charlie sitting against the tree across from me, his head down, and his bony knees drawn to his chin. He rocked back and forth, humming the same two notes over and over.

I put a hand to my throat and came away with crusty blood. "Charlie?" I rasped out.

Tears streaked down his face. "You're not dead."

My Charlie was back.

I shook my head and stood up, steadying myself against the tree, then walked over and pulled him up along with the knife and belt resting at his feet. The dizziness eased and I glanced around the woods. We were alone with no way of knowing who or what would come for us next.

"I hurt you, Joshua … and the awful things I said." Charlie wiped his face.

"It wasn't you. Artemis put you under a hypnotic spell back at her castle, and Leandro triggered it with his words. 'Hold the key.' "

"You broke the spell." His tears slowed.

I remembered the last words I spoke. "Release the key." I'd figured it out! Power swelled inside me. I'd saved myself and Charlie all on my own.

"It's all over now. We can go," I said, as I wound the fire belt and clipped it to my belt loop, but Charlie didn't move.

We stood in silence until he spoke again. "Would you believe that I was a hero to my little brother?"

"Yes. You've been a hero to me, to the kids you saved in the Lost Realm and in the cave … to Apollo."

"Some good it did." He rocked on his toes and gazed up at the purple twilight sky. "I wish the river had taken me too."

"Don't say that."

The skin bunched up around his bright blue eyes. "Family's not supposed to let you down."

Maybe another way could get through to him. I rapped the handle of the knife to his chest and he jumped. "Aren't you letting them down too?"

He looked shocked at the thought. "How?"

"Your family didn't abandon you. But you are if we don't work together to get back to Earth."

His face sagged. "Like I abandoned you when I ran

from the cretan after us in the Wild Lands. I should have stayed and helped you fight."

"That's not what I meant! I meant, so what if your parents do get divorced? Lots of people do. You still have each other. I don't have a mother or a father or a brother. You do. You can't forget them and make up a whole new family just because you want to."

Charlie stooped over and stared at his fists.

He pressed his lips together, the tears rolling again. "I let you down big time. I should have been stronger. Not given in to hypnosis like you!'"

"Yeah, well, I forgive you. Isn't that what brothers do?" I attempted a smile.

"I'm no brother. I don't deserve any brother!"

He jerked around and ran through the trees.

"Charlie, wait!"

I stumbled after him, but the dizziness flared again. I fell to my knees. I tried to stand but slipped on damp leaves and fell again, jabbing the knife handle painfully in my gut. Charlie's black hair bobbed through the woods and was gone. Shadows crawled over me from the setting sun.

"Come back," I whispered to myself.

Alone. Again. Abandoned.

Everyone I'd trusted betrayed me. Ash, Leandro, Charlie—even Apollo with his lack of faith. Now it didn't matter.

Everything I'd taken a leap of faith to trust in failed me: leaving Earth to come here again, believing I was the Oracle, and that I was going to save this world and all enslaved. Laughter bubbled inside over how ridiculous it sounded, but the laughter soon turned to great big sobs.

I ran like a crazed person, pumping my arms to fly

through the woods. I didn't care to where. Light grew beyond the trees. The Great Beyond. One jump. Fly into space and float in peace. Surrender to the nothing. I tripped on a tree root and fell with a *whump* to my knees, coming to my senses.

I didn't want to die—I wanted to forget.

The endless forest pressed around me, comforting me, offering me the chance to hide. No one needed me. As an only child growing up with only a grandfather, I'd never felt lonely. Here, now, abandoned by everyone I knew, loneliness stabbed at my heart.

Waves of tiredness overcame me. I curled up alongside a tree to rest but my mind wouldn't quiet. In the final light of day, I pulled out Leandro's journal, seeking answers and comfort in what used to be.

My Homeland
Journal Entry 55
By Leandro of the Arrow Realm

I have befriended a Wild Child. I did not mean for this to occur, but occur it did nonetheless. If I did not know any better, I think she planned our meeting. Her name is Ash.

On my weekly patrol of the Wild Lands borders, I became separated from my crew with my trusted hound, Lore, and came upon this wispy tall girl. I nearly shot her through the heart with an arrow as she sat in the shadow of a tree atop a giant agrius beast.

I calmed Lore down after it became

apparent this girl's beast was a trained pet and would do no harm.

"Why are you down here?" I asked her. "Don't you know the queen will use you as bait?"

She was not afraid of me and spoke words I will never forget. "I claim my own freedom and what keeps me here is nothing you people do. It won't always be like this. Change is coming."

How could a Wild Child of the treetops know this? Her words lit the truth I knew all along: the Earth boy had a purpose in our world. My heart welled with emptiness after saying goodbye to him in the Lost Realm, adding to the loss of my wife and son.

She said no more as she led me back to my party, then disappeared in a flash before they saw her. I told no one of our meeting. Artemis could no longer be trusted nor could her men. And so the girl and I continued to meet, by chance—or not—it did not matter.

As she opened up, she gave me hope that the Oracle was no myth but the savior to bring our world out of darkness. She wanted to give her people, the Wild Childs, a choice: go home to Earth or remain a Wild Child. Either way they would be free to choose, but only if there was an end to mortal slavery. I knew in my heart who the Oracle was: Joshua.

I asked her, "What do you choose?"

"To stay. This is where I feel most free."

With that, a plan began to form: send her to Earth on the Lightning Road to bring Joshua back. My Child Collector belt would get her there, but we needed a plan to sneak her through the Lightning Gate. I'd be missed if I went. No one would miss a Wild Child.

Fear grips my heart as I now wait for Ash's return from Earth.

What if bringing Joshua here is a death sentence? The myth professes the Oracle will sicken and die if they cross realms, claiming too many Olympian powers at once. How can I control this? What if he is merely a mortal boy and nothing else? Then what? I've tried to analyze my motives. Do I truly do this to free all mortal slaves and restore goodness to our world ... or do I do this with the ultimate goal to get my wife and son back? I'm tormented by my selfish desires and kneel here asking the gods for guidance.

If I must die to save the one who can save us all, I can live with this.

Joshua, I will never betray you. By the Arrow of Artemis, I swear this to be true.

Yours in service, Leandro.

What a bunch of bull!
I threw the journal hard at the trunk.

How I wanted to face Leandro and scream at him. *You did betray me, Leandro! Your wife is dead. Probably your son. Why help this world? No one wants to help me!*

But the Wild Childs could help me disappear.

Ash's words came back to me. *Trust only those you know in your heart.* I once knew Leandro and Charlie by heart. I'd trusted them. Yet they betrayed me. Funny how Oak and Ash, strangers, were now ones to count on.

In the dusk, the words on my slave brand caught my eye. *No escape. Your armor of flesh and bone fuels us on!* I spit on it, scrubbing hard with the hem of my shirt until my arm burned raw. My tears fueled the need to un-brand myself, but the black words engulfed in a ring of flame still taunted me. *No escape.*

A snap of branches nearby reminded me of the danger roaming the Perimeter Lands. Wild beasts, bandits, Artemis ... Leandro. I summoned the strength to leave the ground and pull myself into the branches of a tree. The thought of Leandro's journal being shredded and used as nest material made me glad, but at the last moment, I shoved it back in my pocket. Perhaps there was a sliver of information in it to help me survive.

A dozen feet up, I tucked into a warm tree hollow and ate Ash's remaining squirrel mash and ache cakes before sleep chased me down. I dreamed of Bo Chez again. He stood in the sun, towering over me with stern eyes, the kind for getting bad grades and not using common sense.

"One for the many." He echoed Oak's words but added his own. "*You* are the one."

He grew bigger and blocked out the sun, his giant silhouette shadowing me in darkness.

"Not the one," I yelled. "No one!"

I turned and ran to hide amongst the many.

Chapter Thirty-One

The sky had grown lighter when I awoke. My fifth day in the Arrow Realm. I must have passed the night in my tree. My stiff legs and neck confirmed it. Shaking off sleep, I climbed higher, hoping to see the Wild Childs' houses. If the Wild Childs could survive in a tree world so could I, and no one would look for me there. No one would look for me anywhere.

I pulled myself up faster with urgent purpose. Muted stars winked as they faded with the rising sun. I stopped to stare at them. I clung to the tree, closed my eyes, and visualized staring up at the Big Dipper back home. Holding on to that memory meant holding on to the tiny shreds of the old Joshua. I opened my eyes. The Nostos stars were gone, erased by the blue ball of the rising sun.

I shook myself out of my daze and climbed higher. The limb I stood on cracked in half beneath me, but I sidestepped to another branch in time to watch the wood crash down. At one point, Artemis and her men galloped below. I froze amongst the leaves in hiding, but the army never looked up. From tree to tree, I moved until the great hedge appeared, signaling the border into the Wild Lands.

Was I crazy to head back to the Wild Childs? They could escape but didn't. They survived on their own terms. Leaving it all behind to start a new life sounded good to me.

I snatched up a vine and swung over the wall, and slammed into a tree, the breath knocked out of me. The scent of smoke hung in the air as if left over from the rain. The Wild Childs camp.

Rough bark scraped my arms and face. I pressed myself against a trunk, thankful to still be alive when growls rumbled below. An agrius beast paced the forest floor, pawing the ground. With each snarl, giant billows of steam blew from its flared nostrils. Not Ash's pet for sure. It stood up on its hind legs, attacking the tree, trying to climb but sliding down, howling in anger. I scrambled higher.

From tree to tree I jumped, following the smoke trail. The agrius beast kept pace. Sap stuck to my fingers and clothes, attracting tiny black bugs that buzzed around me, biting my neck and hands. I swatted at them while brushing the sweat off my forehead. The blue sun burned my eyes between patches of sky above. Water dripped from dewy leaves and I drank each drop greedily, my throat parched and my canteen long empty. The leaves formed letters but I bashed them away before reading their words. "No more messages!"

Pale gray sticks scattered across the trails below. More twig messages from my mysterious friend? No. My breath quickened in tight spurts. Not sticks. Bones. Of kids hunted down.

NEVER … GIVE … UP.

Had they? Didn't matter. They were the unlucky ones who hadn't survived to become a Wild Child. Or perhaps they *were* the lucky ones. Their suffering had ended. A skull leaned against a boulder, it blank eyes staring up from its hollow face. I lunged to another tree, tearing my eyes away from the path of death. My dread grew into spears of rage. A primitive cry burst from my lungs. My skin rippled. My muscles bulged. The bark bit into me as my body swelled against the tree trunk. A shock of black fur sprung from my hands.

No! This couldn't be happening—not a beast!

A power this big comes with great responsibility, Oak had said.

The power of the Oracle. Who would teach me how to use it?

Trembling, I willed away this terrifying transformation. My body deflated. The hair on my hands faded to ghostly wisps and then *poof* disappeared.

I hugged the tree, wetting the bark with tears of relief, and looked at the sky. Could I become a bird and fly away or a cadmean beast and torch my enemies? The thought was too frightening. It bound me to Nostos. My tears turned to ones of desperation and the sun held no answers.

Every few minutes, I looked for evidence of the Wild Childs. The thought of finding refuge with others, and the agrius beast's hungry moans below as it hunted me, kept me going. I may die here, but it wouldn't be from being eaten. I fingered Leandro's fire belt, wondering how it could help me, then pulled my hands away, not wanting a connection to him.

Exhaustion sank into my every bone. I hung on to a tree in the nook of its two branches and closed my eyes. One moment of rest. A breeze chilled my skin. As I shivered, my eyes twitched open. The largest tree in the wood appeared through the thick of the forest. The Grand Tree! The protector of the Wild Childs. A beacon of light in this dark Arrow Realm.

My strength was sucked away from lack of food and sleep. I hugged the tree tighter with my remaining strength. If I made it to the Grand Tree, its giant arms would hold me up until the Wild Childs found me.

My foot slipped. I caught a branch but my trembling hands slid off it, finger by finger.

The Grand Tree stomped toward me. Ancient limbs curved and soared upwards with crooked fingers. Closer it grew as the agrius beast paced below, now joined by a cadmean beast. They snapped at one another, battling for breakfast—me. My desperate fingers clung tighter to the branch as I scrabbled to get a foothold on a knotted burl.

"The Reeker is mine, fire-devil!"

"Back off beast! Your stench sickens me."

The growls and grunts of the standoff grew louder. Then the Grand Tree loomed beside me. I willed my body to hang on and take one final leap. I reached out and, with my heart rapping in my chest, launched myself toward it. Stiff hands reached out for me but I faltered, leaned back, and fell.

I screamed as tree branches whipped my arms and legs. Flames from the cadmean beast blasted my feet and heat surged up my body. I fell toward death, but instead of landing on teeth, I slammed into hard wood. The Grand Tree cupped me to safety. The beasts roared but the Grand Tree roared back louder with ear-splitting creaks. It slapped two of its limbs down with balled fingers and flung the creatures away. They howled in pain and dashed off through the forest to find another meal.

Clinging to the sides of the Grand Tree's hand, I peered down. The massive Oak uprooted itself, one root at a time, and strode through the woods on knobby feet. The forest swayed back to let it pass as it forged a trail, twisting wooden fingers around its fellow trunk mates, pushing onward. I held on, amazed to be alive.

Sunlight glimmered and I lifted my face to it. The great tree's leaves curled into cones and dripped water into my throat. I rode this woodland giant until the treetops were filled with huts spread out amongst a meadow of leaves. Figures appeared amongst branches. The Wild Childs. I recognized one of them standing on the big tree house platform.

Ash.

She didn't look happy to see me at all.

Chapter Thirty-Two

"Great one," Ash whispered in awe as she bowed to the Grand Tree with all of the kids. My ride came to an end as the old oak uncurled its slatted palm to set me on the platform.

"Thank you." I nodded to the ancient one. It shook its limbs and a thousand green leaves rustled a wind song. With creaking groans, the Grand Tree lifted it roots and marched back to where it came from.

"It's true then," Ash said, staring at me with ice green eyes. "He goes runabout on Nostos."

"He saved my life," I said.

"The Grand Tree is the one good thing in this world we believe in. It's a symbol of peace. You *are* the one."

I said nothing. The memory of my body bulging into a wild animal paralyzed me with the terrifying—and thrilling—memory.

"And if you *are* this Oracle, then you need to go—

now," Ash said, crossing her arms. A low murmur grew among the Wild Childs with her words.

"What if I don't want to be the Oracle? I risked my life to come back here and be a Wild Child," I said. "I survived the hunt. Don't I belong?"

"You put us in danger. Queen Artemis wants you. She'll keep searching for you. She'll know you'll be hiding with us. The soldiers came searching for you. They'll come again. She'll round us up and stick us like her mother did. We'll all be dead Goners and Leandro will help her."

Yes, he would.

"I don't have anyone."

"Where is your tall, skinny friend and King Apollo? What did you do with them?" Her eyes were accusing.

"Charlie tried to kill me … and ran off."

"Why would your friend want to stick you?" Ash demanded.

"He was under a spell or something. I don't know! Artemis did something to him."

"And Apollo?"

The mad river flashed through my mind. The broken crate. Apollo's face behind me as we navigated the racing rapids. "He's dead."

Ash pointed her knife at me. I stumbled back into the platform's rails.

"Now the Lost Realm will be after us as well with the royal one dead. We'll all be grounded, Oracle. Take your powers and leave now. They're no good to us!"

The Wild Childs swarmed onto the platform and stood behind Ash, jagged spears pointed at me.

I gripped the rough railing, splinters gouging into my hands. "I'd never hurt Apollo! The river got him. Oak helped us escape with the other slave kids from a secret cave, but Apollo didn't make it out."

Ash lowered her knife. "Oak helped you …"

"He risked his life for us."

"Like he does giving us news of Nostos," she said quietly. "Did he survive?"

"I-I don't know. He stayed behind to face off with the soldiers who'd found us."

"And the other kids?"

"They scram and crammed to the Perimeter Lands."

"They have a runabout chance then."

I nodded. The spears dropped and I let out the huge breath I'd been holding, telling her everything that had happened. When I finished, she and all the Wild Childs were quiet. The forest seemed to wait for her words as if she commanded them too. Every branch, every leaf, lay still as water on a windless lake.

A final plea. "Ash, I have nowhere else to go."

She slid her knife away. "Oak helped you. I'll help you." The Wild Childs gave a collective sigh. "You can stay. For now, Oracle. We'll figure something out."

I mumbled thanks.

"You'll have to work." She tossed her head at a Wild Child nearby. "Take him to haul."

Soon enough I discovered the meaning of *haul* and found my arms aching with the strain of pulling up water. My trainer showed me how to lower the big barrel on a pulley through the forest canopy into the bubbling springs far below. The vine rope rubbed my hands raw, but over and over I dipped the bucket in and pulled it up hundreds of feet to my world in the trees. All afternoon I delivered water for washing and cooking and drinking to the tree community. So much easier to turn on a faucet.

But my day wasn't over. The Wild Childs taught me to whittle my own arrows, and I soon filled my quiver with them. Next came hunting dinner. There were two groups of two kids each. The ground team shot the evening meal and the sky team was the lookout.

Lucky me. I got assigned to the sky team with a skinny girl whose only words were, "Don't get us stuck."

After being trusted with a bow and arrow, I slid along tree branches behind her as two boys with animal hide bags navigated the forest floor ahead of us.

The memory of the gaunt cretan and its hunger-stricken face pumped renewed adrenaline through my limbs.

"How do you haul the huge animals up to your tree houses?" I said.

"We don't unless we catch a big one that Artemis and her men take down and can't find," she said glancing back at me. "Then we steal it, butcher it on the ground, and haul it up, but it's risky. We like to stick the small animals."

"What happens if the big beasts hunt the kids down there?"

She stopped as the boys slowed down, letting them get a bit farther ahead of us, and raised an eyebrow at me as if it were obvious. "They scram and cram up here with us."

"How will they know they're being hunted?"

"You and I. We're their eyes up here." She swept a hand out.

"What if we don't see anything?"

"Better hope we do." She pushed back her long knotted hair, leaving a streak of dirt behind on her cheek and turned back to our vigilant watch.

I grabbed a branch to balance on and swallowed the sawdust in my throat, wishing I could haul water instead of being the reason someone lived or died. "Has anyone ... got grounded?"

I didn't think she heard me, but she stopped again and glared back. "Yeah." Her face crumpled and she wasn't a hunter anymore, but just a kid. "The worst day of my life ... after being stolen."

The bones of the dead flashed through my head. A shiver overtook me and I asked no more questions, focusing on the deadly quiet of the empty forest. Not empty for long. Small creatures scuttled in and out of holes and around trees. My legs and back soon cramped from crouching and balancing myself on limbs with every muscle on alert. The girl let me trade with a boy on the ground for practice. My first kill was a large rabbit.

"Stick it, Joshua," the boy whispered, his eyes glowing like two moons in the shadows of the leaves.

For a brief second, an image of firing arrows at Hekate's army alongside Bo Chez and my friends replaced the woods before me—a painful reminder of all I'd lost. My vision cleared and the rabbit's body came back into focus. I calmly put an arrow to my bow and aimed it at my prey.

Zing! The rabbit went down with a squeal, shooting a thrill through my veins, and my partner bagged our first kill.

"Good stick, new boy," the girl above said with an appreciative nod.

Several more rabbits were ours, along with some furry hedgehog animals and a small pig. We'd circled around to make it back to the tree houses, our dinner bags full. Tiredness ached in every muscle, but a feeling of belonging surged in my heart, overriding exhaustion.

Our hunting paradise disappeared when the bash of a giant beast from behind in the brush drove us to swing up in the trees. We crossed the forest back to the Wild Child community, and I used the last of my strength to climb toward home.

Chapter Thirty-Three

We delivered dinner to the kitchen house where a crooked spit hung over a fire blazing on a massive stone in the center of the floor. Rocks had been plastered together with clay and leaves to create a primitive chimney through the roof.

"Won't Artemis or the korax see the smoke?"

The cook, a short boy about my age, gave me a tight smile. "We have a watch who scans the sky, and we have ears in the trees. We know when the queen's got it in for us. She leaves us alone most of the time. We only stick the small stuff, and that leaves the big beasts hungrier than ever. That's good for her hunt."

Not good for the kids Artemis used as bait to hunt.

"Doesn't much matter." The boy sighed. "She knows where we live."

Free in your prison.

He unloaded the bags, admiring our catch. "Pot roast

tonight! We've got a new batch of potatoes and carrots from the garden house."

Who knew kids could grow—and want to eat—their own vegetables? I guess when you don't have grown-ups around you have to be a grown-up yourself.

Dinner was a noisy event in the main tree house and the time of day for the kids to catch up.

My team boasted about my luck with a bow and arrow.

"Good mash, newbie."

"You stuck 'em good."

The warm feeling of belonging to something bigger than me washed away a tiny bit of the sadness over losing my friends—and never getting home again.

Darkness came on fast, and after cleaning up, everyone headed off to bed where they slept two to a house. At the door, a kid handed each group a jar from a cabinet. Every jar had a different shape scavenged from those tossed on the forest floor in a Wilds Lands hunt or from risky treks into the Perimeter Lands, I guessed, and when shaken, they turned on like flashlights. Up close, tiny bugs swirled around in each one, like glow sticks.

Ash gestured for me to come with her, and I followed her across planks through the forest canopy, holding tight to the netted rope. The sky meadow unfolded before me, filled with dancing fireflies as the kids weaved between trees toward bed. One by one, the lights disappeared until the only light was our own and the moon bathed us in its orange glow. It painted glittery dew stars on the swaying leaves that swept back and forth like waves lapping at a dark shore.

Ash brought me to a small cabin next to hers and set me up on a wooden slat cot padded with fresh leaves. The other items in the room were a rough-made table with a jagged slice of a mirror hanging over it, a stool, a jug, and a pot. All found, no doubt, from a treasure hunt.

"The leaves will keep you warm, but this is better." She threw an animal hide on my bed. "The weather's changing. Cold and snow are coming."

I'd never thought of it snowing here. Did they have seasons like on Earth? It made me think of Christmas with Bo Chez. How we'd cut down our tree and carry it home in the snow, then come in to warm up by the woodstove in the kitchen with hot chocolate. As a young kid, we'd make monster shaped sugar cookies and I'd bite off their heads. Monsters weren't real then.

"I have to go to a leader meeting. There's water in the jug if you get thirsty. Will you be okay alone?"

The small room was not much bigger than my bathroom back home, and I nodded as Ash pointed at the pot. "The bathroom. If you have to go, you know. Otherwise, feel free to pee outside off the tree. Everyone's up for the night. Be careful. You can get confused in the dark. I'd hate to find you grounded on the forest floor when I check on you before bed."

Yeah, me too.

She flicked an animal skin down to cover the one window. "It's our coziest house, good for one. The boy who last lived here liked it." Her head fell and reflected next to mine in the cracked mirror. Even in the green light, I could see her dirty dishwater hair next to my dirty blond nearly matched. We could be family saying good night to each other. Had the boy who'd once slept here been like a brother to Ash? I didn't ask. Shaking the lantern, she promised me a few more hours of light with it, saying she could navigate these treetops blindfolded, then she left.

The room seemed cold without her, and for a brief moment, she felt like a big sister. Would I ever get the chance to meet my real big brother? I tucked myself under the blanket, my big feet barely covered. No matter how I tried, there was no escaping my thoughts. Was I doing the right thing? I pulled out Leandro's journal and read it by the crackling green lantern glow.

My Homeland
Journal Entry 57 on Nostos
By Leandro of the Arrow Realm

As of late, Artemis is suspicious of me. I sense it. She looks at me strangely and sends me off on lowly duties the new guards should do. I pray to the gods that the boy accepts Ash's plea to return to Nostos, can prove he is the Oracle, and lead our world into a new era.

If Artemis discovers my plan to thwart her, will I live to see my family or Joshua again? Strange how my one adventure with this mixed mortal boy could be so much more vivid in my mind than the memory of my wife and son who drive my purpose. My ruminations overwhelm me.

Joshua is a boy whose loyal, sturdy heart is more courageous than most soldiers I've met. He showed me what true sacrifice is by risking everything to not merely save his friend, but all the mortal slaves in the Lost Realm.

> If I ever find my son, I wish with all
> my heart for him to be like this boy—and
> that I can dare be as good a father to him
> as he is a son. However, I fear the seed of
> cynicism and hate has festered too long
> in my soul to be of any good to anyone.
>
> I hope Joshua proves me wrong … if
> I live to see the day.

"You were good enough for me," I whispered to myself.

I understood about not being any good to anyone.

My thoughts chipped at my heart and loneliness swept over me. A bittersweet ache melted inside. Carrying Leandro's journal kept him alive—as the good man he'd once been. I held his words to my chest, never wanting to forget.

Exhaustion drove the memories away and the sounds of the forest night swept around the cabin in the trees. Owls screeched and birds trilled to one another, and one by one the kids called out goodnight. My lantern's bugs flitted about and the whisper of their wings carried me to sleep until Ash broke through my doze.

Her silhouette filled the tiny window. "I can stay for a while if you want."

I nodded and closed my eyes again.

Comforted she was there, sleep drew me back in when she said, "You don't belong here, Joshua."

I pretended to be asleep.

"You're destined for bigger things. To change worlds. Make a difference. You can't go runabout from destiny. No matter how much you want to."

I remained silent, tears forcing their way under my lids.

"I know you're still awake, Joshua."

She was a new friend who'd saved me; she deserved a response. "I'm destined for nothing. I couldn't save my friends who'd once saved me." I rolled over and slid Leandro's journal back in my pocket where it kept the memories from crushing me.

"Everyone deserves a second chance," Ash said. "Maybe your friends will get one. Maybe you will. I did by surviving the stick and I have a new family now. Maybe someday I'll runabout to Earth, but that life for me is gone. My home is here. One for the many."

"That's what I want."

"You still have one waiting for you back home. It's not too late for you." I'd told Charlie something similar before he'd run off and now I was doing the same thing.

I didn't answer so she went on. "You can stay with us for now, but soon you'll understand where you need to be, and it isn't with us. Family is where you call home and this isn't it." Her voice sounded harsh, but she had to be wrong. If I didn't belong with them, then where? "Give yourself a second chance to make things right. I gave Oak a second chance when I cured him and his wife."

"But Oak's wife is dead and he could be too!"

"I won't believe Oak is dead unless I see his body. The point is, I gave second chances to people who needed them. If you are who some believe you are then you can free everyone." Her blunt words cracked open my tears full force. She was right. Guilt consumed me. *One for the many.* My motto for life if I accepted the role of Oracle, and I would finally belong. I might not live long as the Oracle, but how could I live with myself if I ignored helping free all the stolen kids?

"Nothing is ever as it seems here," Ash said in a softer

tone from the shadows. "Neither are people."

She was right about that.

"Not all Nostos people are evil … I used to be friends with Livia, Queen Artemis's daughter, when I worked in the castle."

"How?"

"I was assigned to serve her when I got sold here. She was younger than me, but we'd play together when her mother wasn't around. Mostly hide-and-seek. We'd hide from each other in the castle walls." She laughed at the memory. "Hidden tunnels run between the rooms and hallways. Anyway, Liv had the rare, ancient power to turn into animals and she turned into all sorts of them to hide. A mouse. A squirrel. A bird. All she did was will it." She sighed. "She wanted us both to be birds and fly away together …"

I wanted the same. "What happened?"

"It all ended. Liv's grandmother, the queen mother, discovered our friendship and threw me in the hunting pit."

"That's how you got here."

"Yes." She spoke in a stony voice. "It's hard to believe."

"Believe what?"

"Liv's dead. A hunting accident. The queen mother took her hunting. She'd often take Liv out hunting, something Artemis couldn't do. One day they got trapped in a ring of cretans." She rubbed a thumb to her trembling bottom lip. "Only their bones were found."

Grounded into mash for good. Artemis lost her mother and daughter all in one day. I almost felt sorry for her.

"Liv wanted her mother to free all the children. It was our plan." She sighed again. "Silly to think two kids could change the world."

Silly. Yeah. The same thing once occurred to me.

"People change, Joshua, and you can't ever really know someone."

Yeah, everyone I knew.

Like Leandro. He'd risked his life to save me.

Like Apollo. Who once lost faith.

Like Charlie. Who vaped those guards in the Lost Realm to save us. *It's not our day to die*, he'd said then. Could it be now?

Ash whispered goodnight and went off to her own house and bed. Soon, I drifted off to sleep and dreamt of my bedroom on Earth where nothing could hurt me. The safety of home covered me as thick as the quilt on my bed. All too soon it faded to black and cold crept over my body, leaving me with a lonely ache gnawing at my insides.

Chapter Thirty-Four

I spent the next two days working harder than ever. My time was spent hauling water, hunting, washing, whittling arrows, and sewing my own outfit of a shirt, pants, and moccasins from animal skins. My fingers were dotted with sores from poking myself with a wooden needle, but my helper said my work was decent. By the end of the second afternoon, I dressed like everyone else.

Blisters covered the insides of my hands, and every muscle hurt from manual labor, but I was too tired to care, crashing on my cot each night. Here I was a Wild Child. I'd survived the hunt. These kids were my family now—until my Leaving Day.

On the evening of my eighth day in the Arrow Realm, we were eating squirrel stew in the main house when a kid burst in. "Strangers!"

"Scram and cram!" Ash ordered. "Keep on the runabout and stick whatever moves."

The kids jumped up, nabbed bows and arrows from the wall, and eased out the windows and door. I picked up my bow and pulled out an arrow from the new ones I'd crafted that day, as Ash put a finger to her lips and urged me to follow her. I felt strong and ready to fight.

The kid who'd called out the intruders pointed off to the right. Ash nodded and waved at the others to spread out. Like silent ghosts, they melted into the trees.

Over the planks, Ash and I crept into the murk.

"Keep on the runabout," she murmured to me. Wild Child eyes darted from the trees around us, waiting for a sign to attack.

A whisper signaled danger ahead. Ash hunkered lower and fit an arrow to her bow. I did the same with shaky hands. This was no rabbit hunt. A cutting wind sliced across my face, bringing the chill of the night while sweat rose under my new animal skins. My heart throbbed faster with each deliberate creak of a branch by someone—or something—out there. A faint moan snatched my breath.

"Show yourselves!" Ash drew back her bow.

Bodies carved themselves between the leaves, moving closer.

"Tree Girl!" a familiar voice called out.

Two faces appeared before us.

Oak and Charlie! They staggered sideways toward us on the planks between trees—and they carried someone in their arms—Apollo!

"Need Moria plant!" Oak rasped out.

Ash sprang into action on a new mission, shouting orders. "Take them to the empty house. I'll bring the plant!"

The Wild Childs swarmed in to help as Ash grasped a branch and swung into the darkness.

Stunned my friends were alive, I gripped the rope rails and watched them being led away. Charlie's eyes met mine for a brief moment. He raised his hand but I held on to the rope harder, unable to greet my friend. He dropped his head, illuminated by a shaft of moonlight, before getting folded into the mass of kids.

***

Apollo lay still as death on a cot when I entered the house where he rested. Lanterns shed a sick green glow in the room. Oak grabbed me in a big hug, smelling of sweat and mud. "Joshua, you're alive!"

"How'd you get here?" I squeaked out as he squeezed my ribs.

"I hid in a hole in the cave wall when the soldiers came, heard their talk of blowing up the cave, and knew I had one way out of there."

He let me go and I glanced at Charlie, who avoided my eyes and shifted on his feet as Ash knelt next to Apollo, working on his injuries. "The river?"

"Yep. One guard caught me but I bribed him with Apollo's coins and jumped right in!"

"How'd you survive?"

He rapped his chest with a grin. "I'm strong as oak and oak floats!"

"For a flippin' blockhead," Ash said with a snort.

"Better than being a flippin' spudhead like you," Oak teased back, tugging her ponytail.

"I'd be happy to be a spudhead if we could go back home."

"O Canada, our home and native land," Oak sang in a low voice.

"Keep our land, glorious and free," Ash sang softly back.

"As waiting for the better day, we ever stand on guard … " Oak's song faded off, and quiet filled the room as he and Ash smiled at each other with a look only a shared country could inspire.

I broke the silence. "And Apollo?"

Oak's face sagged and he tugged on his moustache. "Smashed up pretty bad."

"He's not grounded yet," Ash said as she stood. "There. I've packed all his wounds with the Moria plant. Now we wait."

I took Ash's spot by Apollo's side and put a hand on my friend's chest. A gash tore down his forehead. A mottled bruise painted his left cheek and jaw. His pale skin felt like ice and he shivered as he dreamed.

"Don't die on me again," I whispered.

Charlie cleared his throat. "Joshua, I-I'm sorry. I shouldn't have run away—"

I nodded. "I get it. I ran away too."

"I couldn't live with what I'd done." His voice cracked and he swallowed hard.

"I know."

"I've abandoned two brothers."

He was right. A great canyon filled the space between me and Charlie. Was there any crossing it? Uncomfortable feelings came with seeing my friends again—and shame for giving up on them and myself.

"Evil is hard to fight," Oak said. "You don't always win but you don't give up."

"I won't give up again," Charlie said, knocking his

knuckles together, an appeal for forgiveness on his face. "Promise."

A promise is a promise. I guess sometimes friends let each other down, but it's what you do in the end that matters. If you can't stand up for your friends, what can you up stand for?

My heart chinked open, letting our friendship back in, and I smiled at him. "Brothers."

"Friends." He smiled back.

"Heroes," a faint voice said.

"King-man," Charlie yelled.

We all helped Apollo sit. Even in the green light, there appeared new color in his cheeks.

"We thought you died in the river!" I said.

"I almost did. If it hadn't been for Oak and Charlie here, I'd be dead by now."

"Sorry ... and about your flute," Charlie said.

"I told you before, it's all right, Charlie." Apollo gave him a tired smile. "The flute saved you and that's what matters."

"But it was the one thing you had of your mother's."

"Not so. I have my memories." He looked at me. "I got to hear it make music again through Joshua in my kingdom—and I got to see you both again."

"How the heck did you survive the river?" I said.

"My crate smashed to pieces, and I was hanging on a ledge at the fork when Oak came racing down river and grabbed me—"

"See, told ya this Oak floats!" Oak rapped his chest with a grin.

Oak patted Apollo on the shoulder. "We were lucky to get out of the river alive. I helped Apollo along for a ways, heading for the Lost Realm, but it was slow going trying to keep undercover from rough folks roaming the Perimeter Lands. We holed up for two nights in a cave, hoping Apollo would recover. Instead, he grew worse. We needed the Moria plant to heal him, and the Wild Lands were the one place I knew that had it."

"How'd you find Charlie?" I said.

"I ran right into him," Oak said. "He told me what happened and, after I shook some sense into him for running away, said he must come with us."

Charlie rolled his eyes. "Ha! More like grabbed me by my neck and dragged me with them."

"I couldn't have gotten Apollo up and across the treetops without you, Charlie."

Charlie half-smiled.

"I never thought I'd see any of you again," I said.

"Second chances," Ash said looking at me.

"Meant to be," Oak said with a nod.

"That outfit wasn't meant to be, Joshua," Charlie said. "Why wear it?"

I ran my hands over the soft hide of my new shirt, not sure how to answer.

"You'd only wear it if you planned to stay," Apollo said, sitting up taller. "Wouldn't you?"

Everyone looked at me.

"You can't stay here!" Charlie threw a hand out, then let his hand fall and said in a quieter voice. "We're all together again. You. Me. King-man. Apollo is freed like we wanted. Now we can go back home. Don't you want to go home? It's our second chance."

They'd found their way back to me while I hid away here to forget my old life, including them. In wanting to forget my friends, I'd abandoned them too. I wouldn't again.

"Sometimes we have to get lost to find our way, right, Joshua?" Oak bent his head to me. "I thought I was dead for sure, by soldier or by river. But here I am."

"All of us got second chances," Apollo said. "I can make my way to the Sea Realm now and convince Poseidon to raise an army and defeat Artemis. It's not far." He stood and put a hand on my arm to steady himself. "We've stopped evil before. You and me, Joshua. We can do it again. Then perhaps my people can see me as their true king. Will you help?"

I didn't want to let my friends down but couldn't will myself to respond.

Ash frowned at me. "Are you so lucky, blockhead, that you throw second chances away?"

I shook my head but couldn't answer.

Apollo squeezed my arm. "You believed in me when I didn't. Let's believe in each other now."

"I do," I said with truth in my words but doubt in my heart that it could make a difference.

Chapter Thirty-Five

Apollo quickly grew stronger from the Moria plant's magic, and we stayed up late making plans to get to the Sea Realm. The days here had been a blur, but in counting them, we'd been here well over a week. It'd be less time on Earth as time moved faster here.

The planning continued. Apollo believed that Poseidon and the people of the Sea Realm would be inspired by me, the Oracle, and band together to attack the Arrow Realm. Meanwhile, this hero business sat heavy on my shoulders. I didn't deny I was the Oracle but nor did I share my recent experience of animal transformation. I pretended to listen to their planning as a different plan formed in my head.

After making the decision to head out in the morning, Charlie and Oak bunked in with Apollo, and Ash went off to a leader meeting to report the new events.

Charlie followed me onto the platform. "I could stay in your house, Joshua."

I shook my head, wanting to be alone and figure things out. "I'm really tired. I just want to sleep."

He nodded but caught my arm as I turned. The lantern light through the window behind us cast him as a hulking figure. "How can you do it?"

I pulled away, not understanding. "Do what?"

"Go on?"

"What's the other choice?"

"Run away."

"I did. There is nowhere to run *to* on this world. This is everywhere. You told me in the Lost Realm there was no getting home."

"I was wrong. You got us home."

"Not anymore. There's no getting home this time."

"I want you to be wrong."

Silence fell from the little house as Ash and Oak stopped talking.

Charlie leaned against the building and shoved his hands in his pockets. In the moonlight, his squinted eyes bled a sick orange. "I think about someone else being a big brother to my brother, you know? At first it made me mad but now I think … if it were someone like you, I'd be all right with that."

I breathed in the scent of dewy wood and leaves. "Thanks, Charlie."

He nodded and went back inside. I headed down the plank path to my guesthouse and tucked myself under the blanket, listening to the goodnights of the Wild Childs. It struck me that fitting in and belonging were two separate things. I fit in here but I didn't belong here, like Ash said. I was hiding here. Hiding meant avoiding. We weren't so different, Nostos and Earth people. We all wanted the same things: freedom, family, friendship.

My friends may have gotten second chances ... but would they get a third? I couldn't risk their lives again. Leandro's journal said the Oracle alone must save Nostos. I must deal with Artemis. There was only one way: command my powers and stop her.

I'd steal the lightning orb back from Artemis, end the spell she was under, and end this evil that plagued Nostos and Earth. Somehow.

Sometimes we have to get lost to find our way, Oak said.

I wasn't lost anymore.

I opened Leandro's journal for a sign of what to do. The book fell open to a short passage.

My Homeland
Journal Entry 63 on Nostos
By Leandro of the Arrow Realm

I wear armor from head to toe, my impenetrable Armor that neither sword nor the sharpest of arrow can penetrate. My Armor is as hard as the strongest steel ever forged by a master blacksmith. With this Armor, I march willingly to battle—my fearlessness is resolute. Tough triumphs in the wearing of this Armor— this Armor is my Faith!

With Leandro stripped of his armor, faith would be my armor. I'd claim it for both of us. I threw back the cover and scribbled a short note on bark using Ash's quill dipped in berry juice. *I can't be the hero you want me to be. Go. Raise an army against Artemis. Don't try and find me.*

My chest ached to write it but I had no choice. They'd

have to believe I deserted them. They couldn't think I planned to face off with Artemis alone. If so, they'd follow and face death again.

I left the note on Ash's desk along with Leandro's fire belt. She'd find a good use for it. I changed back into my Earth clothes, took my bow and quiver of arrows, filled my canteen from the jug on the desk, and left the comfort of my friends behind. The dark rushed around me. I dug into a branch while my eyes adjusted to the night, estimating which way to head based on the direction Charlie, Apollo, and I'd first come from out of the castle's pit.

I couldn't risk taking the lantern with me. I had to trust my new abilities to navigate the woods to get into Artemis's castle from up high.

All the tree houses sat dark except the house where Ash held her meeting. A lantern shone from it, and Ash paced back and forth in front of the small window, talking with her hands. She'd get my friends to safety in the Sea Realm.

"Time to scram and cram," I whispered to no one.

With those final words, I crept away through the treetops. Memory told me it was a few hours journey. After a while, I huddled in the crook of a tree, exhausted from navigating my way across the Wild Lands and Perimeter Lands. I'd slept fitfully for a few hours, waking up to daylight with a huge pain in my neck from curling up against rough wood.

Twigs filled my lap. In my fuzzy sleep-filled state, I went to shove them off when the words they spelled caught my eye: POWER … WITHIN.

Awake now, I stared at them, filled with comfort. My aloneness seeped away a bit.

Every muscle ached and my head throbbed, but it was time to move on. I drank my remaining water and set off in the canopy of green. I backtracked several times, finding myself near The Great Beyond.

The spires of Artemis's castle finally poked through the trees in the distance, and a road appeared below. I trusted it'd lead me to the castle and it did. I clung to a tree and watched Artemis ride across the moat bridge with her army into the castle's courtyard. I searched through the group but didn't see Leandro. Villagers moved back to let them pass, steering clear of the angry queen who cursed at them as she dismounted. A girl my age peered around the edge of a doorway to watch the royal arrival. She reminded me that Artemis used to have a daughter with the ancient power to transform into animals. Ash's words came back to me. *All she had to do was will it. She wanted us both to be birds and fly away together.*

A line of cadmean beasts trotted in behind the soldiers on horseback. I flicked my eyes between them and the girl in the doorway, my idea for a disguise forming. I twisted my way down the tree. The castle grew larger. Its towers pierced the leaves below and the trees curled away from them, as if not wanting to touch such evil stone. Soldiers patrolled the walking bridges between the towers, but no one stood watch on the towers themselves. Hiding behind a burst of leaves, the closest tower revealed a round balcony with a wooden doorway. My way in.

Chapter Thirty-Six

When the patrol faced away from me, I leaped and landed hard on rough flagstone. I rolled to a shadowy corner, waiting for shouts or a warning that an intruder was here. Nothing. My heart slowed and I crept toward the door, trying to lift the heavy iron latch but the wood didn't budge.

Could I will myself to be a bird like Livia and fly down one of the chimneys? They all chugged out smoke and I'd be a toasted sparrow. Only one way to get through it—with fire—and only one way to make it—become a cadmean beast. I trembled, remembering my hands covered in strange fur. What if there was no changing back?

I knelt on the cold rock, seeking answers.

I had no magical weapons. I only had me.

Power within.

I. Was. The. Oracle.

Anger at Nostos drove spikes in me. After all my

friends and I had been through in our deadly adventures, still nothing on Nostos changed. I had to become the thing I feared most to fight this evil.

I closed my eyes, willing it. My skin blistered. Knuckles cracked. Fur ripped along my hands. A moan boiled up from deep inside me. I stood on four legs with power like a train rushing through me. I opened my eyes. The world stood in black and white. Scents punched up my nose from everywhere: earthy moss clinging to trees, smoke wafting from the wall torches at the castle gate. Sounds blared in my ears. Birds chattered in trees miles away. Squirrels thumped along branches. Whispers of the villagers in the courtyard voicing their trepidation of Artemis shouted in my head. I grew dizzy with the overwhelming attack on my senses and forced myself to move forward on heavy, padded feet, my tail swishing behind me.

With a snap of my jaws, I commanded the very fire that once tried to kill me. It roared from my mouth in an angry blaze. The door crackled as fire surged across it, gorging on wood. Within moments, its timber split apart and crumbled to ash. Urgency powered me to dash through the door and jet down the stone steps, tumbling into walls with my new four-footed body flying beneath me.

I soon reached a dank, cobwebby hallway, my beast eyes taking in every detail, my senses alive. There was a definite advantage to being a beast than a boy right now. Around a corner, voices jumbled together. I paused, listening with twitchy ears.

"I'm off to her chambers to light the fire before she gets back from the hunt," said a scratchy woman's voice.

"I've got it worse in the kitchen," Scratchy's companion

whined. "She'll likely blast me to bits if I ruin her dinner. She's sending those Reekers to the Wild Lands now for sport, not just food."

"Things sure have changed around here. Death is everywhere. Now her and Leandro are trying to get the Oracle for their own use. Wait 'til Zeus finds out! Indeed! As if a mixed mortal could solve our world's problems. Humph."

"Who cares about the Reekers?" Whiny shot back. "I've got my own problems to worry about, much less all of Nostos. Like getting extra food rations to feed my family."

"Or like serving fatty meat and undercooked potatoes to her highness. You better watch your back. Vapes go off around here like fireworks."

The voices of Scratchy and Whiny grew closer. I shoved my hard-muscled brutish body up against cold rock in the blackest well of shadows. Pushing deeper into it, the wall gave way and, muffling a yelp, I fell into complete darkness. My canine eyes switched to night vision as the hidden door closed shut. A tunnel opened between the walls like Ash said! The voices moved away. I followed the sound as I sprang along my new hideaway.

"She vaped a Reeker yesterday and didn't even use a vape." Scratchy's voice lowered but my sharp hearing picked it up perfectly.

"You mean like ancient magic?"

"Yes. She shot blue right out of her fingers! The poor Reeker."

Like that evil Hekate vaped folks to death with her fingers in the Lost Realm!

"What'd the stupid mortal do to get vaped?" Whiny said.

"He hung her dress too close by the fire to dry after washing and singed the back of it."

"Serves the ignorant Barbaros right. Dumb lot they are. They should stay on Earth among their own kind."

"Not the Oracle," Scratchy said. "He's the wise one to fix us up right. Give those nasty heirs back their powers and make 'em do good with them. Give us choices. I could've run my own business, you know. Been rich, if I weren't made to work for Artemis."

"You'd be nothing of the kind, you lazy bum. You'd end up living in a ditch in the Perimeter Lands like your ancestors, eating acorn paste and washing clothes for the outlaws. Rich. Bah! Take your dreams and bag 'em."

"Oh, bugger off," Scratchy said. "Get to the kitchen or you'll be next in line for a vaping—after me, if I don't light her majesty's fire!"

"I'm going. I'm going," Whiny grumbled.

Footsteps clomped away. A light pierced my eye through a hole in the rock. A peephole set in a door! A fat woman with a torch headed my way. I jumped back before I realized that the woman couldn't see me, and she passed right by. She was Scratchy the fire starter, and this had to be Artemis's chambers! I watched her as she did her work, complaining the entire time. She waddled off and shut the ornate door behind her. Taking a deep breath, I pushed hard against the tunnel door. It creaked open and I slunk through, my beast senses on high alert.

Giant arches rose up in a cathedral ceiling, and firelight flickered across the queen's chambers from the walk-in fireplace. In the center rose a massive bed with Greek columns at each edge. Gold curtains fell from the ceiling all around it. I moved into the royal room, and the overwhelming scent of roses exploded up my nose.

The smell shocked my body stiff. My every limb trembled and I collapsed on the floor.

Only one person had that smell.

Hekate! She had returned, posing as Artemis! How did she do it? Using the queen's body as she'd done before to keep her nasty brother alive, Cronag the Child Collector? I clenched every muscle. A sick dread snaked through my stomach, and I retched in the shadows until nothing more came up.

I shook off my sickness and stood on all fours.

Focus, Joshua!

Apollo had killed Hekate with her own curse in the Lost Realm and Bo Chez's words came to me. *Let's hope she doesn't find magic to come back.* But she had, and she'd put a spell over Leandro and Artemis to follow her commands. Now to find the orb!

I dashed around the room, pawing open drawers and closets until my eye caught a box on her dresser. Would she keep it in plain sight? I ripped the lock apart with my teeth. The top clicked open. The lightning orb glimmered inside. Clouds swirled inside the giant gumball-sized crystal. Lightning dashed across the tiny storm. I scooped it up in my giant jaws when a shape moved next to me. My reflection in a mirror. In shock, I dropped the crystal. I faced my worst nightmare. Red eyes burned into mine. Slicked-back fur like arrows sprung all over my monstrous body while muscles rippled across my chest and haunches. A thick tongue panted from my snout as foam dripped in points from dagger teeth. A giant murderous flame-breathing fox stared back at me. Where was I in there?

The loss of my world dunked my heart in a well of sorrow. The beast melted away. Joshua the boy faced me again. I dropped my bow and quiver and gasped. Stunned to see my return, I didn't hear the soft footfalls outside in the hall or a knock at the door.

"My queen?"

The door ripped open. I lunged for the orb but two words stopped me.

"Stand down!"

I jerked around to Leandro's fierce face and a sword pointed at my chest.

Chapter Thirty-Seven

"Well, well," Leandro said darkly. "I came to report that my party still hadn't found the Oracle, and now I have you."

No chance to scram and cram. Soon rope chafed my wrists as Leandro led me alongside his horse in a throng of soldiers through the dusty, noisy village that filled the castle's courtyard. I considered willing myself into a bird to fly away, but Leandro would know for sure I was the Oracle. I couldn't risk it yet.

"I'm not the Oracle. I'm just a kid."

He gave me a sidelong glance. "You'll prove it soon enough."

I feared how as I stumbled along. Thatched huts wound down alleyways and into the shadows of the towering castle. Stray dogs ran about and rough riders drove squeaky wagons carrying crates of clucking chickens and grunting pigs. Tethered goats *baahhed* near smoking pots where women stirred their contents over open fires. Roasting meat and thick stews invaded my nose and my stomach griped in hunger.

Quiet soon fell over the square, the clop of our horses the one sound cutting the air as we passed the Arrow Realm folk. They stopped their daily market business to watch us pass. Some spit at my feet. Some stared at me with pity. *You're all kept by Artemis too*, I wanted to shout. "Your journal," I said. "You should read it." It bumped into my side with each step.

"Means nothing to me now. Artemis helped me see that. If you don't give us your powers, it'll burn with you."

"You'll never get my powers."

Leandro stopped fast and pulled my chin to face him. "Those may be your last words, Reeker."

I matched his stare-off until he threw his head back and laughed. "No need for you to submit. We have you now. Soon to be all of you."

I held my breath. "What do you mean?"

"Your body. Could be useful. Hypnosis or maybe possession. My queen will decide."

"No way."

"Oh, there is always a way. Trust me."

I did once.

"You can't make me!"

"You'll change your mind."

He dismissed me and resumed his horse's trot while I ran to keep pace. Much more of this and my body wouldn't be worth anything.

I willed my feet over muddy ruts. "Leandro, why?"

He flung his hair back with a frown. "A means to an end—or rather a new beginning for some of us."

"Don't you remember us?" I tried another way.

Leandro looked straight ahead. "There is no us."

"Release the key."

He laughed. "You think I'm under some spell you can remove? I've never been under a spell. You've been my target all along."

"It's a lie!"

"I do not lie."

"You lied to Hekate to save me. You and Bo Chez. Don't you remember? In the Lost Realm?"

"Irrelevant. It's payback time."

The Child Collector had said the same thing to me in the Lost Realm.

"For what?"

"My sister."

"Sister?"

"Hekate."

"Cronag?" I croaked out.

"Not so dumb after all, are you, Reeker?" He threw his head back and laughed. "Of course it's Cronag the Child Collector, only much better looking thanks to this body!"

No! Cronag was dead and gone. He'd been no Ancient Immortal like his sister. She'd kept his spirit alive for centuries in the bodies of others.

"How?" I whispered.

"Hekate's ancient magic."

I wanted to turn away, not see the ugly insides of the Child Collector who'd murdered my mother, but the face of Leandro froze me with this awful truth.

"What about Ash?"

"I sent her to get you under the guise of rescuing Apollo. All part of the plan for Artemis—excuse me, Hekate—to get your powers and rule Nostos."

"You're a liar and a traitor!" I stumbled back, pain shooting through my tired legs. "I don't believe you! You changed after I saw you in the dungeon."

He came to a halt, falling behind the others, and thrust a knife in my face. "When I'm the queen's head advisor that tongue will get you killed."

He shoved me back and continued his trot as I struggled to keep up.

"You gave me the bow you made for your son." I tugged on my rope to force him to look at me. He turned, his eyes crinkling as if with a long lost memory. His nostrils widened then he faced front again, pulling my rope so hard I staggered to the left, barely missing a hoof to my head. "You'll never know your father."

His words cut deep. How could he know this? Not so long ago it was true, but now I had hope he was alive and someday we'd meet. No one could take away that hope, not even my fallen hero.

I walked faster to keep up. "Where are you taking me?"

"The Great Bog. Once the queen proves your powers and acquires them with her magic, you are no longer needed." He picked up speed, catching up behind his men and the queen. "Keep up, boy. If the queen finds no use for your body, you'll need to run when we dump you in the Wild Lands, like you dumped me. I doubt you'll fare as well as I did." He laughed, sending a chill through me.

We passed under the arches of the castle and words cut clear into the stone over them. *Leave these doors in honor of Queen Artemis. Return with plenty and we shall live forever. May your hand be steady and your arrow find its mark! Hunt on!*

The hunt *was* on as we cantered into the forest and I was the delivered prey. Leandro picked up speed and I ran to keep up, terrified of being dragged by his black stallion.

We stopped at a clearing in the woods. Artemis shouted out orders, and her men split into two ranks encircling a great bog before us, then she ordered Leandro to bring me to the edge of the water.

He untied me and pushed me to Artemis, handing her my lightning orb. She grasped it as she sat on her horse, watching me with triumph on her face. The rotten vegetation smell of the bubbling water made me gag. Moss and vines hung from trees, fading in and out of the curling mist that rose from the brackish water. Movement caught my eye. Did my blurry, tired vision deceive me? No. The water rippled. A tusk poked up from the sludge. And another. Deadly hydriads. A swarm of them. They'd nearly killed me in the Lost Realm. Leandro had saved me then. Not now.

Twigs fell in the water, swirling into shapes. FRIENDS ... ARE ... HERE ... FOR ... YOU.

"No one is here for me," I whispered to myself.

The water swirled again. ONE ... FOR ... THE ... MANY.

"I'm the one," I said to myself.

"It's time to prove you're the one, Oracle," Artemis said, answering my whisper, her black sunglasses twin pits to hell.

Leandro dismounted and pushed me into the bog, the water just above my knees. The tusks paused in their movement before racing toward me. Adrenaline rushed through me, and I pushed through the water toward a boulder, scrambling up on it. The monstrous fish bashed against my rock, eager to lance me and suck the water from my body.

"Go on. Fight back, Oracle! Become the beast you want to be!" Artemis threw up an arm.

No. I wouldn't do it. Not for her! Not this way.

Leandro raised his bow and nocked an arrow to it. The other soldiers followed. An army stood against me. The arrows flew. I slid off the rock and grabbed the fallen weapons, fleeing into the bog. The hydriads came fast. Their snouts banged into me and I stabbed them with the arrows. Blood swirled around me. I dragged myself up on another rock.

My hand shook over the water. A part of me wanted to make the water rise with my new power. *Drown them all! No!* I wouldn't kill many to save only me—the one. *The Oracle.*

Artemis's laughter rang out. "Why don't you fight back with your powers, boy? Or are you helpless without this?" She held up the lightning orb. In the sun's blue haze, it shone like a crystal ball with a terrifying future to tell. "I can kill with it too."

She flung the orb.

I slammed face down on the rock, and the orb exploded beside me in the water, killing a slew of hydriads. *Missed!* The orb sailed back to her hand. Rage funneled dark inside me. I stood, battling my body's want to become what she desired. I willed the animal inside me down.

"You think you can force me to show powers?" I shouted across the water. "I didn't before, why would I now?"

She held up the orb. "You'll have no choice where we're headed. The Black Heart Tree has the power to hypnotize far stronger than Hypnos. That idiot escaped, and his people will suffer because of it. Now you shall suffer by the hand of your own friend." She handed the orb back to Leandro who held it high.

"Reveal your powers and I will eliminate you without pain," Artemis said.

I shook my head and shivered in my wet clothes. "N-never."

"You've proven resourceful with your mortal skills. Let's see how you are now. Move the water and release your beast!" Artemis said, slapping the reins at her horse.

My heart jumped at every splash in the misty, bubbling bog, expecting death from all sides. A giant roar cut across the water. Through the rising fog, a yellow mass of teeth and muscle and mane launched at me. A cretan.

If there was ever a time to reveal my Nostos powers, now was it—but there was one hope left. I clutched a tree vine and started climbing. My arms screamed with the effort. Up I went, inch by inch, aiming for the first tree branch to grab. The soldiers stopped shooting their arrows and began chanting. "Oracle. Oracle."

Leandro pulled his hand back to throw the orb, but Artemis stopped him and the chants died down. "Fight beast with beast, boy. End this battle of wills. Show your powers. I must know for sure."

She'd own me if I did. Evil would live and good would die. Earth kids would keep getting kidnapped. The Wild Childs would never get home. All in the WC would remain enslaved. And I'd be dead. Myth said another one hundred years would pass before an Oracle came again. This was my role. Here. Now.

I. Am. The. Oracle.

The time to make a decision was now. I hung on for dear life, my chest threatening to splice in two as my legs gripped the fraying rope. *Pling.* A thread shot off the vine. *Pling-pling.* More popped. The vine grew thinner and the cretan roared below, shaking the vine between its teeth. My hands slipped. Farther I slid down, my legs hugging the vine as I prayed it didn't break. My enemies watched and waited.

Artemis couldn't have my powers if I didn't command them. But I was losing the battle of the vine and would soon be cretan chow. The beast flung its mane, moaning with hunger. Despite its need to eat me, my heart went out to it.

"Let me live and I'll take her down. I'll fight to save you and all the animals," I pleaded with it.

My hands grew numb. Down I slid. The cretan's tongue panted faster as it pawed at my life line.

"You. Killed. Brotherrrr," it groaned in a piercing wail that rose in pitch.

"I'm sorry," I whispered. "He tried to kill my friend."

"Sad. Mad. Hungrrrry."

"It's Artemis's fault! We're her victims."

The lion shook its mane and let go of my vine. "No victim."

The shaggy beast jumped around and raced toward Artemis. Before it reached her, it stood on its hind legs and roared an agonizing cry of loss and suffering.

Arrows flew. They took the beast down. The great, sad lion-bull stumbled and fell with a watery *whoomph* in the bog. The mist rolled over the massive cretan, shrouding it from view.

I clung to my vine, heartbeats away from death.

Chapter Thirty-Eight

My hands bled from the rough vine. If I let go, I'd fall into the bog with the swarm of hydriads waiting to feed unless I commanded the water in time. Death by hydriad or Artemis. Not good choices.

"You won't give in?" She spread her hands out. Leandro cocked his head at me with a questioning look, as if why not?

I shook my head and closed my eyes, hanging on with my final spare energy and waited for death by witch or tusk. Minutes ticked by like fingernails tapping a table. The air grew cold. My hands slipped again, I adjusted my legs that cracked as they squeezed the rope.

"Perhaps they'll change your mind," she said.

I opened my eyes to see dozens of kids packed in wagons making their way to the bog. Their wide eyes and hands grasping prison bars, revealing their fear at what new terror awaited them. My arms shook, unable to hold on much longer.

"Last chance to show your powers or all my slaves die."

Her soldiers raised their arrows. The hydriads circled, waiting for my decision.

"Why?" I said the one word my energy could muster.

"I've been waiting centuries to lead Nostos!"

"Hekate!" I called her out.

She smiled and flung her fingers at me. Blue sparks rippled along the tips. "Yes, I've come back. My ashes still had life and blew here. Lucky me to take up residence in the Black Heart Tree. Poor scaredy-cat Queen Artemis should be glad. I lured her weak spirit to the tree. It was so easy to snake my spirit inside her body, and in her body we can rule Nostos. She no longer has to be afraid of the woods ... or use her heart to lead." She glanced at Leandro, but he stared at me without expression.

"How could you make Leandro into your nasty brother?"

"It's as Artemis wished—and I. Two wishes granted for the price of one. I planted my memories of Cronag in Leandro's body, but my brother's live spirit will never return, thanks to you." She smiled grimly.

"You can't replace family!"

"Why not? It's perfect. Artemis can love Leandro like a brother again and I have my brother back."

"He's not your brother. He's my friend!"

"Enough! So what will it be, Oracle? Sacrifice yourself and none die. Don't and they all die. Then I'll round up the Wild Childs for execution."

One for the many.

One choice to make now.

My hands let go.

I fell into the bog of thrashing monsters and swept the churning water and beasts up with my last dregs of power to fling a tidal wave at the enemy. The giant wave crashed over Artemis and her men, dashing them aside like dolls. Screams shredded the air as soldiers rode a river cast through the forest. Some escaped death and clung to branches—Artemis was one of them.

Trembling with exhaustion, I collapsed in the water. Tusks raced toward me in a blur, but instead of being pierced to death, a nudge tossed me in the air. I landed on the back of an agrius beast and clamped a hand to its fur with a renewed surge of energy.

"Agri," I cried out as he charged out of the bog, stomping on hydriads. We reached the edge and he plunged into the woods. Faces poked out overhead. Wild Childs!

Ash appeared and threw me my bow and quiver I'd left behind in Artemis's chambers. They meant nothing to Leandro now. I was glad he'd left them there. I caught them by surprise. "I followed you after I found you gone and snuck in the castle's passageways. I found them on the queen's room's floor. I knew you'd go there to get your orb. And I know how to sneak in!"

She grinned at me. She brought her Wild Child family here to risk everything for the hope of something better. They were betting on me.

Across the bog, Artemis stood with her remaining men. Gray clouds boiled above and the air turned glacial.

Wild beasts came from the woods. Cretans. Agrius beasts. Cadmean beasts. I clung to Agri and begged him to flee but he snorted. "Friends."

With all of the Wild Lands behind me, I faced Artemis and death across the bog, and Leandro with the bow he'd carved for his son. Could I save him from Hekate's evil spell before we killed each other? Could I convince her to release Leandro from his spell? There'd be one chance to steal the orb from him.

Through the hoard of warriors, Apollo, Ash, Charlie, and Oak flashed between the tree branches. My heart swelled with the power of friendship. I was no longer alone—I never really had been.

"Free-dom. Re-lease us," the animals grunted.

Artemis adjusted her sunglasses and swung up on a nearby horse, pushing her men through the dangerous waters. Swords slashed the hydriads. The water churned with red foam. The kids cheered us on from their wagon cages on the bog shore. Agri stomped at the bog's edge as the other wild beasts raced toward the enemy.

"We've got you covered, *mon ami*!" Charlie yelled down from his tree, shooting arrows as I did. His hair flopped about wildly as his crazed eyes darted about.

Through the misty bog, Leandro headed right for me on his horse.

"Leandro!" Oak's desperate call rang out to stop him, but Leandro didn't hesitate and plunged through the water, dodging arrows and wild animals from all sides.

The decimated army pushed us into the woods. The Wild Childs scrambled back through the trees. Agri turned and fled into the woods with me clinging to him. "Keep. Oracle. Safe," he grunted.

I hung on, peering back at Leandro who still kept coming, his fierce gaze fixed on me. Blue light flew from Artemis's fingertips as she zapped animals with Hekate's ancient evil power. We soon left the madness behind.

The air grew colder and snow swirled down. Flakes fell heavier in white gusts, obscuring the battle in the distance.

"Agri, stop!" I pulled on the great beast's fur, trying to steer him back to help my friends. He slid on snow-covered leaves and skid around. "Agri, go back!"

"Keep. Oracle. Alive," he said.

"My friends need me!" Then Leandro was upon us. Agri dug his feet in the ground to face the man who'd once been my hero and now came at me like an assassin.

Leandro pulled his horse to face me and we circled each other, my bow armed and drawn back against his sword. He shook the snow off his long hair. The blizzard flung its bone-chilling fingers at me. I shuddered and a flash of silver swung at me. I missed death by inches. Agri lunged at Leandro, who dodged the beast's snapping jaws.

How could I fight a sword with a bow?

How could I wound the man I loved?

He'd once told me we must pass over what is evident and search deeper for the truth. And I knew the truth about Leandro the lionheart.

I lowered my bow. "Leandro, don't do this. I know you're in there. I *am* the Oracle. I can find a way to bring you back!"

He kept silent, his fierce gaze ensnaring me with his dark mission. "Artemis says you must surrender your powers and die. I will rule by her side as brother and king."

The blizzard raged, enclosing us. We sidestepped around each other in the blowing snow. A gust of wind blew a clear view open behind Leandro to see my friends take on a group of soldiers from the treetops while an agrius beast nipped at Artemis as she dodged her horse left and right. The window closed and my friends disappeared in the white.

Snow clawed at my face, throwing sleet in my eyes, and I didn't see the sword swing—but Agri did. He tossed me off his back and took the knife to his own heart. Leandro's sword plunged into the beast's chest as I crashed to the ground.

"Noooo!" I crawled to Agri who lay on his side, panting in distress.

"Be. Who. You. Are." The great beast's chest slowed its pumping and fell still.

Leandro ripped his sword from Agri and pointed it at me. Blood dripped down the shaft onto the newly fallen snow, painting a crimson ring.

I knew what I must do.

Fight lion with lion.

Chapter Thirty-Nine

My bones cracked and stretched into beast. My muscles exploded into massive limbs of rock and power. Rough fur rippled along my skin.

Leandro stumbled back, fear cutting his face.

I shook my mane and lunged at him with a great roar, curling back my lips to reveal spiked teeth.

He dodged aside and sliced at me with his sword. It flew past my ear. Snow bashed angrily at us with mad flakes. The pounding of my lion heart pumped loud in my ears. We circled one another. Man and beast.

Slice. Dodge. Slice.

I backed up to a tree and lost my balance. The second I caught my footing, Leandro swung—and so did I. My hefty paw swiped his sword away, but I overshot, slashing his chest with a mighty blow. He fell. And didn't get up.

My massive knees buckled, and I dropped to Leandro's side in the snow. He gasped for air, palm to his heart. He pulled away a shaky hand red with blood.

"Kill me now, beast or boy, whatever you may be."

I became the boy again. Tears ran down my cheeks as I bent over him, the wet snow shooting ice through my clothes that had returned to me. "Hekate came back. Like you warned! She put you under a spell. Fight it, Leandro!"

He couldn't die. Not now. Because of me.

He shook all over, his hand dropped to his side. "No fight left. I am what Artemis created me to be. Nothing more."

My tears fell harder. "So much more."

I pulled my mother's picture from my wallet, crumbled and worn, and held it up to Leandro. The one photo I possessed of her face forever smiling at me. "My mother. Your wife."

Something passed across his face. A memory. A spark of recognition. I saw the glimpse of the man I knew but it faded. "I am no one. An instrument of war. My battle is over." He pulled the orb from his pocket with a grimace and handed it to me. "Use it on me. Quickly."

He inhaled a deep breath and arched his back. A great groan rose from him. He tried to sit up, grasped my arms, and looked deep into my eyes with pain and regret—a look of the lost Leandro. "Joshua ... you *are* the Oracle ... forgive me." He closed his eyes and fell back.

"No. No!"

Don't die now!

The snow melted on his eyelashes and cheeks, so white in the cold. I pressed my hands to his chest. It rose once. *Rise again!* I bent down to hear his breath, but only the shouts of battle and the *scritch-scratch* of biting snow filled my ears. I thought of the last time I'd pressed my head to his chest, waiting for him to come back to me. The lonely wind screeched around me as I inhaled his chocolate leather smell, wanting to hold on to it—to him.

The battle cries died away and so did my friend.

Ash! She had the Moria plant. There was just one way to save Leandro—become the lion that killed him.

With giant paws, I scooped him up and carried him across the snow as he'd once carried me to safety.

Snow swirled gently around us, then stopped. The sun came out. Through the woods, it was clear my friends won the battle. Artemis and her handful of men hung over the bog from vines lassoed around their waists, handiwork of the Wild Childs who sat in the branches above with arrows aimed. Artemis dangled in the middle, writhing about, unable to free her murderous Hekate-vape fingers. Hydriads poked their tusks in the air at the soldier snacks wriggling an arms-length out of reach.

Ash paced the bog shoreline while Oak yelled at Artemis. "Where's Joshua and Leandro?"

"My brother drove him to the Black Heart Tree where he'll be cut down forever," Artemis gloated.

"That better be a lie or Ash here will cut *you* down," Oak growled, shaking a fist at her. "The hydriads can feast on your evil flesh!"

Ash stopped pacing and aimed her arrow above Artemis's head at the vine keeping her from death. Charlie dashed about between the trees calling my name, and Apollo worked to unlatch the wagon cages and free the kid slaves. He'd removed his Wild Child clothing and shone out in his kingly garb.

They all stopped when they saw me staggering along

on my two back feet as I carried Leandro.

"Ash! Help!" I roared from my lion chest.

Charlie ran toward me and slid to a stop. "Joshua?"

Why didn't they understand me?

"The Oracle is mine!" Artemis shook her head, twisting in her vine net. "Help me, Wild Childs! You'll never need to go to the WC again. I can make it so. Not Artemis but me, Hekate!"

They laughed at her and shook her vine from above, sending the hydriads in a frenzy as they tossed their tusks closer to her. She shrieked and twisted her legs up.

I placed Leandro on the ground before them, careful to lay him on his cloak as protection from the snow, and willed myself to be a boy again. The gasps of my friends cut through the silence.

"Need the Moria plant to bring him back!" I said.

Ash shook her head. "It dies in the cold and loses its power." She stood fast and looked around. "Maybe Agri can find some elsewhere—"

"Agri died to save me … from Leandro."

Ash's face fell and she knelt beside me, tears ran down her face. My own sobs engulfed me as I stared down at Leandro's still face. *Open your eyes!*

"If you're the Oracle, Joshua, you can bring him back," Oak said quietly.

"Maybe the true Leandro will return to us," Ash said to me in a broken voice. "He would never have killed Agri, or you."

But we had no Moria plant to save Leandro. We only had me.

I put my hands on his chest, willing him to wake. I thought of his organs healing inside and his lungs breathing in and out and his heart—his good lion heart—pumping with life. I thought of all his words of wisdom along the way. *You must trust on faith. Believe in yourself and you will have the power to be whatever destiny drives you to be.*

Destiny sent me here on a lightning road.

I looked up at my audience who watched and waited and believed.

Even Artemis was silent. I felt her hateful eyes glaring at me from behind her sunglasses.

Chapter Forty

I clasped Leandro's strong hand and pushed his shirt up, revealing the broken arrow scar on his arm that the queen mother had fire branded him with long ago. It pressed against the arrow slave mark on my arm. His brand, a more permanent reminder of his refusal to kill human slaves for the thrill of the hunt. He couldn't refuse the powerful spell that marked him here, though. Marks on the outside do not always make the man on the inside, he'd once told me. Even with all he'd done to hurt me, those acts weren't committed by the man inside. Hekate used my hero to take me down. Was her ancient immortal evil so great no one could defy it?

I cried at the unfairness of my friend dying when we'd been brought together again. "By the gods, come back to me, Leandro!"

Fingers touched my arm.

Leandro smiled up at me with his green-blue eyes,

and his one eye bluer than the other twinkled in the bright sun that chased the storm away. The air in my lungs seized as I choked with gladness. A rippling murmur ran through the crowd before us.

I took Leandro's hand to help him up, but he held me down. "I saw all while under the spell." His voice caught in a tormented whisper, and he clutched my hand tighter. "I had no control. The things I said … the things I did." He looked up at Ash. "And Agri … "

"I knew it wasn't you," Ash said in a quiet voice.

"Hekate did this to you," I said. "She did it to Charlie too. She's taken over Artemis and put a spell on you and the soldiers. But how did the spell leave—"

"Death ends it. You brought me back."

I nodded. He gripped my hand harder. "Thank you." He glanced at Artemis and her men hanging from the vine. I pulled at him again, but he kept me down. "My wife."

I opened my mouth but couldn't begin to express all that boomed in my heart.

"The photo," he whispered.

I tugged it out. He held it up and stroked the corner with his calloused thumb, then looked at me with shiny eyes. "Your mother. My Dee Dee … you called her Diana. Of course! Dee Dee was a nickname … yet you're not my—"

I shook my head. "I'd wished though."

"So had I, Joshua." He pinched his lips together. "My wife … she loved another. But who?"

"I don't know." All my life I'd wished I known, and, until recently, I'd wished my father were Leandro. Wishing didn't get you much.

He nodded once and stared at the photo again before handing it back to me. "You look like her. How come I never saw it?" His eyes grew shinier, holding my gaze. "She's dead."

I swallowed hard. "Yes."

His mournful cry cut through the bog. After he'd let it go, he blew out a shuddery breath, staring at the pendant hanging out of my shirt. He reached for it and we opened it together. "My wife ... my son."

His shoulders heaved as a great sob burst from him, raging against the gods. He closed his eyes. When he opened them, it seemed a great peace fell around him and he spoke calmly. "A lost wife and mother. A lost son and brother. Now we have them between us."

I closed up the pendant and slid it back under my shirt, afraid I'd cry if I spoke.

He squeezed my hand. "We must find our family."

We now shared a mission to find our missing family. The words floated in my head new all over again. I had a brother!

Guilt swept through me. "I'm sorry, Leandro."

"Sorry? For what?" He looked up at me, astonished.

"I killed you."

"You saved me in doing so. Destiny." He smiled. "I'm the one who's ashamed. You were doing what a hero should do. You must never feel guilt over that. One for the many, right?"

"One for the many," the Wild Childs chanted.

"Oak told me that a long time ago." Leandro glanced at Oak, who nodded. "You were right to try and stop me, Joshua. I see now that Hekate hypnotized me soon after she released you into the Wild Lands. I told her everything about me and you. Then she planted her brother's memories in me." He shivered. "I can never erase those."

"Not your fault."

Leandro bowed his head. "You are growing into your prophesied role, Joshua, as the Oracle. Destiny—again."

I understood now that being a leader—and a hero—meant having to make tough decisions.

I pulled out his journal. "When you were under the spell, this helped me remember how you were so I wouldn't forget … I didn't want to forget."

"You helped me find my way back."

"Tough triumphs," I recited back his words.

He smiled. "Neither sword nor arrow stopped my faith."

"Stronger than steel," I said, returning his smile.

He pushed the journal back in my hands. "You keep it. Add your own adventures. Then we'll have them together even if we're apart."

I liked this idea so I slid it back in my pocket.

Leandro said no more but let me help him up, and Oak rushed to offer a hand. Silence hung thick in the air as the rest of the audience, my friends—and enemies—stared at me with new awe confirming the truth in my heart.

Apollo knelt to me. To my surprise, Ash, Oak, and Charlie did the same. "Joshua, you have the ancient power to heal like Apollo. The power to transform like Artemis. The power to command water like Poseidon. The Oracle has come!"

The Wild Childs banged their bows and arrows on the trees. Power filled me inside. I *was* the Oracle. My destiny. No questioning. No turning back.

Leandro swept a great bow before me and clapped a hand to my shoulder, surveying the scene. "What now … Oracle?"

I pulled the lightning orb from my pocket. "We send

Hekate's spirit away for good."

Artemis struggled in her ropes, cursing me. Her soldiers hung helplessly. The freed kid slaves huddled and watched the show, unsure where to go now.

I held up the orb. It crackled with electric power in the blue sun. Artemis stopped struggling and fixated on it, as did her men. Even the hydriads slowed their pace.

"Like brother, like sister."

The Wild Childs chanted in a steady beat. "Stick her good!"

"No, that's too good for her," I said.

A great wail rose from Artemis. Her legs kicked and her head flopped from side to side. Her head fell forward and was still. The soldiers flopped in their vine nooses, then froze as well.

"My queen!" Leandro drew his sword in one hand and his dagger in the other and dashed into the bog toward Artemis, slashing hydriads on either side. He scaled a rock under her and cut her vine down. She clung to him with a smile, then grabbed his dagger and stabbed him. She aimed for his heart but he jerked away. The knife sank into his shoulder. He shouted in pain and fell back into the bog, pulling the knife out with a great groan.

"Leandro!" Rage fired the animal in me and I roared through the water toward him, this time willed as a cadmean beast. The wild animals leaped in behind me, and the bog surged forward with us. I reached Leandro, who clung to a rock as Artemis stood nearby on hers, laughing.

"Get on!" I growled to him.

He clambered up my back to grab my fur tight as I breathed fire on the hydriads and dodged Artemis's vape fire. Cretans and agrius beasts bound away. Some didn't make it and vanished into the air. Her lightning bullets hit her own soldiers dangling helplessly in the firing zone, and many exploded in a swirl of dust, their broken vines left swinging empty.

I lunged through the muck around her rock as she fired at me. The Wild Childs filled the branches above, their arrows aimed at her. The queen was trapped!

Leandro whispered in my ear, "Artemis is still in there. We must save her like you saved me!"

"You can't stop me!" Artemis continued to smile at us. "If you do, you kill the queen. I'll make sure she can never be brought back."

The ferocious growls of the wild beasts rumbled around the bog as Artemis rose taller to face off with me. I urged them to stand down and they moved back. From the shore, Charlie, Oak, and Apollo watched with wide eyes.

"I don't intend to let the queen die," I said, snapping my jaws at her.

"Oracle! Oracle!" The chants of the Wild Childs echoed around the bog. In the second I glanced at them, Artemis flung her blue bullets at me. I catapulted over a rock and barely missed getting vaped. The wild beasts thumped the water in a thunderous beat. Leandro slipped off my back with a shout. "Get to shore!" I nudged him to a cretan that tossed him on his back and got him safe to land.

Now it was me and Artemis in a fight to the death.

Chapter Forty-One

Artemis and I paced around the rock step by step. She tossed her hand in the air, and her braided bracelet gleamed with polished wood.

The bracelet! It must hold Hekate's spirit still!

Her fingers flashed blue and I leaped high, aiming for her hand. With one flick of a claw, I scraped her bracelet off, tossed it in the air, and torched the braided band with my fire breath. It exploded in ash. Artemis sucked in the gray cloud then fell into the water. A black funnel rose from her gasping mouth. It spewed into the air as a monstrous cloud, buzzing like a drone of angry wasps, and shot out of her, fleeing into the woods with a shriek. I snatched her cloak in my teeth, hauling her body from the water, and raced through the bog.

Leandro waited at the water's edge. He slipped off his cloak, and I placed Artemis gently down on it and became a boy again.

"Leandro?" She turned her head to him.

"I am here, my queen … Temi. You've returned!" He thrust my bow and quiver into my hands and knelt to his queen. He placed a hand to her cheek and kissed her forehead while placing her crown back on that had fallen on the ground. In his softness, Leandro revealed how my mother must've seen him.

"As have you," Artemis said. He tugged off her glasses. Her eyes were as bright blue as his. Their sharp, angled faces next to one another revealed that they looked like brother and sister.

She grazed the wound she'd given him, and I quickly placed my hand on it to heal it. A tear ran down her cheek. "I've hurt you. So much hurt I've caused."

"It wasn't you, Temi."

"The Black Heart Tree wooed me. Hekate's evil spirit was in it. It's how she made it back. When Apollo took her down, her ash blew from the Lost Realm to here and settled in that tree, forging it in new evil." She turned away from him. "I told her my secrets. Told her about you being like a brother. About wanting to end slavery and change our Nostos ways. About standing up to Zeus and bringing the boy that you believed to be … the one. And he is. And I made you do all those terrible things … such evil."

"It's not your fault, Temi. Hekate took the good things in your heart and twisted them into her own sick need."

"I loved you as a brother, my lionhearted one."

He bowed to her. "As did I, my sister."

"A long time ago," she whispered.

"Never forgotten." He clasped her hand, revealing the royal tattoo on the inside of her wrist, the same spot as

Apollo's. Hers flared like the flag over her castle, an arrow of fire with a fancy "A" on it. Slave or queen. Everyone on Nostos was marked.

"I thought I was destined to be alone. Everyone leaves me. My mother, my love, my daughter … all dead. You left me too."

"I'm here now."

She nodded. "I'm truly sorry about your wife."

Leandro touched his forehead to hers and we both helped her stand. She looked around in a daze at her soldiers who'd been awakened from their spell and peered at us from their vine traps, then she gained command. "Release them, Wild Childs. They'll cause you no harm."

The Wild Childs didn't move but turned to me for confirmation. I raised my bow to them. "Hekate scram and crammed for good. It's okay."

One by one the soldiers were hauled up into the trees, untied, and left to climb across the trees and bog to safe ground.

Artemis held my hand with her trembling one and gazed about with wide eyes. "So bright. Like a whole new world."

"It can be," Leandro said solemnly.

Artemis fell to her knees, her head down, clawing at moss and leaves.

"Your terror of the woods, m'lady," Leandro said, putting a hand to her shoulder. "It's come back with the spell gone."

Ironic how the queen of the hunt was terrified of trees and a memory of facing my past fears came to me. "Find the calm," I told Artemis.

Her face was stricken. "How do I do this? Hekate never needed the glasses. She kept them on to instill fear in my people. Now I need them … need something … "

I knelt beside her and put a hand on her arm. "You have it already. It's the place inside you no one can touch."

She balled leaves in her hand. "Not my mother?"

"Not anyone."

"And not Hekate."

"Right."

"How do you know this, mortal boy?"

"Lightning used to scare me. I didn't know why until I found out a Child Collector had killed my mother with lightning. Then I got the chance to stop him and my fears."

She shook all over. "But I don't know why the woods terrify me. My mother forced me to sleep in them at night under the Black Heart Tree—alone—to get over it. It was before Hekate's spirit controlled it." She spat the words out. "I hated my mother for that. Hated her for making me like all of our ancestors."

Leandro stepped closer. "Perhaps your fear of the woods was your mind's way of resisting your ancestor's dark legacy to hunt mortal children. You told me once as younglings you wanted to free them all, remember?"

"I did," she whispered, her chin touching her chest. "I do."

"Perhaps if you change your legacy, you'll lose your anxiety."

She looked up with teary eyes. "Do you believe so, Leandro?"

"I want to, my queen."

"I fought off my fear of lightning," I said.

"It's the fight inside that's the hardest battle, isn't it?" she said.

"Sometimes we must keep fighting to find our true

legacy," Leandro said, handing her sunglasses back. "And sometimes we need a little help."

She put the glasses on with a trembling hand and stood taller, breathing deeply.

"It's okay to be different," I said.

"It's hard to find your way when you're different," Leandro said looking at me.

How right he was.

Artemis took Apollo's hand and put it to her chest. "Please forgive me for the terrible things I've done, my kin."

"All is forgiven when it comes to family."

Artemis directed a group of men to take the dead back and another group to send the slaves home through the Lightning Gate. Leandro broke through the calm. "How can we know we truly vanquished Hekate? We thought we had once before."

Artemis put a hand on his arm. "Hekate put her spirit in me with that bracelet. The Black-Heart Tree placed it on my wrist. Some terrible things I remember but much is a blur." She darted an apology to me with her eyes. "If Hekate's spirit possessed the Black Heart Tree, her black cloud could have returned there. We must burn it, sink its ash in the sea, and hope her spirit cannot revive from a watery grave."

"*Allons*! Let's go burn down the evil tree and send the witch away for good," Charlie said, punching the air.

"To the Black Heart Tree," I said.

We darted between the trees on the backs of beasts as the Wild Childs raced above. On and on we ran, over patches of melting snow when cramps struck my every limb. I lurched over the back of Agri, not wanting to fail now with so much on the line. But my body was failing me and I had no idea why. Exhaustion, hunger ... or something else. It all spun in my head as pain spiraled through me.

I braced myself to sit up straight and hide my condition from my friends. Suddenly, Artemis caught the reins of the agrius beast from Apollo's hands and skidded to a stop, horror on her face. "The Black Heart Tree is gone."

She pointed to a dark hole in the earth that looked like a monster had clawed its way out of hell. Roots and clumps of dirt were thrown about as if mighty hands flung them away in fury. A wide path of destruction spread ahead. Trees were violently uprooted, cast aside. Between them, a road cut into the ground with big holes stomped in it from giant feet.

The Wild Childs above us hollered a mighty chant. "One for the many!" They launched themselves from tree to tree ahead of us.

The ear-splitting crash of wood struck me with fear of what waited for us through the thick of the trees, but we had to follow these children of the woods to the next fight of our lives.

Chapter Forty-Two

In the middle of a clearing, the Black Heart Tree and the Grand Tree battled.

The two ancient ones lashed at each other in a frenzied fury. Massive limbs swung about in the ultimate face-off. The clash of wood smashed the air and arrows rained down from the Wild Childs who targeted the Black Heart Tree. Their arrows stabbed the enemy, but it pulled them out with gnarled fingers and flung them back. The Wild Childs dodged the wooden bullets. Not all made it. The cries of the fallen pierced the air.

The worst horror faced us. The Black Heart Tree.

Its trunk convulsed in a serpentine mass that slithered through it with each smack of its gargantuan limbs at the Grand Tree. The molded faces of children screamed along its hardened skin in a nightmare, their bones broken and crushed in the bark: a foot poised to kick, a hand fisted, fingers begging to live. With each punch the monster tree wielded, the dead writhed and moaned in its thrashing wood. A ghoulish vision that would haunt me forever.

The Black Heart Tree grabbed a Wild Child nearby. I rushed forward with the other kids but we couldn't save her. A great creaking threatened to split my skull open. The branches at the top of the evil tree curled outward, and the trunk spread open like a carnivorous mouth. Gray leaves tinged with blood red lapped the air hungrily. With a flick of its branches, the monster threw its captive in the air and swallowed her whole. The girl's screams echoed as she fell down the death tunnel. Her face and hands bulged from the tree's innards, cast in its wood, her mouth petrified in a wide *O*.

The beasts rushed the Black Heart Tree, gnawing at its branches, slashing the trunk with their claws, and cracking limbs in pieces, but they couldn't take it down. The tree's great arms tossed the animals away. The Grand Tree battled bravely but stumbled back after one sweeping blow. It bent its boughs, clutching itself in agony.

"No!" I threw my lightning orb with every ounce of strength left. Anger pumped thick inside me while my body throbbed with deepening pain. The orb exploded on the coiled snake bark of the Black Heart Tree, leaving a scorched hole. The tree broke off a branch and thrust it at me. I dodged left and just missed getting speared.

Charlie, Leandro, Oak, and Ash joined the Wild Childs in the Grand Tree's branches to help the oaken elder fight. Apollo and Artemis rode their agrius beast around the two timber giants, firing arrows at our enemy. I was all out of arrows but I had the orb. I blasted the Black Heart Tree with it, wounding it but nothing more, when something pinched me. Wooden fingers scratched at me, digging in. The Black Heart Tree's branches caged me with Hekate's evil spirit. I shook wildly.

"Joshua!" Charlie tried to pull me free but splinters dug into me. Blood oozed.

Using my feet, I kicked at the arms trapping me. "Let me go!"

The limbs relaxed and I busted free, crawling backward. Hollow moans of laughter heckled us as the tree shook its arms in a mocking dance. It rose, a black witch of darkness, blacker than any tree in these woods and twice as tall.

The ground shook like an earthquake as the two trees smashed in combat, and the splitting shriek of wood ripped the air as they tore limbs from one another. The Grand Tree's boughs sank lower and lower, its tired body growing weary from the attack. It staggered back and fell.

A familiar voice cut through the chaos.

"Joshua." It floated down from the sky.

A trick of the Black Heart Tree?

It called again, this time clear and strong. "Joshua!"

Bo Chez!

Chapter Forty-Three

I flattened myself against the craggy bark of a nearby tree, searching desperately for my grandfather amongst the leaves above me. There! His face appeared through the canopy shadows. The branches spread apart more, revealing his location, and horror streaked through me. He hung from a vine high over the heart of the Black Heart Tree. His arms and legs were bound tight to his body, leaving him helpless to use his hands to fight with his Storm Master power. But he'd come for me!

I grabbed the Black Heart Tree's trunk and pulled myself up on knotty footholds, trying to avoid stepping on the bones and faces of the dead.

"Joshua, no!" Charlie tried to pull me down. Branches snagged at us and I kicked them away.

"Charlie, it's Bo Chez!"

He fell back with wide eyes, scrambling out of the hooks of the Black Heart Tree.

I pulled myself up higher. Splintered fingers scratched at me. I broke them off and kept climbing. I had to free Bo Chez.

A final glance down showed the terrified faces of my friends on the ground.

Joshua, oh, Joshua.

The words sing-songed in my head, vibrating through the trunk I climbed. Hekate!

Your powers are mine. You die or your friends die. Your grandfather dies. A hero would choose the many over the one. Be a hero—and die!

I clung to my enemy and willed her voice away. It came through stronger.

Give yourself to me. It is your destiny, Oracle.

"No! I won't!" I pushed myself up faster toward the top of the Black Heart Tree. Its branches snatched at me but I smacked them away. Wooden fingers pierced me with their ragged nails. I groaned with each lance. Blood welled, dripping down my arms and neck. I had to end this now. Hekate would keep coming back—keep enslaving people from both worlds.

"Joshua, here!" From another tree, Ash threw me Leandro's fire belt I'd left behind. I caught it midair. Instinct told me to throw it up. It zipped upward, defying gravity, then twisted around a branch near Bo Chez. I grabbed on and hauled myself up, my body fired on adrenaline.

"Go back, Joshua," Bo Chez yelled, swinging his whole body back and forth to break free.

"No," I yelled back. "Not without you!"

The Grand Tree stooped lower and lower, and still I climbed. Finally, I stood gasping for breath on a branch right below Bo Chez. His chest heaved for air against the vine that cut into his burly body. It encircled him from his shoulders to ankles. Exhaustion wrung through me, and one foot slipped off the branch as the sickness in me grew like a poison seeping through my veins. Must keep strong!

The Black Heart Tree stopped moving. Its arms leaned in as if watching and listening.

"I would've never stopped looking for you," Bo Chez said in a hoarse voice, his eyes full of sorrow.

"I knew you'd come." I clenched a knobby branch. "How'd you get here?"

"Artemis kidnapped me and threw me in the dungeon. Except it wasn't Artemis."

"Hekate."

"Yes. She put Leandro under her spell too. He told her our home location. She wanted to use me as blackmail to persuade you to give up your powers." He wriggled in his ropes to no use.

"You've been in the dungeon this whole time! The dreams. The messages!"

He gave me a weary smile. "Hypnos entranced me so I had the power to seek you out with my mind in exchange for helping him escape with my storm powers. I used my powers to get you messages, but they tied me up and I was limited ... so limited. I almost lost you again." His voice broke. "I couldn't live with myself if ... you're the only family I've got."

"You sent the lightning to help me and Charlie survive in the Wild Lands."

"It was all I could manage with my powers so out of reach."

"It was everything."

"I told you I'd always come for you," he said.

I'd never doubt it again—if we survived this day.

"Bo Chez ... Hypnos mentioned my father in the dungeon. He said my father would die if I didn't give my powers to the queen. He's not dead ... whoever he is."

"Perhaps you will meet with Hypnos again and find out."

We hung in silence for a moment as the battle raged below.

"But it's not your time to stay—yet," Bo Chez said, echoing Leandro's words. The truth hit hard. I'd always be an outsider to both worlds, but if this was the consequence for saving both, I must do it. I belonged in the role I was destined to fill, and belonging starts with belonging to yourself first.

"I have faith in you," he said. My heart swelled with his. "You must do whatever necessary to complete your mission."

I said nothing.

"Even if it means leaving me behind on future adventures."

His gaze held mine, unblinking, his eyebrows great mountains. I shook my head.

"And never seeing me again," he finished.

One word came to me. "No!" I climbed above Bo Chez until I could climb no farther.

"I'm going to cut you down," I shouted down. "Jump to the left and land on that branch!"

I sawed at the vine with the edge of an arrow, but it shook in my hands and I dropped it. *Ping. Ping.* It bounced down to Bo Chez who managed to grab it with one finger. He began sawing at his vine cage.

I pulled out my last arrow. Make it count! Soon a string ripped off the vine that held Bo Chez, then another.

Bo Chez cut through one of his ropes. Faster and faster I sawed.

The fire belt! I reached to uncurl it from the branch when something slithered around my ankles and up my leg. It was like a giant hand squeezing me into stone. The same vine I'd been sawing away to free Bo Chez now ensnared me! I screamed with the last breath I could push out before the vine tied me up like a spider would a fly. My bow pressed hard into my back as the vine tightened, and my arrow fell through the mist to my friends below.

"Joshua, hang on!" Bo Chez worked faster at his rope. "Aha!" Another vine popped and he dropped like a sack down a chute, banging into the trunk below, perilously close to the gaping mouth of the Black Heart Tree. The branch we swung from creaked with our weight. The vine and branch holding us up wouldn't hold much longer. The fire belt hung so close but out of reach. Through the eerie silence, laughter cracked the air like wood cymbals smashing together.

"It's going to break, Bo Chez!"

Wider the trunk mouth gaped, breathing in and out like fire bellows. Bo Chez hung over it like an appetizer, with me as the first course.

"She's wanted to take me down ever since I stopped her evil plot centuries ago," Bo Chez said between ragged breaths.

"How can we stop her? The orb couldn't when I blasted this tree!"

The branch that held our lives in its fingers cracked. We slipped farther. The gasping mouth inhaled deeper, pulling at my legs, sucking me down.

"She wants your powers and mine, Joshua. Don't give her both!"

I shook my head. "What do you mean?"

"You have the orb, don't you?"

I nodded, my stiff fingers rubbing the top of it in my pocket.

"Can you get it?"

"I don't know!"

"Try!"

I wiggled my weak, pain-riddled fingers to no use. We jerked down another foot.

"Throw it in the heart of the beast, Joshua. It's the only way!"

The branch snapped again, splintering in two.

"I can't get it, Bo Chez!" My tears rained down on him.

Here. Today. We'd die together, dragged down into the beating belly of the Black Heart Tree. I must will myself to become a beast! But then the vine around me would bust open. I'd land on Bo Chez and we'd both fall to our death. There must be another way!

"Throw it Joshua." His voice grew harsh now, an order. "You must sacrifice me."

"No, Bo Chez!" Tears burst out. "We'll get home. Never come back!"

"That's not your destiny, grandson. You know what you are in this world, don't you?"

I nodded, crying harder, clawing at the orb but my fingers were wrapped in iron.

"A second chance."

"You got a second chance too, Bo Chez. You can again!"

"My chances are up."

Snap! We shot farther down.

"It's not your day to die a hero, Joshua." Leandro

once said the same thing to me in the Lost Realm. "But it is mine."

He sawed through the last rope. *Pop!*

Then he fell—a hand reaching out in farewell, eyes begging for forgiveness—and disappeared into the yawing jaws that swallowed him whole.

"No!"

The branch that carried only me now snapped, but it didn't break; it held—and I hung helplessly in the arms of my enemy and wept.

Chapter Forty-Four

Bo Chez was gone. Really gone! I swallowed hard, forcing my tears away, but I couldn't break my stare from the evil tree's cracked throat where it fed on humans and hope—and my grandfather.

Cloud cover pushed down on me and the trees became swallowed up by fog as snow softly swirled again. My friends remained lost in the misty canopy below. Their voices faded into muffled shouts as the creaking moan of the Grand Tree filled the air with its pain. A death cry shook the air as the great elder crashed down. The whole world shook with its fall.

The Black Heart Tree swayed with its splintered laughter. By chance, the vine trapping me slid up, providing me enough space to grip the lightning orb in my pocket. I held it tight, but exhaustion, grief, and pain sliced through me.

Throw it, Joshua, you must sacrifice me.

But Bo Chez was already dead! Or was he? What if he

was still alive and I killed him with the blast?

One for the many.

Oak believed it. The Wild Childs believed it.

Could I sacrifice my own grandfather?

With aching fingers, I drew the lightning orb out of my pocket when the soothing voice filled me once again.

Surrender to me. Your life is so hard. Aren't you tired of fighting your destiny?

Yes, so tired of being a hero, of losing my home, my family. Tired of being made to sacrifice. My eyes drooped. The vine unwrapped from me. I grabbed a branch before I fell and held on tight, pressing my body against the evil trunk. Branches floated in, and their twig hands gently cradled me.

So easy. Jump in to my soul.

Yes, so easy. Easy was good. Easy was painless.

I will become you. Carry on your legacy. These are my people. Not yours. Mine to rule. You don't belong here.

I never wanted to be a hero.

My mind uncurled. Bo Chez, Leandro, Charlie, Apollo, Ash, Oak. They all floated away.

Yes, let those simple creatures go. Now for your magic. Give it to me, Oracle. You were only the vessel, never the intended. I've been patient enough for thousands of years. My time is now!

Loneliness stabbed me again like when my friends abandoned me, but this flared a different kind of lonely. This loneliness came from being the one person to save your friends—and a whole world. Time to embrace it.

The Black Heart Tree's neck widened, its great mouth craving me. The branches pushed me closer to its gaping jaws.

I possessed what it wanted.

Be. Who. You. Are. The words of the dying Agri

echoed in my head.

I wanted a chance to discover the real me. Invisible fingers pulled at my spirit, seeking to suck me away.

The Black Heart Tree's mouth breathed in and out.

Come.

It called to me, inhaling deeply.

Leandro's journal poked out from the top of my other pocket, reminding me I had a brother out there. I could find my father. Leandro and his people—my people—believed the Oracle would save them one day.

The Oracle. Me.

I could not crush the dreams of a whole world.

I raised my orb. The jaws of the Black Heart Tree stretched wider. Below it spun a black funnel pumping in and out with a pounding heartbeat.

No! Vines slithered in, twisting around my wrist. *Nasty Reeker! You killed my brother. It's time to pay for what you've done! Give me what I deserve.*

"Not me," I whispered. My hand shook, growing numb as the vine tightened.

The tree hissed. *Your body is mine! Your powers are mine!*

I sucked in a big breath, and with my final strength, ripped the vine off my wrist and threw the orb into the heart of Hekate.

"For Bo Chez!"

A great rumble swelled in the belly of the Black Heart Tree. The branches that held me in safety let go. I seized the fire belt before I fell. My head cleared, freed from the trap of Hekate's spirit. The giant tree shook. I slid down the belt, banging into the tree as I went. Shards of bark ripped into my hands and arms. I cried out but held on.

The sky went white with fire. A great flaming ball erupted from the top of the Black Heart Tree. Fire burst along the wooden canopy hanging over me. Wood fingers clawed at the air in a final protest and crumbled into ash. The fire raced down the tree toward me and I scrambled to climb down the fire belt that grew with magic.

I die. You die!

My feet pushed off the screaming faces of the dead as I propelled myself down, banging into the monster's trunk. Bo Chez's face flashed before me. I jerked back, not wanting to touch him carved into the flesh of his murderer, but the fire belt twirled me into his frozen form. His eyes stared into mine, his mouth a firm line of determination and a hand still up in farewell. I placed my palm to his—giant sobs wrenching through me.

With a final heave, the tree belched out a great tongue of fire and threw me from its limbs—and from the man who'd raised me. Down I fell through the cloud cover, bouncing off branches. Pain struck everywhere. I grabbed on to a limb, dangling high above the ground. My friends circled the tree below like toy figures. I called to them, but only a lone whisper puffed out.

"Joshua!" Leandro shouted. Explosion after explosion shook the Black Heart Tree. Smoke blew thick and my friends disappeared. A wrenching scream split the air as wood crackled and crashed down. I flattened myself against the trunk. Burning branches smashed around me. The monstrous tree tilted and I scrabbled down it.

A fierce sting struck my chest as a jagged branch pierced my skin. My feeble fingers couldn't pull it out, and my chest burned like the fire raging overhead. Embers bit my flesh. Leaves of fire spun in the air, and the ground reached up to pull me down. The world became a silent tomb shutting me into a dark cave.

The evil giant fell, taking me with it.

Chapter Forty-Five

Snow blew down on my face. I tried to open my eyes but they were stuck. The world had disappeared. Was I dead? I lay alone surrounded by darkness. A clap of cold wind carried voices to me.

"Joshua, wake up," Leandro said. His voice cracked open my lonely world.

Why's he telling me this? I am awake.

"Joshua, don't die, please," Charlie said with a moan. "*Mon ami* ... my brother."

"He got stuck bad," Ash said.

"He's leaving us," Oak said with a wretched sigh.

I'm right here, I protested. But my mouth wouldn't move.

"No. He's still with us," Leandro said.

"He has to be ... after all we've been through and all we've got to do," Apollo said in a low voice. "Look, he's still holding your son's bow."

Something cold and smooth fell into my hand.

"The orb," Charlie said. "It's glowing!"

Fingers pushed my bangs back. They felt so cool, driving away the heat and pain that racked my body. "It's chosen to heal him," Leandro said, a chink in his voice I'd never heard before. "It's claimed him as its master now."

"It can do that?" Charlie said.

"Once its master is dead."

"But Joshua isn't a Storm Master."

"Only one mixed mortal could be the greatest Storm Master there is—the Oracle. He is here to battle the greatest storm of our world."

"What does that mean?"

"It belonged to his grandfather, a Storm Master. Now it belongs to Joshua."

Thanks, Bo Chez. Wetness trickled down my throat. It tasted of soothing honey.

"Joshua, we'll get you and Charlie to the Lightning Gate," Apollo said. "You're going home!"

My voice came to me again. "No home. Bo Chez is gone!"

Silence encased me. "Sorry, my friend," Leandro said in a mournful voice.

"So alone."

"Bo Chez is gone but you're not alone."

"Tired ... so tired," I mumbled.

Fingers hooked mine. "There is no sleeping today, young Joshua," Leandro said, his voice rising. "We must get you back to Earth. Your job may not be done yet, but it is done for today."

"No job ... I didn't do anything."

"Yes, you did. Your job is to vanquish evil—and you did. Artemis's army is carting the ash of the evil Black

Heart Tree in a metal box right now to sink in Poseidon's lake. Hekate won't rise from that. If she does, I'll take her down myself!"

"Bo Chez is in that ash." I tried to sit but fell back. "Bo Chez!" His name was a knife to my heart.

I tightened my fingers around Leandro's, my eyes still glued shut, but I'd know him blindfolded. His rich, earthy chocolate scent made me feel safe. "Come back to us, son."

He called me son.

The burning sensation crept back. Pain, such pain, it shot through me everywhere. Something was ripped from my chest. A great suction let loose and I inhaled great gulps of air.

"It hurts," I whispered.

"Pain is good," Leandro said with a sigh. "It means you're alive. And you're alive, aren't you, Joshua?

A muscled hand covered mine and held it tight. My shivers melted away with the warmth of Leandro's cloak.

I don't want to go. I want to live.

My friends needed me. This world needed me. Bo Chez wanted me to stay—I wanted to stay.

I opened my eyes and blinked in the bright world. My friends stood next to horses chuffing clouds of steam in the cold air that had brought the snow back. It fell in a slow dream.

"My chest hurts," I said. The pain receded as my skin knotted up and the glow of the lightning orb in my hand faded.

"Well, it would with this in it." Leandro knelt beside me with a bloody stick in his hand.

"Yeah, I remember now. The Black Heart Tree shot me."

I healed myself! But not Bo Chez. The grief was too raw to bear.

"You sure took care of Hekate," Ash said, coming forward.

"That witch tree is toast with you around," Oak boomed.

"For sure," Apollo said and Artemis agreed.

I stood with Leandro's help and slung his bow across my chest. Even with my wound healed, my every muscle ached and nausea swept through me. The orb couldn't heal my permanent sickness that had taken over.

Leandro's fire belt sprawled on the ground. I picked an end up and handed it to him.

"Thanks for getting it back to me," he said, winding it up on his belt. "It's been useful in our adventures."

It couldn't save Bo Chez.

I stumbled with the thought and Leandro caught my elbow.

"How'd I get here? I was falling and—"

"The Grand Tree saved you, right Tree Girl?" Charlie said.

Ash nodded. "It caught you in the palm of its hand on a blanket of leaves before it crashed."

The Grand Tree. The orb. My friends. They'd all been there for me.

"Strong as oak you are too, like your grandfather," Oak said with crinkled eyes sparkling like tarnished gold. "Now this old tree must say goodbye."

"Where are you going?"

"Back to the Wild Child camp. The others are already there." He jerked a thumb at Ash and they mounted a horse each. "I need to figure out a plan to find the children of the slaves and relocate them with their parents. First,

I've got to get their parents out of the WC."

"But Hekate's spirit is gone and Queen Artemis has returned. She'll let the WC slaves go, right?" I said.

"Yes, but let's see how this bodes with Zeus," Artemis said. "He has the might to stop anyone. If we could bond the realms together, we may have a chance. It'll be a challenge. Not all rulers are so easy to deal with, like Ares of the Dred Realm. If Zeus discovers an Oracle lives, he'll seek to crush him, like Hekate. Not to get his power—to end it. Now that Zeus has shut down all the Lightning Roads to Earth except to the Arrow Realm, and the WC is located here, his eye is on this realm. It's what keeps him in wealth and slaves."

Oak nodded. "He wants to keep things the way they are, with him as head ruler and his minions with ancient powers at his disposal. You'll have to fear him coming for you now, Joshua."

Ash steered her horse to me, the mystery girl who got us here, and looked down at me with a serious face. "Whenever you're in trouble, Joshua, you don't always have to be brave. Just scram and cram. Promise me?"

"I promise."

"And don't get stuck, you hear?"

"You either."

"Family is all we've got. Blood or not. When it's gone, it's never really gone." She put a hand to her heart. "Remember this."

I pinched my lips, the lump in my throat too thick to form words. She shook her reins and trotted back to Oak's side.

"Family," Oak said gruffly, then cleared his throat. He and Ash melted away together in the woods.

I gripped the pendant in my hand. Somewhere out

there I had a brother. It barely soothed the pain inside me.

"Time to go home, boys," Leandro said and we each mounted a horse. It took several tries to lug my legs up and over. This world was killing me slowly. The myth's reality sank in. I couldn't stay and gain all the Oracle's powers at once. Leandro helped me get on, the white streak in his hair blazed down as he bent to secure my shoe in the stirrups. The details in this fleeting moment would be forever seared in my memory, along with knowledge that he was a good man.

"I have no home. No one, no—" I choked up inside.

"You have me, *mon ami*," Charlie said, nudging his horse into mine. "Come home with me. We'll figure it out. My dad really isn't all that bad."

I stared at the ground my head spinning along with the pain coursing through me.

Stay. Go. Come back.

My life now bridged two worlds.

"Home is where you're wanted," Leandro said quietly to me, tapping the reins on his horse and sharing a look with Artemis.

"Wherever home is," Apollo said.

Resolve set in and I nodded at my friend turned king. He'd appeared older since I got here days ago. The line of his jaw, how he carried himself, and the confident way he controlled his horse all told me the king had returned. He opened his mouth to say something when trumpets blared and sleet beat down on us. Charlie yanked the reins of his horse and nearly got tossed.

"Zeus and his Storm Masters! He must know the Oracle is here. He's after you!" Leandro said. He thrust a hand to Artemis and Apollo. "Get to the castle. Be safe!"

"Not without you," Artemis protested, her horse jigging side to side as hail the size of gumballs suddenly battered us.

"Our people need you to fight together. Find a way to change Nostos!"

Apollo put a hand on Artemis's arm. "He's right." He had to shout to be heard over the pounding ice balls.

Artemis nodded and turned her horse around. "We'll take the back way in!" Her horse lunged forward, eager to race, but she held it back. "Leandro, take great care."

He bowed his head and flung his fingers at her. "Go, my queen. I'll find you!"

She dug her heels in and galloped away, and with a final glance back, she rounded the trees and disappeared. Apollo gave me and Charlie a hardened smile. "Thank you."

We came here for him and we'd done our job. He'd been rescued—for now.

"Bo Chez will always be with you." Apollo put a hand on his heart. His king's ring *pinged* with hail. "Light of Sol go with you, my friends!"

"Go with arrow fire, my king," Leandro said, raising his bow in the air. Apollo nodded and sped off after his Olympian sister.

"To the Lightning Gate!" Leandro wasted no time. He reined his horse in and raced off with us close behind.

We were wanted—again.

Chapter Forty-Six

The trumpets blared again, fainter this time.

Hail pummeled us from Zeus's Storm Masters, as we thundered toward the Lightning Gate. If Hekate terrified me, the idea of meeting Zeus terrified me more. My every limb ached with each jolt of the horse as my sickness worsened.

"I can stay," I yelled to Leandro.

"You will die."

"You don't know that."

"I see you suffering. Your body is shutting down."

"I can fight it! Send Charlie home. Keep me here. Together we'll fight Zeus!"

My purpose grew stronger in me even as the pain rocketed.

To save this world, my world.

To find my brother, his son.

"If you stay and activate all the lost Olympian powers

at once, it'll be too much for your mortal body. You will die."

"I'll survive. I'll change this myth. I'm ready to be the Oracle." The intense pain that speared my body told me otherwise as I wobbled on my horse. Death came for me now on this world. Time to get to Earth before it got me.

"No!" His voice sliced into me, then grew quiet. "We need you to survive. You can't stay yet."

"Joshua, I can't go home without you!" Charlie looked sick at the thought as he leaned over his horse, his bangs flattened in black spikes down his forehead from the pelting hail.

We flew around a bush, and the massive Lightning Gate blasted up before us in a clearing. Its giant presence thrust through the crowded woods like a spaceship to take us home. Its bronze columns gleamed with power.

Leandro dragged me off his horse. The gate stood deserted. No need for guards with all the slaves sent home. Charlie stumbled behind me, and Leandro shoved us both under the portal.

"Get home! I'll come for you another time."

"Promise," I said.

"By the gods, I promise."

"Promise by *you*, not *them*."

He squeezed my shoulder, his face streaked with sleet. "For the love of Olympus and all who have fallen, I swear I will find you again." He said in a softer voice. "For the love of my son, your brother … I'll find him for both of us."

I looked into his eyes and believed him.

He pressed his gate key into the gate and jabbed in the Earth code from his scroll.

Rough voices slashed the air from the road leading to the gate. The ground trembled. Hooves pounded toward us. Wind swirled, shooting down branches at us. The sky darkened and thunder boomed. The hail magically stopped like a switch turned off, but tornadoes funneled toward us, ripping trees from the ground as Zeus's Storm Masters closed in.

"Run, Leandro!"

A golden glow wrapped around me. Sparks bit my fingers and toes, my whole body electrified. Charlie clutched my shirt in his hands.

Leandro's face twisted in a grimace. "Arrow speed to you."

He punched a fist to his chest and held it up.

He didn't want me to go either.

But he did as I said. He ran.

***

Faster and faster we rushed down the Lightning Road, bolted to its white fire. Stars streamed like comets in the dark around us as the wind snatched at my clothes and hair. Charlie's hand bit hard into me from fear of falling off, but the pain meant I wasn't alone. We burst from the black and blazed into my kitchen, the pain in my body gone in an instant but the pain in my heart intense.

The tick-tick of the stove clock screamed in the sudden silence. How many Earth days had we been gone? The snow still blew outside in a white welcome. The life I had before was sucked from me in a flash. My knees buckled as I swayed. Charlie grabbed my arm to keep me standing, but my legs gave way, and I fell on the cold kitchen tile.

Bo Chez was dead.

His words came to me. *You must do whatever necessary to complete your mission.*

The lightning orb throbbed against my thigh. I pulled it out with a jittery hand. All Bo Chez had been and stood for stormed inside this electrified weapon he'd earned. He'd left that life behind to be thrust into it again by me. The orb glowed blue then faded.

Charlie knelt beside me and shook me with a mournful face. "*Mon ami*, we're home."

I let loose a pained laugh, staring at the black arrow that blazed across his arm and mine. *No escape.* But we had … yet home no longer claimed me in this old world I'd so easily forgotten. I understood now the word home had many meanings, and you don't abandon one family by seeking another. Even when families are separated, they still have each other, no matter how far apart. I pressed the pendant to my heart. Its metal warmed in my hand.

Charlie tried to replace his brother with me.

Hekate tried to replace her brother with Leandro.

I could not replace Bo Chez—I could only bring him back. And find my lost brother and father while trying to save two worlds as the Oracle.

One day I might die trying.

The day would come very soon.

The battle on Nostos had begun. With me.

ACKNOWLEDGEMENTS

As always, my first reader and dear friend, Lisa Green, continues to shine her enthusiasm and light on Joshua's adventures. Her insight drove me to breathe fiery life into this story and these characters. I am also grateful to have had an amazing editor throughout this series, Tara Creel. She has guided me in enriching these stories (along with the pesky grammar stuff!). And to my favorite person in the world who started it all, the real Joshua Cooper Galanti, whose adventurous imagination fuels my own and whose faith in my storytelling never wavers.

DONNA GALANTI

Donna Galanti is the author of the *Joshua and The Lightning Road* series (Month9Books). She attended an English school housed in a magical castle, where her wild imagination was held back only by her itchy uniform (bowler hat and tie included!). There she fell in love with the worlds of C.S. Lewis and Roald Dahl, and wrote her first fantasy about Dodo birds, wizards, and a flying ship. She's lived in other exotic locations, including Hawaii where she served as a U.S. Navy photographer. She lives with her family and two crazy cats in an old farmhouse, and dreams of returning one day to a castle. She is a contributing editor to International Thriller Writers the *Big Thrill* magazine and blogs at Project Middle Grade Mayhem. Visit her at www.donnagalanti.com

OTHER MONTH9BOOKS TITLES YOU MIGHT LIKE

JOSHUA AND THE LIGHTNING ROAD
KING OF THE MUTANTS
ARTIFACTS
HAIR IN ALL THE WRONG PLACES

Find more books like this at Month9Books.com

Connect with Month9Books online:

Facebook: www.Facebook.com/Month9Books
Twitter: https://twitter.com/Month9Books
You Tube: www.youtube.com/user/Month9Books
Blog: http://month9books.tumblr.com/

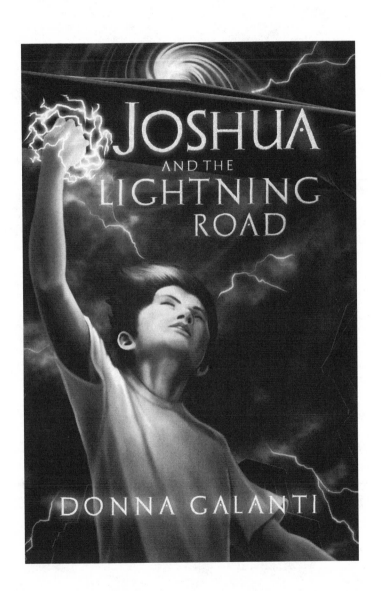

KING
of the
MUTANTS
SAMANTHA VERANT

ANDREW BUCKLEY

HAIR
IN ALL THE
WRONG
PLACES

WHAT'S HAPPENING TO HIM? WHAT HAS HE DONE?
AND WHAT ON EARTH IS THAT SMELL?